The PURPLE PTERODACTYLS

The PURPLE PTERODACTYLS

The Adventures of
W. Wilson Newbury, Ensorcelled Financier

by

L. SPRAGUE de CAMP

PHANTASIA PRESS
HUNTINGTON WOODS, MICHIGAN

1979

THE PURPLE PTERODACTYLS

Published by
Phantasia Press
13101 Lincoln
Huntington Woods, Michigan 48070

The Lamp first appeared in the March 1975 issue of *The Magazine of Fantasy & Science Fiction;* copyright© 1975 by Mercury Press, Inc.

Balsamo's Mirror first appeared in the June 1976 issue, The Purple Pterodactyls in the August 1976 issue, and Tiki in the February 1977 issue of *The Magazine of Fantasy & Science Fiction; copyright©* 1976 by Mercury Press, Inc.

Far Babylon first appeared in the May 1976 issue of *Fantasy Crossroads;* copyright© 1976 by Jonathan Bacon.

Algy first appeared in the August 1976 issue of *Fantastic Stories;* copyright© 1976 by Ultimate Publishing Company, Inc.

The Menhir first appeared in the May 1977 issue, Dead Man's Chest in the September 1977 issue, and United Imp in the December 1977 issue of *The Magazine of Fantasy & Science Fiction;* copyright© 1977 by Mercury Press, Inc.

The Figurine first appeared in the February 1977 issue, and Priapus in the December 1977 issue of *Fantastic Stories;* copyright© 1977 by Ultimate Publishing Company, Inc.

Darius first appeared in the Fall 1977 issue of *Escape!;* copyright© 1977 by Charles W. Melvin.

The Huns first appeared in the May 1978 issue, and The Yellow Man in the December 1978 issue of *The Magazine of Fantasy & Science Fiction;* copyright© 1978 by Mercury Press, Inc.

A Sending of Serpents first appeared in the August 1979 issue of *The Magazine of Fantasy & Science Fiction;* copyright© 1979 by Mercury Press, Inc.

FIRST EDITION

MANUFACTURED IN THE UNITED STATES OF AMERICA

ISBN 0-932096-02-6

To *Jocelyn Hazard Darling,*
whose Pink Panther
inspired the title story

Contents

Foreword

W. Wilson Newbury is younger than I, and he plays a far better game of tennis. Moreover, while I have made my living as a lumberjack, naval officer, teacher, lecturer, and scrivener, he selected his profession soon after leaving college and has remained faithful to it ever since.

Willy is a banker—not one of those faceless fellows who peer out of tellers' windows—but a dark-suited, well-brushed, short-haired type who jockeys a desk behind a row of marble pillars in one of the city's largest banks. And Willy, as all his friends call him to keep him from getting a swelled head, is smart.

Although we are different in many ways, Willy and I, we have always had one thing in common: a lively interest in the occult. And the occult seems to have a strange affinity for Willy.

Just why the esoteric seeks out a conventional, upright family man like W. Wilson Newbury, I cannot imagine; but somehow dwellers from the realms of metaphysical worlds beyond worlds keep tangling up the strands of his life. It may be that whatever prescience or intuition lets him separate a trustworthy loan applicant from a dead beat opens the shutters of his mind wider and makes him more psychically aware than the rest of us; but this gift—or curse—is not something a banker can discuss with the average run of mankind.

Bankers are supposed to be sane and sensible—the backbone of the community. A financier who talks of his involvement in fey happenings might cause a run on the bank, or trigger a recession, or at the very least lose his job. Since I hunch over my typewriter all day and am not given to gossip, I have been one of the few people in whom Willy could confide.

Willy was an avid reader of *Weird Tales,* that long-lamented record of the fantastic; and some of the unworldly happenings chronicled therein and the writers who set them down must have had a great influence on Willy.

The unnamed friend in "Balsamo's Mirror" is Howard Phillips Lovecraft, the fantasist of Providence, Rhode Island. In a letter to his Aunt Lillian Clark, Lovecraft told of buying a little pottery oil lamp from ancient Greece. He wrote: "It sits before me now, enchanting in its glamour, & has already suggested at least one weird story plot to my imagination: a plot in which it will figure as an *Atlantean* rather than Hellenic survival." Although Lovecraft never composed the tale, Willy in some inexplicable way experienced it.

In the story "Far Babylon," *aficionados* of fantasy will recognize the man in the cowboy hat as Robert E. Howard, the versatile poet and writer of Cross Plains, Texas. In a letter to Lovecraft, Howard mentioned a "sending of serpents" as the germ of a possible plot. And here again the occult broke through. That idea, combined with certain experiences of my peripatetic banker friend, became the aventure recounted here as "A Sending of Serpents." In the same story, Willy's remarks about "Zikkarf" allude to the fictional planet Xiccarph, on which Clark Ashton Smith laid several of his tales.

I, for one, am grateful to Willy Newbury for sharing adventures that are occasionally frightening, always amusing and sometimes unforgettable. I hope you will enjoy them, too.

L. Sprague de Camp
Villanova, Pennsylvania

Balsamo's Mirror

My friend in Providence took long walks, especially at night. He loved to end up at a graveyard, an abandoned church, or some such site. Since he earned a meager living by writing for *Creepy Stories,* he claimed that these walks inspired him with ideas. In any case, one such walk that he took with me gave him some ideas he had not foreseen.

When I was an undergraduate at M.I.T., my people lived too far away, in upstate New York, for frequent visits home. So on week ends, when up on my studies, I rattled over from Cambridge in my Model A to see my friend. We had become pen pals through the letters column of *Creepy Stories.* I had invited myself over, and we had found each other congenial in spite of differences of outlook, age, and temperament.

I used to love to argue. A thing I liked about my friend was that he could argue intelligently and always good-naturedly on more subjects than anyone I ever knew. Some of his ideas were brilliant; some I thought were crazy but later came to agree with; some I still think were crazy.

We found plenty to debate about. Politics was hot stuff, with the Depression still in full swing the year after Roosevelt had closed the banks. I was pretty conservative still, while my friend had just been converted from a Mesozoic conservative to an ardent New Dealer. Another young student, who sometimes dropped in, was a red-hot Communist sympathizer. So we went at it hot and heavy.

We also disputed religion. My friend was a scientific materialist and atheist; I was still a believing Christian. We argued esthetics. He defended art for art's sake; I thought that philosophy a pretext for indolence and had no use for idlers, whether rich, arty, or plain lazy.

We wrangled over international affairs. He wanted America to rejoin the British Empire; I was for splendid isolation. We argued history. He was devoted to the eighteenth century; I thought that men wearing wigs over

9

good heads of hair looked silly.

"Willy," he said, "you are looking at the superficies only. The perukes are not significant. What is important is that this was the last period before the Industrial Revolution, with all its smoke and rattling machinery and hypertrophied cities and other horrors. Therefore, in a sense, this was the most gracious, elegant, civilized time we have ever seen or shall ever see."

"What," I said, "would you do with the surplus nine tenths of humanity, whom you'd have to get rid of if we went back to eighteenth-century technology? Starve them? Shoot them? Eat them?"

"I didn't say we could or should go back to pre-industrial technology. The changes since then were inevitable and irreversible. I only said..."

We were still arguing when we set out on one of our nocturnal prowls. My friend could always find something to show the visitor. *This*, he would explain, was the house once owned by a famous Colonial pirate; *that* was the site of the tavern where he was seized before being hanged; and so on.

This balmy May evening, under a gibbous moon, my friend was on the track of a piece of Colonial architecture on Federal Hill. We hiked down the steep incline of Angell Street to the center of Providence. Thence we continued west up the gentler slope of Westminster Avenue, where the restaurants were called trattorias. Near Dexter Street, we turned off and trudged around little back streets until we found the Colonial house.

The doorway was still there, but the rest of the ground floor had been eviscerated to make room for a small machine shop. My friend clucked. "Damned Dagoes!" he muttered. "A pox on 'em." His ethnic prejudices, although weakening, were still pretty strong.

We examined the doorway with my pocket flashlight, my friend being too absent-minded to think of bringing his own. At last we started back. We had already walked two miles, and the climb back up Angell promised a rigorous workout. Since it was night, we could not use the elevators in the County Court House, at the foot of the slope, to save

10

ourselves some of the climb.

In this tangle of alleys, my friend took a wrong turn. He quickly realized his error, saying: "No, Willy, it's this way. This should take us back to Westminster. I don't think I know this street."

As we neared the avenue, we passed a row of little shops, including a Chinese laundry. Nearly all were closed, although ahead we could see the lights of restaurants, bars, and a movie house on Westminster. My friend put out a hand to stop me before one place, still lit, in the row of darkened shops.

"What's this?" he said. "Damme, sirrah, it hath the look of a den of unholy mysteries!" He talked like that when in his eighteenth-century mood.

The dim-lit sign in the window said: MADAME FATIMA NOSI. FORTUNES TOLD. SPEAK WITH YOUR DEAR DEPARTED. OCCULT WISDOM SHARED. A crude painting beneath the legend showed a gypsylike woman bent over a crystal ball.

"I can just imagine," said my friend. "This is the cener of a secret, sinister cult. They're a gang of illegal immigrants from Kafiristan, where the ancient paganism survives. They worship a chthonian deity, which is in fact a gelatinous being that oozes its way through solid rock..."

"Why not go in and see?" I said. "Madame Nosi seems open for business."

"Oh, you're so practical, Willy!" said my friend. "I had rather gaze upon this cryptic lair from afar and let my imagination soar. Inside, it is probably dirty, squalid, and altogether prosaic. Besides, our sibyl will expect remuneration, and I am badly straitened just now."

"I've got enough dough for both," I said. "Come on!"

It required urging, because my friend was a shy man and sensitive about his perennial poverty. This indigence was curious, considering his gifts and intellect. A few minutes later, however, we were in Madame Nosi's oratory.

The place was as dingy as my friend had predicted. Fatima Nosi proved a tall, strongly built, bony woman of middle age, with a big hooked nose and graying black hair hanging down from under her head scarf.

"Well," said she, "what can I do for you gentlemans?" She

11

spoke with an accent, which did not sound Italian. She looked hard at me. "You are college student, no?"

"Yes."

"At the—um—the Massachusett Institute of the Technology, yes?"

"Yes."

"And you expect to graduation in—umm—two year, no?"

"That's right," I said, surprised at her prescience.

"Name, please?"

"Wilson Newbury."

She wrote in a little notebook. "And you!" she turned to my friend. When she had written his name, she said: "You are writer, no?"

"I," said my friend, "am a gentleman who sometimes writes for his own amusement and that of his friends." His face tensed with the effort of trying to speak a foreign language without stuttering. "*P-parlate italiano?*" He got it out slowly, with a pronounced down-east accent.

She looked puzzled; then her face cleared. "*Così, così.* But I am not Italian, me, even though I was born in Italy."

"What are you, then, if I may be so bold?" asked my friend.

"I am Tosk."

"Oh, Albanian!" he exclaimed. He said aside to me: "It fits. She's a perfect example of the Dinaric racial type, and that name didn't sound quite Italian." He turned back. "I am honored; *sono—sono onorato.*"

"Tank you. Is many Albanians in Italy," said Madame Nosi. "They went there two, tree hundred years ago to excape the Turks. And now, what can I do for you? Horoscope? Séance? Crystal ball? I tink, you smart gentlemans no care for simple occult manifestations. You tell me what you most want. You, please." She indicated my friend.

He thought a long moment and said: "Madame, the thing whereof I am most desirous is to view the world as it was at the climax of Western civilization—that is to say, in the eighteenth century. No, permit me to amend that. It is to witness the most civilized part of that world—England—at that period."

"Umm." Madame Nosi looked doubtful. "Is difficult. But then, maybe I get chance to use the mirror of Balsamo. You got to come upstairs to inner sanctum."

She led us up creaking steps to a shabby little sitting room. Stepping to the side of the room, she pulled a cloth cover off a mirror on the wall. This mirror, otherwise ordinary-looking, had an ornately carven frame whence most of the gilding had worn off.

My friend leaned towards me and murmured: "This should be interesting. Giuseppe Balsamo, alias Count Alessandro di Cagliostro, was the most egregious faker and charlatan of the eighteenth century. Wonder what she'll do?"

"This," said Madame Nosi, "will cost you ten dollars. Is a very powerful spell. It exhaust my weak heart. If your friend want to go along with you, it cost him ten buck, too."

My friend looked stricken, as well he might. For ten dollars, one could then eat in a good restaurant for a week. Twenty sounded steep to me, also; but I had lately received a check from home and did not like to back out. Had I been older and bolder, I might have haggled—something I knew my friend could never bring himself to do. I pulled out my wallet.

"Tank you," said Madame Nosi. "Now, you sit here facing the mirror. You, too. I will light candles on this ting behind you. Look at reflections of the candles in glass."

She lit a sconce on the opposite wall. In the dimness, the reflections of my friend and me were little more than shapes. I took my eyes off the image of my gaunt, lantern-jawed friend and raised them to that of the cluster of wavering lights.

Madame Nosi bustled about behind us. A sweetish smell told me that she had lit incense. She began to croon a song in a language I did not recognize.

I cannot tell exactly when her spell, or whatever it was, took effect, any more than one can tell exactly when one drops off to sleep and begins to dream. But I presently found myself trudging a dirt road, overgrown with foot-high grass between two deep, narrow ruts.

This experience, I soon discovered, was not a simple case of time travel, such as one reads about. In stories, the time traveler arrives in another time *in propria persona,* able to act and function as he would in his own time. I, however, found myself in someone's else body, seeing and hearing with his

13

organs and able to follow his thoughts but helpless to affect my host's actions. I could not even crane his neck or roll his eyes to see anything that he did not wish to look at. Now his gaze was fixed on the ground before him to avoid a stumble.

This situation avoided the familiar time-travel paradox. While I partook of all my host's experiences, mental and physical, I could not do anything that would change an event that had already taken place. Whether this adventure should be explained as a return to a former time, or the vision of former events imposed upon my present-day mind, or sheer illusion, I cannot judge.

I could only sense the thoughts that ran through my host's conscious mind; I could not plumb his store of memories. Hence I had no way of finding out who or where or when I was, until my host happened to think of such things or until someone or something else gave me a clue.

"Now remember, lad," said a creaky voice in my ear, "no gangling after the trollops, to the peril of thy immortal soul. And if we meet the squire and his Macaroni zon, keep thy temper no matter what they zay."

At least, this is what I think he said. So strong was his unfamiliar dialect that, until I got used to it, I caught only half his words.

My host did me the favor of turning his head to look at his companion. He said: "Oh, hold thy water, Vayther. I' faith, I'm a grown man, can take care o' meself."

"Childhood and youth are vanity. Ecclesiastes eleven," said the other. "Thy loose tongue'll get us hanged yet."

"Unless thy poaching doth it virst," replied my host.

"I do but take that dominion over the vowls of the air and the beasts of the vield, which God hath given me. Zee Genesis one. 'Tis wrong o' Sir Roger to deny us poor volk the use of 'em..."

My companion, evidently my host's father, continued grumbling before relapsing into silence. He was a man of mature years, with the gnarled brown hands and deeply creased brown neck of a lifelong outdoor worker. He wore the knee breeches and full-skirted coat of the eighteenth century, but these were of coarse, self-colored homespun, patched and darned. His calves were clad in a pair of baggy,

14

soiled cotton stockings, and his big, shapeless shoes did not differ as to right and left.

On his head rode a large, full-bottomed, mouse-colored wig, which hung to his shoulders but from which half the hair had fallen out. On top of the wig was a stained, battered, wide-brimmed felt hat, turned up in back but otherwise allowed to droop in scallops.

Besides the wig, he also flaunted a full if straggly gray beard. I had thought that all men in this era were shaven.

I wondered if my friend was imprisoned in the body of the father, as I was in that of the son. If so, the beard was a good joke on him. As a devotee of the eighteenth century, my friend detested all hair on the face. He had long nagged me about my harmless little mustache. If indeed my friend was there, though, there was no way for me to communicate with him.

Then I thought: was I, too, wearing a wig? I could not tell. It would be an equally good joke on me, who despised wigs.

The pair subsided into silence, save for an occasional muttered remark. They were not great talkers. I could follow the thoughts of the son, but these did little to orient me. The jumble of names, faces, and scenes flickered past me too quickly to analyze.

I did learn that my host's name was William, that his father was a yeoman farmer, and that they were the only surviving members of their family. I also learned that the father had a feud with the local squire, and that they were on their way to a fair. From an allusion to Bristol, I gathered that we were somewhere in the Southwest of England. From the look of the vegetation, I surmised that it was springtime.

The open fields and woodlots gave way to a straggle of small houses, and these thickened into a village. From the height of the dim, ruddy orb that passes for sun in England, I judged that the time was about midday.

On the edge of the village roared the fair. There were swarms of rustics, clad more or less like my father (for so I had come to think of him). There were a few ladies and gentlemen in more photogenic eighteenth-century attire, with high heels and powdered wigs. Some younger men, I

15

noted, wore their own hair in pigtails instead of wigs. My father's beard, however, was the only one in sight.

When we got into the crowd, the stink of unwashed humankind was overpowering. Although I, who smelled with his olifactory nerves, found it horrible, William seemed not to notice. I suppose he was pretty ripe himself. From the itches in various parts of his body, I suspected that he harbored a whole fauna of parasites.

Two teams were playing cricket. Beyond, young men were running and jumping in competition. There was a primitive merry-go-round, powered by an old horse. A boy followed the beast round and round, beating it to keep it moving. There were edibles and drinkables for sale; of the fairgoers, some were already drunk.

There were games of chance and skill: throwing balls and quoits at targets, guessing which walnut shell the pea was under, cards, dice, and a wheel of fortune. A row of tents housed human freaks and a large one, a camel. A cockfight and a puppet show, striving to outshout each other, were going on at the further end of the grounds.

My father would not let me squander our few pence on most of these diversions, but he paid tuppence for us to see the camel. This mangy-looking beast loftily chewed its cud while a man in an "Arab costume" made of old sheeting lectured on the camel's qualities. Most of what he said was wrong.

"Hola there!" cried a voice. I—or rather the William whose body I shared—turned. One of the gentlemen was addressing us—a well-set-up man of middle years, with a lady on his arm.

"Stap me vitals," said this man, "if it beant old Phil!"

My father and I took off our hats and bowed. My father said: "God give you good day, Mayster Bradford! Good day, your la'ship! 'Tis an unexpected pleasure."

Bradford came up and shook my father's hand. " 'Tis good for the optics to see you again, Philip. You, too, Will. Zookers, but ye've grown!"

"Aye, he's a good lad," said Philip. "The earth hath zwallowed all my hopes but un."

"The Lord giveth and the Lord taketh away. Tell me, Phil,

16

how goes it betwixt you and Sir Roger?"

"Ill enough," said my father. "E'er since the enclosure, he hath been at me to sell out me poor little patch to add to his grand acres."

"Why don't ye sell?" said Bradford. "I hear he hath offered a good price."

"Nay, zir, with all due respect, that I won't. Shirlaws ha' been there zince memory runneth not to the contrary, and I'll not be the virst to gi' it up. And if I did, 'twould not be to a titled villain who rides his damned vox hunt across me crops. Clean ruined last year's barley, he did."

"Same stubborn old Phil! Roger Stanwyck's not so bad a cully if ye get on's good side. For all's glouting humors, he doth good works of charity." Bradford lowered his voice. "Harkee, Phil, we're old friends, and ne'er mind the distinctions o' rank. Sell out to Sir Roger for the best price ye can get, but quit this contention. Otherwise, I shan't be able to answer for your well-being. *Verbum sat sapienti.*"

"What mean ye, zir?"

"In's cups, which is oft enough, he boasts that he'll have your land or have you dancing on the nubbing cheat ere the twelvemonth be out."

"Aye, zir?" said Philip.

"Aye verily, no question. I was there, at a party at Colonel Armitage's. Roger's the magistrate and can do't."

"He must needs ge' me dited and convicted virst."

"I' fackins, man, talk sense! With all the hanging offenses on the books, they can string you up for auft more heinous than spitting on the floor."

"Fie! Juries won't convict in such cases."

"If they happen to like you. I needn't tell you ye be not the most popular man hereabouts."

"Aye, Mayster Bradford, but wherefore? I lead a good Christian life."

"Imprimus, ye foft against the enclosure."

"Sartainly I did. 'Tis the doom o' the independent farmer."

"Me good Philip, the day of the old English yeoman is past. The country needs corn, and the only way to get it is to carve up all these wasteful commons and put 'em to grain crops. Secundus, ye are a Methodist, and to these folk

17

that's worse nor a Papist or a Jew. They'd be tickled to see a wicked heretic swing, specially since we haven't had a hanging in o'er a year."

"I believe what the Almighty and the Good Book tell me."

"Tertius, ye wear that damned beard."

"I do but obey the divine commands, zir. Zee Leviticus nineteen."

"And quartus, ye are learned beyond your station. I don't mind; I like to see the lower orders better themselves— within reason, o' course. But the villagers think ye give yourself airs and hate you for't."

"I only strive to obey God the more wisely by me little larning. Zee Proverbs one, vifth verse. As for zelling out to Zir Roger, I'll come to the parish virst."

Bradford sighed and threw up his hands. "Well, say not that I failed to warn you. But hark, if ye do sell, ye shall have a good place with me for the asking. 'Twon't be arra clodhopping chore, neither, but a responsible post with good pay. Ask me sarvents if I beant a good master."

"Well, thankee, zir, but—"

"Think it o'er." Bradford clapped Philip on the shoulder and went away with his wife.

We strolled about, bought a snack of bread and cheese, and watched the contests. William would have liked to spend money on the freak shows and the gambling games, but Philip sternly forbade. Then a shout brought us about.

"Hey, Shirlaw! Philip Shirlaw!"

We were addressed by a stout, red-faced man with a strip of gold lace on his three-cornered hat. He came swiftly towards us, poling himself along with a four-foot, gold-headed walking stick. With him was a gorgeously dressed young man, tall and slender. The young man carried his hat beneath his arm, because it could never have been fitted over his wig. This wig, besides the curls at the sides and the queue at the back, shot up in a foot-high pompadour in front.

The youth was as pale as the older one was ruddy and had black beauty spots glued to cheek and jaw. He languidly waved a pale, slender hand as he spoke.

"I'll have a word with thee, sarrah," said the red-faced one.

"Aye, your honor?" replied Philip.

18

"Not here, not here. Come to my house this afternoon—after dinner-time will do."

"Father!" said the youth. "You forget, Mr. Harcourt and's wife are dining with us." I noted that the young man dropped his final r's, like a modern Englishman, whereas the others with whom we had spoken did not.

"So he doth, so he doth," grumbled Sir Roger Stanwyck. "Make it within the hour, Shirlaw. We're about to depart the fair, so tarry not!"

It was a long walk back from the fair to Sir Roger's mansion, but the squire would never have thought to offer us a lift in his coach.

Stanwyck House so swarmed with servants that it was a wonder they did not fall over one another. One of them ushered us into Sir Roger's study. I had little chance to observe the surroundings, save as William's vision happened to light on things; and he had been here before. There was, for instance, a pair of swords crossed behind a shield on the wall—but all made of glass, not steel.

Sir Roger, wineglass in hand, glowered at us from a big wing chair, then put on a forced smile. His son, seated at a harpsichord and playing something by Händel, left off his strumming and swung around.

"Now, Shirlaw!" barked Sir Roger. "I have argued with thee and pleaded with thee, to no avail. Art a stubborn old fart; s'bud, I'll give thee credit. To show me heart's in the right place, I'll raise me last offer to an hundred guineas even. 'Tis thrice what thy lousy patch is worth and will set thee up for life. But that's all; not a brass farden more. What say ye? What say ye?"

"Zorry, zir," said Philip. "I ha' gi'en you mine answer, and that's that. Me land stays mine."

They argued some more, while the son patted yawns. Sir Roger got redder and redder. At last he jumped up, roaring:

"All right, get out, thou Hanoverian son of a bitch! I'll Methodist thee! If one method won't sarve, there's a mort more in me locker. Get out!"

"Your honor may kiss mine arse," said Philip as he turned away.

19

Behind us, Sir Roger hurled his wineglass at us but missed. The glass shattered, and Sir Roger screamed: "John! Abraham! Throw me these rascals out! Fetch me sword, somebody! I'll qualify them to run for the geldings' plate! Charles, ye mincing milksop, why don't ye drub me these runagates?"

"La, Father, you know that I—" began the young man. The rest was lost in the distance as Philip and William walked briskly out, before the hired help could organize a posse. Behind us, the clock struck four.

I was myself filled with rage, both from that I got from William's mind and on my own account. If I had been in charge of William's body, I might have tried something foolish. It is just as well that I was not. In those days, a peasant simply did not punch a knight or baronet (whichever Sir Roger was) in the nose, no matter what the provocation.

We left the grounds by another path, which led across a spacious lawn. At the edge of this lawn, the ground dropped sharply. There was a retaining wall, where the surface descended almost vertically for six or eight feet into a shallow ditch. From this depression, the earth sloped gently up on the other side, almost to the level on the inner lawn. This structure, like a miniature fortification, was called a ha-ha. Its purpose was to afford those in the house a distant, unobstructed grassy vista and at the same time keep the deer and other wild life away from the inner lawns and flower beds.

We descended a flight of steps, which cut through the ha-ha, and continued along a winding path. This path led over a brook and through a wood. On the edge of the brook, workmen were building a tea house in Chinese style, with red and black paint and gilding. As we followed the winding path through the wood, a rabbit hopped away.

"Hm," said Philip Shirlaw. "That o'erweening blackguard ... And us wi' noft but bread and turnips in the house. Harkee, Will, Zir Roger dines at vive, doth he not?"

"Aye," said William. " 'Twas vour, but that craichy zon o' his hath broft the new vashion vrom London."

"Well, now," said Philip, "meseems that God hath put us in the way of a bit o' flesh to spice our regiment. Wi' guests at

Stanwyck House, the Stanwycks'll be close to home from vive to nigh unto midnight. Those ungodly gluttons dawdle vive or zix hours o'er their meat, and the pack o' zarvents'll be clustered round to uphold Zir Roger's hospitality. By the time they're throf, Zir Roger'll be too drunk to know what betides."

"Dost plan to nab one o' his honor's coneys?"

"Aye, thof it an't Zir Roger's but God's."

"Oh, Vayther, have a care! Remember Mayster Bradford's warning—"

"The Almighty will take care of us."

Another half hour brought us to our own farm and house. The house was little more than a shack, not much above the level of the houses of comic-strip hillbillies. Furnishings were minimal, save that a shelf along one wall bore a surprising lot of books. This must be what Bradford had meant when he spoke of Philip Shirlaw's being learned above his station.

Since William did not fix his eyes on this shelf for more than a few seconds at a time, I could not tell much about Philip's choice of books. I caught a glimpse of several volumes of sermons by John Wesley and George Whitefield. There were also, I think, a Bible, a Shakespeare, and a Plutarch.

Philip Shirlaw climbed up into the loft and came down with a pair of small crossbows. I was astonished, supposing these medieval weapons to have been long obsolete. I later learned that they were used for poaching as late as the time of our adventure, being favored for their silence.

William unhappily tried again to dissuade his sire: "Don't let thy grudge against Zir Roger lead thee into risking our necks. Colonel Armitage's vootman, Jemmy Thorne, hath told me 'tis a hanging offence to 'trespass with intent to kill rabbits.' Them are the words o' the statute."

I followed the argument with growing apprehension. What would happen to me if William were killed while I shared his body?

But Philip Shirlaw was not to be swayed. "Pooh! Put thy trust in Providence, zon, and vear noft. Nor do I, as a good Christian, bear Zir Roger a grudge. I do but take my vair

21

share o' the vruits o' the earth, which God hath provided for all mankind. Zee the ninth chapter o' Genesis."

The steel crossbow bolts were about the size of a modern pencil. With a pocket full of these and a crossbow under his arm, William set out behind his father.

They scouted the woods between the Stanwyck estate and the Shirlaw farm, seeing and hearing none. The sun sank lower and disappeared behind the clouds, which thickened with a promise of rain.

As Philip had surmised, all the service personnel of Stanwyck House had gone to the mansion to wait upon the master and his guests.

At last—it must have been nearly six—we roused a rabbit, which went hippety-hoppity through the big old oaks. William made a quick motion, but Philip stayed him with a geture. Carefully, they cocked their weapons, placed their bolts in the grooves, and scouted forward.

They raised the rabbit again, but again it bolted before they got within range. Being old hands at this, they spread out and continued their stalk.

The woods thinned, and they reached the edge of the outer lawns, not far from the ha-ha. In the depression that ran along the foot of the ha-ha sat their rabbit, nibbling.

Philip's crossbow twanged. The quarrel whined. The rabbit tumbled over.

"Got un!" said William.

The Shirlaws ran out from the wood to seize the game, when a bellow halted them. Atop the ha-ha stood Sir Roger Stanwyck and his son Charles. Sir Roger held a musket trained upon them; Charles, a pistol.

"Ha!" roared Sir Roger. "Said I not I'd have you? The divil set upon me if I don't see you twain dangling from the hempseed caudle!"

"O Gemini, they mean it!" muttered William. "Get ready to vlee!"

"Drop those crossbows!" came the high voice of Charles Stanwyck.

William's bow was still cocked and loaded. Without thinking, the young man whipped up the weapon and discharged it at Sir Roger. He missed, and the whistle of the

22

bolt was drowned by the roar of the musket. I heard the ball strike Philip, who fell backwards with a piercing scream. William dropped his crossbow and ran for the woods.

Another flash lit up the evening landscape. The report came to William's ears just as a terrific blow struck him in the back....

And then I was back in Madame Nosi's room, on my feet but staggering back from the wall. About the floor lay the shattered remains of Balsamo's mirror. To my left lay my friend. Madame Nosi was not to be seen, but I had a dim memory of terrible shrieks and crashes just before my "awakening."

I dashed to the head of the stair. At the foot, in an unlovely sprawl, lay Madame Nosi.

After a second's hesitation, I went back to the room. My friend was sitting up on the floor, mumbling: "Wha—what hath happened? I thought I was shot...."

"Come, help me!" I said. We descended to Madame Nosi.

"Pull her up," said my friend. "It's not decent for her to be lying upside down like that."

"Don't touch her!" I said. "Shouldn't move an injured person until the doctor comes." I felt for her pulse but found none.

A policeman appeared, followed by a couple of neighbors. The cop asked: "What goes on? What's the screaming and crashing—oh!" He sighted Fatima Nosi.

In due course, the ambulance came and took Madame Nosi. For the next few days, my friend and I spent hours answering questions by the coroner and other officials.

As nearly as we could reconstruct the events, my friend and I had leaped out of our chairs at the moment when, in our eighteenth-century lives, we were shot by the Stanwycks. I had blundered into the wall and broken the mirror. Whether in sudden panic at the success of her spell, or for some other reason, Madame Nosi had run out of the room. She had died, not from the effects of the fall, as we at first supposed, but from heart failure before she fell. Her physician testified that she had suffered from heart disease.

The officials, although puzzled and suspicious, let us go.

They swept up the fragments of Balsamo's mirror for "evidence," but I could never find out what became of the pieces. I had some vague idea of putting them together but let it go in the rush of cramming for spring finals. I suppose the pieces were thrown out with the trash.

When it was over, my friend sighed and said: "I fear me that the eighteenth century, which I have idealized all these years, never really existed. The real one was far dirtier, more narrow-minded, brutal, orthodox, and superstitious than I could have ever conceived without seeing it. Gawd, to be cooped up in the body of a bewhiskered amateur theologian and not be able to say a word to controvert his fallacies! The eighteenth century I visualized was a mere artifact—a product of my imagination, compounded of pictures in books which I saw as a child, things I had read, and bits of Colonial architecture I've seen."

"Then," I asked, "you'll settle down and be reconciled to your own twentieth century?"

"Good heavens, no! Our experience—assuming it to be genuine and not a mere hallucination—only serves to convince me that the real world, anywhere or in any age, is no place for a gentleman of sensitivity. So I shall spend more time in the world of dreams. If you like, Willy, I shall be glad to meet you there. There's a palace of lapis lazuli I must show you, atop a mountain of glass...."

The
Lamp

I stopped at Bill Bugby's Garage in Gahato and got young Bugby to drive me to the landing above the dam. There I found Mike Devlin waiting for me, in an aluminum row-canoe with an outboard motor. I said:

"Hello, Mike! I'm Wilson Newbury. Remember me?"

I dropped my gear into the boat, lowering the suitcase carefully lest I damage the box I was carrying in it.

"Hello, Mr. Newbury!" said Mike. "To be sure, I remember you." He looked much the same as before, save that the wrinkles on his brown face were a little deeper and his curly hair a little grayer. In old-fashioned lumberjack style, he wore a heavy flannel shirt, a sweater, an old jacket, and a hat, although the day was warm. "Have you got that thing with you?"

I sent the car back to Bugby's to keep until I needed it again and got into the boat. "The thing Mr. Ten Eyck wanted me to bring?" I said.

"I do mean that, sir." Mike started the motor, so that we had to shout.

"It's in the big bag," I said, "so don't run us on a stump. After fetching that thing all the way from Europe, and having nightmares the whole time, I don't want it to end up at the bottom of Lower Lake."

"I'll be careful, Mr. Newbury," said Mike, steering the boat up the winding course of the Channel. "What is that thing, anyhow?"

"It's an antique lamp. He got me to pick it up in Paris from some character he'd been writing to."

"Ah, well, Mr. Ten Eyck is always buying funny things. After his troubles, that's about all he's interested in."

"What's this about Al's having been married?" I asked.

"Sure, and didn't you know?" Although born and reared in Canada, Mike still sounded more Irish than most native-born Irishmen. I suppose his little home town in Nova Scotia had been solidly Irish-Canadian. "He married the Camaret girl—the daughter of that big lumberjack." Mike chuckled, his faded blue eyes searching the channel ahead for snags. "You remember, when she was a little girl, and the teacher in Gahato asked all the children what they wanted to be when they grew up, she said: 'I want to be a whore!' It broke up the class for fair, it did."

"Well, what happened? Whatever possessed Al—"

"I guess he wanted a husky, hard-working cook and housekeeper, and he figured she'd be so pleased to marry a gentleman that she'd do what he wanted. Trouble was, Mélusine Camaret is a pretty hot piece—always has been. When she found Mr. Ten Eyck couldn't put it to her night and morning regular, she up and ran off with young Larochelle. You know, Pringle's foreman's son."

A big blue heron, disturbed by the racket of the outboard, flapped away up the Channel. Mike asked: "How was the Army, Mr. Newbury?"

I shrugged. "Just manning a desk. Nobody bothered to shoot at me. I sometimes feel I was lucky the war ended when it did, before they found what a nincompoop they'd put into an officer's uniform."

"Ah, sure, you was always the modest one."

The Channel opened out into Lower Lake. The lake was surrounded by the granite ridges of the Adirondacks, thickly clad in hardwoods and evergreens—mostly maple and pine. Here and there, a gray hogback or scar showed through the forest. Most of the marketable timber had been cut out early in the century and its place taken by second growth. The post-war shortages, however, had made it profitable to cut stands that theretofore had stood too far back from transportation to be profitable. While much of the land thereabouts had gone into the Adirondack State Park and so was no longer cuttable, enough remained in private hands to keep the lumber trucks rolling and the saws of Dan Pringle's mill in Gahato screaming.

We cut across Lower Lake to Ten Eyck Island, which separated Lower Lake from Upper Lake. On the map, the two lakes made an hour-glass shape, with the island partly

26

plugging the neck between them.

Alfred Ten Eyck, in khaki shirt and pants, came to the dock with a yell of "Willy!" He had a quick, nervous handshake, with a stronger grip than I expected.

We swapped the usual remarks about our not having changed a bit, although I could not say it sincerely of Alfred. While he had kept his slim, straight shape, he had pouches under his eyes. His sandy hair was graying; although, like me, he was still in his early thirties.

"Have you got it?" he asked.

"Yes, yes. It's in that—"

He had already grabbed my big suitcase and started for the old camp. He went up the slope at a pace that I almost had to run to keep up with. When he saw me lagging, he stopped to wait. Being out of condition, I came up panting.

"Same old place," I said.

"It's run down a bit," he said, "since the days when my folks entertained relays of friends and relatives all summer. In those days, you could hire help to keep it up—not that Mike doesn't do two men's work."

The trail was somewhat overgrown, and I stumbled on a clump of weeds. Alfred gave me a wry grin.

"I have an understanding with Nature," he siad. "I leave her alone, and she leaves me alone. Seriously, any time you want to help us clear out the trails, I'll give you a corn hook and tell you to go to it. It's all you can do here to keep ahead of the natural forces of growth and decay."

Camp Ten Eyck was a big two-story house, made of huge hand-hewn logs, with fifteen or sixteen rooms. There was a tool kit beside the front door, with tools lying about. Mike and Alfred had evidently been replacing a couple of porch boards that had begun to rot.

Most Adirondack camps are of wood, because lumber is relatively cheap there. The Adirondack climate, however, sees to it that a wooden house starts to fall apart almost as soon as it is completed. Some of the big logs that made up the sides of Camp Ten Eyck had spots so soft that you could stick your thumb into them.

While I caught my breath, Alfred said: "Look, I'll show you your room; but first would you please get *it* out? I want to see

27

it."

"Oh, all right," I said. I set the suitcase on one of those old-fashioned window seats, which filled the corners of the living room, and opened it. I handed Alfred the box.

"You'll notice it's properly packed," I said. "My sister once sent us a handsome antique luster vase from England, in just a flimsy carton, and it got smashed to pieces."

Alfred cut the cords with shaking hands. He had to go out to get a chisel from his tool chest to pry up the wooden lid. Then he burrowed into the excelsior.

While he worked, I looked around. There were the same old deerskins on the couches and window seats, the same deer heads staring glassily from the walls, the same stuffed fox and owl, the same silver-birch banisters with the bark on, and the same lichens on whose white nether surfaces amateur artists had scratched sylvan scenes.

I was surprised to see that the big, glass-fronted gun case was empty. As I remembered it from the thirties, the case had held an impressive array of rifles, shotguns, and pistols, mostly inherited by Alfred from his father and grandfather.

"What happened to all your guns?" I said. "Did you sell them?"

"The hell I did!" he said, working away, "You know that no-good cousin of mine, George Vreeland? I rented the place to him one year, and when I got back I found that he had simply sold most of the guns to the *natives*." (Alfred always snarled a little when he said "natives," meaning the year-round residents of the country.)

"What did you do about it?

"Nothing I could do. George was gone before I got back, and the last I heard he was in California. Then, when I was away last winter, one of our local night workers made off with the rest, including my sailing trophy. I know who did it, too."

"Well?"

"Well, what? No matter how good my proof was, do you suppose I could get the goddam *natives* to convict him? After what happened to me with Camaret?"

"What about Camaret? I don't know this story."

"Well, you knew I'd been married?"

28

"Yes. Mike mentioned it."

Alfred Ten Eyck gave me a brief account of his short-lived union with Mélusine Camaret. He said nothing about his own sexual inadequacy, for which I cannot blame him.

"The day after she flew the coop," he said, "I was walking along the street in Gahato, bothering absolutely nobody, when Big Jean comes up and says: 'Hey! What you do wit my leetla girl, *hein?*' And the first thing I know, he knocks me cold, right there in the street."

(That was not quite how the folk in Gahato remembered the event. They say that Alfred answered: "Now look here, you dumb Canuck, I don't know what that floozie of yours has been telling you, but—" and then Camaret hit him.)

"Well," Alfred went on, "when I came to, I swore out a warrant and had the trooper run Jean in. But the jury acquitted him, although half the village had seen him slug me. I heard they figured that if Big Jean wanted to belt his son-in-law, that was a family fight and none of their business."

(The villagers' version was that, since Jean Camaret was built like a truck and had a notoriously violent temper, anyone fool enough to pick a fight with him deserved what he got.)

Waving an arm to indicate the surrounding mountains, Alfred glowered at me. "They can't forget that, fifty years ago, everything you could see from here was Ten Eyck property, and they had to get a Ten Eyck's permission to so much as spit on it. Now the great Ten Eyck holdings are down to this one lousy little island, plus a few lots in Gahato; but they still hate my guts."

(In fact, several members of the Ten Eyck family still held parcels of land in Herkimer County, but that is a minor point. Alfred did not get on well with most of his kin.)

"I think you exaggerate," I said. "Anyway, why stay here if you don't feel comfortable?"

"Where should I go, and how should I earn a living? Jeepers! Here I at least have a roof over my head. By collecting a few rents on those shacks on Hemlock Street in Gahato—when the tenants don't talk me out of them with hard-luck stories—and now and then selling one of the remaining lots, I get by. Since I can't sell them fast enough to get ahead of my expenses and build up some investments, I'm whittling away at my capital; but I don't seem to have any choice. Ah, here we are!"

Alfred had unwrapped the page from *Le Figaro,* which enfolded the lamp. He held up his treasure.

It was one of those hollow, heart-shaped things, about the size of the palm of your hand, which they used for lamps in Greek and Roman times. It had a knob-shaped handle at the round end, a big hole in the center top for refilling, and a little hole for the wick at the pointed or spout end. You can buy any number of them in Europe and the Near East, since they are always digging up more.

Most such lamps are made of cheap pottery. This one looked at first like pottery, too. Actually, it was composed of some sort of metal but had a layer of dried mud all over it. This stuff had flaked off in places, allowing a dull gleam of metal to show through.

"What's it made of?" I asked. "Ionides didn't seem to know, when he gave me the thing in Paris."

"I don't know. Some sort of silver bronze or bell metal, I guess. We'll have to clean it to find out. But we've got to be careful with it. You can't just scrub an antique like this with steel wool, you know."

"I know. If it has a coating of oxide, you leave it in place. Then they can put it in an electrolytic tank and turn the oxide back into the original metal, I understand."

"Something like that," said Alfred.

"But what's so remarkable about this little widget? You're not an archaeologist—"

"No, no, that's not it. I got it for a reason. Did you have any funny dreams while you were bringing this over?"

"You bet I did! But how in hell would you know?"

"Ionides told me that might happen."

"Well then, what's the gag? What's this all about?"

Alfred gave me another glare from his pale-gray eyes. "Just say I'm fed up with being a loser, that's all."

I knew what he meant. If the word "loser" applied to anybody, it was Alfred Ten Eyck. You know the term "Midas touch"? Alfred had the opposite, whatever that is.

He could turn gold into dross by touching it.

Alfred's father died while Alfred was at Princeton, leaving him several thousand acres of Adirondack land but hardly any real money to live on. So Alfred had dropped out of college and come to Herkimer County to try to make a go of the country-squire business. Either he lacked the right touch, however, or he had the most extraordinary run of bad luck. He sold most of the land, but usually on unfavorable terms to some smarter speculator, who thereupon doubled or tripled his money.

Alfred also dabbled in business of various kinds in Gahato. For example, he went partners with a fellow who brought in a stable of riding horses for the summer-visitor trade. It turned out that the fellow really knew very little about horses and imported a troop of untrained crowbaits. One of his first customers got bucked off and broke her leg.

Then Alfred put up a bowling alley, the Iroquois Lanes, with all that expensive machinery for setting up the pins after each strike. He did all right with it and sold out at a handsome profit to Morrie Kaplan. But Morrie was to pay in instalments. He had not had it a month when it burned up; and Morrie, who was no better a businessman than Alfred, had let the insurance lapse. So Morrie was bankrupt, and Alfred was left holding the bag.

Then came the war. Full of patriotic fire, Alfred enlisted as a private. He promptly came down with tuberculosis in training camp. Since antibiotics had come in, they cured him; but that ended his military career. Maybe it was just as well, because Alfred was the kind of fellow who would shoot his own foot off at practice.

"Okay," said Alfred, "let me show you to your room. Mike and I just rattle around in this big old place."

When he had settled me in, he said: "Now what would you really like to do, Willy? Drink? Swim? Hike? Fish? Or just sit in the sun and talk?"

"What I'd really like would be to go for a row in one of those wonderful old guide boats. Remember when we used to frog around the swamps in them, scooping up muck so we could look at the little wigglers under the microscope?"

Alfred heaved a sigh. "I don't have any more of those

boats."

"What happened to them? Sell them?"

"No. Remember when I was in the Army? I rented the island to a family named Strong, and they succeeded in smashing every last boat. Either the women got into them in high heels and punched through the hulls, or their hell-raising kids ran them on rocks."

"You can't get boats like that any more, can you?" I said.

"Oh, there are still one or two old geezers who make them through the winter months. But each boat costs more than I could afford. Besides the outboard, I have only an old flatbottom. We can go out in that."

We spent a couple of very nice hours that afternoon, out in the flatbottom. It was one of those rare days, with the sky crystal-clear except for a few puffy little white cumulus clouds. The old rowboat tended to spin in circles instead of going where you wanted it ot. When, not having rowed for years, I began to get blisters, I gave my place to Alfred, whose hands were horny from hard work.

We caught up on each other's history. I said: "Say, remember the time I pushed you off the dock?" and he said: "Whatever happened to your uncle—the one who had a camp on Raquette Lake?"

And I said: "How come you never married my cousin Agnes? You and she were pretty thick..."

I told Alfred about my inglorious military career, my French fiancee, and my new job with the trust company. He looked sharply at me, saying:

"Willy, explain something to me."

"What?"

"When we took those tests in school, my IQ was every bit as high as yours."

"Yes, you always had more original ideas than I ever did. What about it?"

"Yet here you are, landing on your feet as usual. Me, I can't seem to do anything right. I just don't get the hang of it."

"Hang of what?"

"Of life."

"Maybe you should have gone into some line that didn't demand such practicality—so much realism and adaptability. Something more intellectual, like teaching or writing."

He shook his graying head. "I couldn't join the professorate, on account of I never finished college. I've tried writing stories, but nobody wants them. I've even written poems, but they tell me they're just bad imitations of Tennyson and Kipling, and nobody cares for that sort of thing nowadays."

"Have you tried a headshrinker?" (The term had not yet been whittled down to "Shrink.")

He shook his head. "I saw one in Utica, but I didn't like the guy. Besides, chasing down the line to Utica once or twice a week would have meant more time and expense than I could afford."

A little breeze sprang up, ruffling the glassy lake. "Oh, well," he said, "time we were getting back."

The island was quiet except for the chugging, from the boathouse, of the little Diesel that pumped our water and charged the batteries that gave us light and power. Over drinks before dinner, I asked:

"Now look, Al, you've kept me dangling long enough about that damned lamp. What *is* it? Why should I have nightmares while bringing the thing back from Europe?"

Alfred stared at his scotch. He mostly drank a cheap rye, I learned, but had laid in scotch for his old friend. At last he said:

"Can you remember those nightmares?"

"You bet I can! They scared the living Jesus out of me. Each time, I was standing in front of a kind of chair, or maybe a throne. Something was sitting on the throne, only I couldn't make out details. But, when it reached out toward me, its arms were—well, kind of boneless, like tentacles. And I couldn't yell or run or anything. Each time, I woke up just as the thing got its snaky fingers on me. Over and over."

"Ayup, it figures," he said. "That would be old Yuskejek."

"That would be *what*?"

"Yuskejek. Willy, are you up on the mythology of the lost continent of Atlantis?"

33

"Good lord, no! I've been too busy. As I remember, the occultists try to make out that there really was a sunken continent out in the Atlantic, while the scientists say that's tosh; that Plato really got his ideas from Crete or Egypt or some such place."

"Some favor Tartessos, near modern Cadiz," said Alfred. (This happened before those Greek professors came up with their theory about the eruption of the volcanic island of Thera, north of Crete.) "I don't suppose a hard-headed guy like you believes in anything supernatural, do you?"

"Me? Well, that depends, I believe what I see—at least most of the time, unless I have reason to suspect sleight-of-hand. I know that, just when you think you know it all and can see through any trick, that's when they'll bamboozle you. After all, I was in Gahato when that part-time medium, Miss—what was her name? Scott—Barbara Scott—had that trouble with a band of little bitty Indian spooks, who threw stones at people."

Alfred laughed. "Jeepers Cripus, I'd forgotten that! They never did explain it."

"So what about your goofy lamp?"

"Well, Ionides has good connections in esoteric circles, and he assures me that the lamp is a genuine relic of Atlantis."

"Excuse me if I reserve my opinion. So what's this Yuskejek? The demon-god of Atlantis?"

"Sort of."

"What kind of name is 'Yuskejek,' anyway? Eskimo?"

"Basque, I believe."

"Oh, well, I once read that the Devil had studied Basque for seven years and only learned two words. I can see it all— the sinister Atlantean high priest preparing to sacrifice the beautiful virgin princess of Ongabonga, so the devil-god can feast on her soul-substance—"

"Maybe so, maybe not. You've been reading too many pulps. Anyway, let's go eat before I get too drunk to cook."

"Doesn't Mike cook for you?"

"He's glad to, when I ask him; but then I have to eat the result. So most of the time I'd rather do it myself. Come along. *Mike!*" he roared. "Dinner in twenty minutes!"

By mutual unspoken consent, we stayed off Atlantis and its lamp during dinner. Instead, we incited Mike to tell us of the old lumbering days and of some of the odder lumberjacks he had known. There was one who swore he was being trailed, day and night, by a ghostly cougar, or puma, although there hadn't been one of those animals in the Adirondacks since the last century...

We let Mike wash the dishes while Alfred and I settled down in the living room with the lamp. Alfred said:

"I think our first step is to get this crud off. For that, suppose we try an ordinary washcloth and a little water?"

"It's your gimmick," I said, "but that sounds reasonable."

"We have to be oh-so-careful," he said, wetting his cloth and rubbing gently. "I wish we had a real archaeologist here."

"He'd probably denounce you for buying looted antiquities. Some day, they tell me, governments will clamp down on that sort of thing."

"Maybe so, but that time hasn't come yet. I hear our brave boys looted half the museums in Germany during the occupation. Ah, look here!"

Much of the mud had come off, exposing a white, toothlike projection. Alfred handed me the lamp. "What do you make of it?"

"I need a stronger light. Thanks. You know, Al, what this looks like? A barnacle."

"Let me see! Jeepers Cripus, you're right! that means the lamp must have been under water—"

"That doesn't prove anything about its—its provenience, I think they call it. It could have been a lamp of Greek or Roman times, dropped overboard anywhere in the Mediterranean."

"Oh," said Alfred, dampened. "Well, I wouldn't dare work on it longer this evening. We need full daylight." He put the thing away.

That night I had the same nightmare again. There was this throne, and this dim character—Yuskejek or whatever his name was—sitting on it. And then he stretched out those rubbery arms...

A knocking awoke me. It was Alfred. "Say, Willy, did you hear something?"

"No," I said. "I've been asleep. What is it?"

"I don't know. Sounds like someone—or something—tramping around on the porch."

"Mike?"

"He's been asleep, too. Better put on your bathrobe; it's cold out."

I knew how cold Adirondack nights could get, even in July. Muffled up, I followed Alfred downstairs. There we found Mike, in a long nightshirt of Victorian style, with a lantern, a flashlight the size of a small baseball bat, and an ax. Alfred disappeared and, after fumbling in one of the chests beneath the window seats, reappeared with a .22 rifle.

"Only gun on the place," he said. "I keep it hidden in case the goddam *natives* burgle me again."

We waited, breathing lightly and listening. Then came the sound: a bump—bump—bump—pause, and then bump—bump—bump—bump. It sounded as if someone were tramping on the old porch in heavy boots, the kind everyone used to wear in the woods before the summer people started running round in shorts and sneakers. (I still like such boots; at least, the deer flies can't bite through them.)

Perhaps the sound could have been made by a horse or a moose, although we haven't had moose in the region for nearly a century. Anyhow, I could not imagine what either beast would be doing, swimming to Ten Eyck Island.

The sound was not especially menacing in itself; but in that black night, on that lonely spot, it made my short hair rise. The eyes of Alfred and Mike looked twice their normal size in the lantern light. Alfred handed me the flashlight.

"You fling open the door with your free hand, Willy," he said, "and try to catch whatever-it-is in the beam. Then Mike and I will go after it."

We waited and waited, but the sound did not come again. At last we went out and toured the island with our lights. There was no moon, but the stars shone with that rare brilliance that you get only in clear weather in high country. We found nothing except a raccoon, scuttling up a tree and turning to peer at us through its black bandit's mask, with

36

eyes blazing in the flashlight beam.

"That's Robin Hood," said Alfred. "He's our personal garbage-disposal service. It sure wasn't him that made that racket. Well, we've been over every foot of the island without seeing anything, so I guess..."

There were no more phenomena that night. The next day, we cleaned the lamp some more. It turned out quite a handsome little article, hardly corroded at all. The metal was pale, with a faint ruddy or yellowish tinge, like some grades of white gold.

I also took a swim, more to show that I was not yet middle-aged than for pleasure. I never cared much for swimming in ice water. That is what you get in the Adirondack lakes, even in the hottest weather, when you go down more than a foot or so.

That night, I had another dream. The thing on the throne was in it. This time, however, instead of standing in front of it, I seemed to be off to one side, while Alfred stood in front of it. The two were conversing, but their speech was too muffled for me to make out the words.

At breakfast, while demolishing a huge stack of pancakes that Mike set before me, I asked Alfred about it.

"You're right," he said. "I did dream that I stood before His Tentacular Majesty."

"What happened?"

"Oh, it's Yuskejek, all right—unless we're both crazy. Maybe we are, but I'm assuming the contrary. Yuskejek says he'll make me a winner instead of a loser, only I have to offer him a sacrifice."

"Don't look at me that way!" I said. "I've got to get back to my job Monday—"

"Don't be silly, Willy! I'm not about to cut your throat, or Mike's either. I have few enough friends as it is. I explained to this spook that we have very serious laws against human sacrifice in this country."

"How did he take that?"

"He grumbled but allowed as how we had a right to our own laws and customs. So he'll be satisfied with an animal. It's got to be an animal of real size, though—no mouse or squirrel."

"What have you got on the island? I haven't seen anything bigger than chipmunks, except that 'coon."

"Jeepers, I wouldn't kill Robin Hood! He's a friend. No, I'll take the outboard down to Gahato and buy a pig or something. You'd better come along to help me wrassle the critter."

"Now I know we're nuts," I said. "Did you find out where the real Atlantis was?"

"Nope; didn't think to ask. Maybe we'll come to that later. Let's shove off right after lunch."

"Why not now?"

"I promised to help Mike on some work this morning."

The work was cutting up a dead poplar trunk into firewood lengths. With a powered chain saw, they could have done the job in minutes; but Mike distrusted all newfangled machinery. So they heaved and grunted on an old two-man crosscut saw, one on each end. I spelled Alfred until my blisters from rowing began to hurt.

The weather had other ideas about our afternoon's trip to Gahato. It is a safe rule that, if it rains anywhere in New York State in summer, it also rains in the Adirondacks. I have known it to rain some every day for eight weeks running.

We had had two fine days, and this one started out clear and balmy. By ten, it had clouded over. By eleven, thunder was rumbling. By twelve, it was raining pitchforks with the handles up, interrupting our woodcutting job on the poplar.

Looking out the windows, we could hardly see to the water's edge, save when a particularly lurid flash lit up the scene. The wind roared through the old pines and bent them until you thought that any minute they would be carried away. The thunder drowned half of what we said to one another. The rain sprayed against the windows, almost horizontally, like the blast from a fire hose.

"Yuskejek will have to wait, I guess," I said.

Alfred looked troubled. "He was kind of insistent. I told him there might be a hitch, and he mumbled something about 'Remember what happened last time!' "

The rain continued through the afternoon. The thunder and lightning and wind let up, so that it became just a steady

Adirondack downpour. Alfred said:

"You know, Willy, I think we really ought to take the boat to Gahato—"

"You *are* nuts," I said. "With this typhoon, your boat would fill before you got there."

"No; it's an unsinkable, with buoyancy tanks, and you can bail while I steer."

"Oh, for God's sake! If you're so determined on this silly business, why don't you take Mike?"

"He can't swim. Not that we're likely to have to, but I don't want to take the chance."

We argued a little more, in desultory fashion. Needless to say, neither of us really wanted to go out in that cataract. Alfred, though, had become obsessed with his Atlantean lamp and its attendant spirit. Perhaps the god had been evoked by our rubbing the lamp, like the jinn in the *Arabian Nights.*

Then Alfred grabbed my arm and pointed. "Look at that!"

I jumped as if stuck; the spooky atmosphere had begun to get to me. It was a relief to see that Alfred was pointing, not at the materialized form of Yuskejek, but at an enormous snapping turtle, plodding across the clearing in front of the house.

"There's our sacrifice!" cried Alfred. "Let's get him! *Mike!*"

We tore out the front door and went, slipping and sliding in the wet, down the bank to Lower Lake in pursuit of this turtle. We ringed the beast before it reached the lake. Looking almost like a small dinosaur, it dodged this way and that, showing quite a turn of speed. When we got close, it shot out its head and snapped its jaws. The *glop* of the snap sounded over the noise of the rain.

The turtle was snapping at Mike when Alfred caught it by the tail and hoisted it into the air. This took considerable strength, as it must have weighed at least twenty pounds. Alfred had to hold it almost at arm's length to keep from being bitten. The turtle kept darting that hooked beak in all directions, *glop, glop!* and flailing the air with its legs.

"Watch out!" I yelled. "That thing can castrate you if you're not careful!"

39

"Mike!" shouted Alfred. "Get the ax and the frog spear!"

We were all soaked. Alfred cried: "Hurry up! I can't hold this brute much longer!"

When the tools had been brought, Alfred said: "Now, Mike you get him to snap at the end of the spear and catch the barbs in his beak. Willy, stand by with the ax. When Mike hauls the head as far out of the shell as it'll go, chop it off!"

I had no desire to behead this turtle, which had never done anything to me. But I was a guest, and it was just possible that the lamp and its nightmares were kosher after all.

"Don't you have to do some ritual?" I asked.

"No; that comes later. Yuskejek explained it to me. Ah, got him!"

The turtle had snapped on the frog spear. By twisting the little trident, Mike hauled the head out of the shell. Then—

"Mother of God!" shouted Mike. "He's after biting off the shpear!"

It was true. The turtle had bitten through one of the tines of the trident—which may have been weakened by rust— and freed itself.

Instantly came a wild yell from Alfred. The turtle had fastened its beak on the flesh of his leg, just above the knee. In the excitement, Alfred had forgotten to hold the reptile out away from his body.

As the turtle bit into his leg through his trousers, Alfred danced about, tugging at the spiny tail. Then he and the turtle let go together. Alfred folded up on the ground, clutching his wounded leg, while the turtle scuttled down the slope and disappeared into the rain-beaten waters of Lower Lake.

Mike and I got Alfred back to Camp Ten Eyck, with a big red stain spreading down the front of his soaking pants leg. When we got the pants off, however, it did not look as if a trip to the doctor in Gahato would be needed. The turtle's jaws had broken the skin in four places, but the cuts were of the sort that a little disinfectant and some Band-aids would take care of.

With all the excitement, we more or less forgot about Yuskejek and his sacrifice. Since Alfred was limping, he let Mike get dinner. Afterwards we listened to the radio a bit, read a bit, talked a bit, and went to bed.

The rain was still drumming on the roof when, some hours later, Alfred woke me. "It's that stamping noise again," he said.

As we listened, the bump—bump—bump came again, louder than before. Again we jerked open the door and sprayed the light of the flash and the lantern about. All we saw was the curtain of rain.

When we closed the door, the sound came again, louder. Again we looked out in vain. When we closed the door again, the noise came louder yet: boom—boom—boom. The whole island seemed to shake.

"Hey!" said Alfred. "What the hell's happening? It feels like an earthquake."

"Never heard of an earthquake in this country," I said. "But—"

There came a terrific *boom*, like a near-miss of a lightning bolt. The house shook, and I could hear things falling off shelves.

Mike risked a quick look out and wailed: "Mr. Ten Eyck! The lake's coming up!"

The shaking had become so violent that we could hardly stand. We clutched at the house and at each other to keep our balance. It was like standing in a train going fast on a bad old roadbed. Alfred looked out.

"It *is!*" he shrieked. "Let's get the hell out of here!"

Out we rushed into the merciless rain, just as the water of Lower Lake came foaming up to the porch of Camp Ten Eyck. Actually, it was not the lake that was rising but the island that was sinking. I stumbled off the porch to find myself knee-deep in water. A wave knocked me over, but I somehow shed my bathrobe.

I am, luckily, a fairly good swimmer. Once I was afloat, I had no trouble in keeping on the surface. There were no small waves of the kind that slap you in the face, but big, long, slow surges, which bobbed me up and down.

There was, however, a vast amount of debris, which had floated off the island when it submerged. I kept bumping into crates, shingles, sticks of firewood, tree branches, and

41

other truck. I heard Mike Devlin calling.

"Where are you, Mike?" I yelled.

By shouting back and forth, we found each other, and I swam to him. Remembering that Mike could not swim, I wished that I had had more lifesaving practice. Fortunately, I found Mike clutching a log—part of that poplar they had been sawing up—for a life preserver. With some pushing on my part, we got to shore half an hour later. Mike was sobbing.

"Poor Mr. Ten Eyck!" he said. "Such a nice, kind gentleman, too. There must have been a curse on him."

Whether or not there was a curse on Alfred Ten Eyck, his corpse was recovered the next day. He was, as he had admitted, a loser.

The surges had done many thousands of dollars' damage to other people's docks, boats, and boathouses on Upper and Lower Lakes and the Channel. Because of the downpour, however, all the other camp owners had stayed in and so had not been hurt.

The State geologist said the earthquake was a geological impossibility. "I should have said, an anomaly," he corrected himself. "It was obviously possible, since it happened. We shall have to modify our theories to account for it."

I did not think it would do any good to tell him about Yuskejek. Besides, if the story got around, some camp owner might be screwy enough to sue me for damages to his boathouse. He would have a hell of a time proving anything; but who wants even the silliest lawsuit?

The Atlantean lamp is, I suppose, at the bottom of the lake, and I hope that nobody dredges it up. When Yuskejek threatens to sink an island if disappointed of his sacrifice, he is not fooling. Perhaps he can no longer sink a place so large as Atlantis. A little islet like Ten Eyck is more his present-day speed.

I do not, however, care to needle that testy and sinister old deity to find out just what he can do. One such demonstration is enough. After all, Atlantis is supposed to have been a *continent*. If he got mad enough...

Algy

When I parked behind my aunt's camp on Lake Algonquin, the first face I saw was Mike Devlin's wrinkled brown one. Mike said:

"Hello, Mr. Newbury! Sure, it's good to see you again. Have ye been hearin' about *it*?"

"About what?"

"The monster—the Lake Algonquin monster."

"Good lord, no! I've been in France, getting married. Darling, this is my old friend Mike Devlin. Mike, my wife Denise."

"Me, I am enchanted, Monsieur," said Denise, whose English was still a little uncertain.

"You got yourself a good man, Mrs. Newbury," said Mike. "I'm after knowing him since he was no bigger'n a chipmunk. Gimme them bags."

"I'll take this one," I said. "Now, what's this about a monster?"

Mike scratched his crisp gray curls. "They do be saying that, on dark nights, something comes up in the lake and shticks its head out to look around. But nobody's after getting a good look at it. There's newspaper fellies, and a whole gang of Scotchmen are watching for it, out on Indian Point."

"You mean we have a home-grown version of the Loch Ness monster?"

"I do that."

"How come the Scots came over here? I thought they had their own lake monster. Casing the competition, maybe?"

"It could be that, Mr. Newbury. They're members of some society that tracks down the shtories of sea serpents and all them things."

"Where's my aunt?"

"Mrs. Colton and Miss Colton are out in the rowboat,

43

looking for the monster. If they find it, I'm thinking they'll wish they hadn't."

Mike took us into the camp—a comfortable, three-story house of spruce logs, shaded by huge old pines—and showed us our room. He pointed at the north window. "If you look sharp, you can see the Scotchmen out there on the point."

I got out the binoculars that I had brought for wild-life watching. Near the end of Indian Point was a cluster of figures around some instruments. I handed the glasses to Denise.

The year before, Mike had been left without a job when my old schoolmate, Alfred Ten Eyck, had been drowned in the quake that sank Ten Eyck Island. I recommended Mike to my aunt, whose camp on Lake Algonquin was twenty miles from Gahato. Since my aunt was a widow with children grown and flown, she could not keep up the place without a handy man. Mike—an ex-lumberjack, of Canadian birth despite his brogue—filled the bill. My aunt had invited Denise and me to spend our honeymoon at the camp. Her daughter Linda was also vacating there.

Settled, we went down to the dock to look for my aunt and my cousin. Several boats were out on the lake, but too far away to recognize. We waved without result.

"Let's go call on the Scots," I said. "Are you up to a three-quarter-mile hike?"

"That is about one kilometer, no? *Allons!*"

The trail wanders along the shore from the camp to Indian Point. When I was a kid there in summer, I used to clear the brush out of this trail. It had been neglected, so we had to push through in places or climb over deadfalls. At one point, we passed a little shed, almost hidden among the spruces, standing between us and the water.

"What is that, Willy?" asked Denise.

"There used to be a little hot-air engine there, to pump water up to the attic tank in the camp. When I was a kid, I collected wood and fired up that engine. It was a marvelous little gadget—not efficient, but simple, and it always worked. Now they have an electric pump."

Near the end of Indian Point, the timber thins. There were

44

the Scots around their instruments. As we came closer, I saw four men in tweeds and a battery of cameras and telescopes. They looked around as we approached. I said: "Hello!"

Their first response was reserved. When I identified myself as Mrs. Colton's nephew and guest, however, they became friendly.

"My name's Kintyre," said one of them, thrusting out a hand. He was a big, powerful-looking, weather-beaten man with graying blond hair, a bushy mustache, a monocle screwed into one eye, and the baggiest tweeds of the lot. The only other genuine monocle-wearer I had ever known was a German colonel, captured in the last month of the war.

"And I'm Ian Selkirk," said another, with a beautiful red beard. (This was before anybody but artists wore them) He continued: "Lord Kintyre pays the siller on this safari, so he's the laird. We have to kneel before him and put our hands in his and swear fealty every morning."

Lord Kintyre guffawed and introduced the remaining two: Wallace Farg and James MacLachlan. Kintyre spoke British public-school English; Farg, such strong "braid Scots" that I could hardly understand him. The speech of the other two lay somewhere in between. At their invitation, we peered through the telescopes.

"What about this monster?" I said. "I've been out of the country."

They all started talking at once until Lord Kintyre shouted them down. He told me essentially what Mike Devlin had, adding:

"The bloody thing only comes up at night. Can't say I blame it, with all those damned motorboats buzzing around. Enough to scare any right-thinking monster. I've been trying to get your town fathers to forbid 'em, but no luck. The younger set dotes on 'em. So we may never get a good look at Algy."

"Algae?" I said, thinking he meant the seaweed.

"Surely. You Americans call our monster 'Nessie,' so why shouldn't we call the Lake Algonquin monster 'Algy'? But I'm afraid one of these damned stinkpots will run into the poor creature and injure it. I say, are you and your lovely bride

45

coming to the ball tomorrow at the Lodge?"

"Why, my lordship—I mean your lord—"

"Call me Alec," roared his lordship. "Everyone else does. Short for Alexander Mull, second Baron Kintyre. My old man sold so much scotch whiskey abroad, after you chaps got rid of the weird Prohibition law, that Baldwin figgered he had to do something for him. Now, laddie, how about the dance? I'm footing the bill."

"Sure," I said, "if Denise can put up with my two left feet."

Back at the camp, we met my aunt and her daughter coming back from their row. The sky was clouding over. Linda Colton was a tall, willowy blonde, highly nubile if you didn't mind her washed-out look. Nice girl, but not exactly brilliant. After the introductions, my Aunt Frances said:

"George Vreeland's coming over for dinner tonight. Briggs gave him the time off. Do you know him?"

"I've met him," I said. "He was a cousin of my late friend, Alfred Ten Eyck. I thought Vreeland had gone to California?"

"He's back and working as a desk clerk for Briggs," said Aunt Francis.

Joe Briggs was proprietor of the Algonquin Lodge, a couple of miles around the shore from the Colton camp, the other way from Indian Point. Linda Colton said:

"George says he's going to get one of those frogman's diving suits to go after the monster."

"I doubt if he'll get very far," I said. "The water's so full of vegetable matter, you can't see your hand before your face when you're more than a couple of feet down. When they put in the dam to raise the lake level, they didn't bother to clear all the timber out of the flooded land first."

I could have added that what I had heard about George Vreeland was not good. Alfred Ten Eyck claimed that, when Alfred was away, George had rented the camp on Ten Eyck Island from him. While there, he had sold most of Alfred's big collection of guns in the camp to various locals. He pocketed the money and skipped out before Alfred returned. I wouldn't call Vreeland wicked or vicious—just one of those old unreliables, unable to resist the least temptation.

Instead, I told about our meeting the Scots. Linda said.

46

"Didn't you think Ian Selkirk just the handsomest thing you ever saw?"

"I'm no judge of male beauty," I said. "He looked like a well-set-up-man, with the usual number of everything. I don't know that I'd go for that beard, but that's his business."

"He grew it in the war, when he was on a submarine," said Linda.

Denise said: "If you will excuse me, I looked at Mr. Selkirk, too. But yes, he is handsome. And he knows it— maybe a little too well, *hein?*"

My cousin Linda changed the subject.

At dinner time, George Vreeland came roaring over from the Lodge in an outboard. He did not remember me at first, since I had met the little man only casually, and that back in the thirties when we were mere striplings.

It was plain that Vreeland was sweet on Linda Colton, for all that she was inch taller than he. He talked in grandoise terms of his plans for diving in pursuit of Algy. I said:

"It seems to me that, if there is no monster, you're wasting your time. If there is a monster, and you disturb it, you'll probably end up in its stomach."

"Oh, Willy!" said Linda. "That's the way he always was, George, even as a boy. Whenever we'd get some beautiful, romantic, adventurous idea, he'd come out with some common-sense remark, like a cynical old gentleman, and shoot down our lovely plan in flames."

"Oh, I'll have something to protect myself with," said Vreeland. "A spear-gun or something—that is, if the goddamned Scotchmen don't harpoon the thing first."

"They told me they had no intention of hurting it," I said.

"Don't trust those treacherous Celts. Trying to stop our motorboats, ha! They'd ruin the whole summer-visitor season, just to get a strip of movie film of the monster."

Soon after dinner, my Aunt Frances called our attention to distant lightning. It flared lavender against the clouds, which hung low above the forested Adirondack ridges.

"George," she said, "since you came by water, you'd better be starting back, unless you want Linda to drive you to the Lodge and come back tomorrow for your boat."

47

"No, I'll be going," said Vreeland. "I have the night duty tonight."

After he had gone, we talked family matters for an hour or so. Then an outburst of yells brought us out on the porch.

The noise came from the direction of Indian Point. I could see little flickers of light from the Scottish observation post. Evidently the Scots thought they had seen something.

Between flashes of lightning, the lake was too dark to make out anything. "Wait till I get my glasses," I said.

The glasses proved of no help so long as the lake remained dark. Then a bright flash showed me something—a dark lump—out on the lake. It was perhaps a hundred yards away, although it is hard to estimate such distances.

I kept straining my vision, while the three women buzzed with questions. I picked up the thing in several more lightning flashes. It seemed to be moving across my field of vision. It also seemed to rise and fall. At least, it looked different in successive glimpses. I handed the glasses to my aunt, so that the women could have a look.

Then thunder roared and the rain came down. Soon we could see nothing at all. Even the hardy Scots gave up and went back to the Lodge.

When we awoke next morning, it was still raining. We came late to breakfast. When I started to apologize, Linda Colton said:

"Oh, that's all right, Willy. We know that honeymooners like any excuse to stay in bed."

I grinned sheepishly. Denise, who comes of a somewhat straitlaced French Protestant family, stared hard at her orange juice.

That morning, I studied economics for my trust company job. By noon, the rain had stopped and the skies had begun to clear. When the afternoon turned warm, I suggested a swim. Denise said:

"But, Willy, *mon cher*, if there is a monster there, what if it eats us?"

"Listen, darling, my friends and kinsmen and I have been swimming in these lakes for most of my thirty-two years, and Algy has never bitten any of us. If there is a monster here, it's had plenty of chances.

"Besides, I used to argue with the geology prof at M.I.T. about such monsters. He explained that such a critter needs an area big enough to support the food, such as fish, that it feeds on. Lake Algonquin couldn't have support anything much bigger than a snapping turtle. *Il n'y a rien a craindre.*"

"Well then, how about the alligators and crocodiles that you have in the Florida? They do not need a whole sea to live in," she said.

"In the first place," I explained, "they live in interconnected bodies of water, so they can move around from one to another. You need, not just enough area for one, but fifty or a hundred times that much, to support a breeding population. Otherwise, the species dies out. So don't look for a *Plesiosaurus* or a *Mosasaurus* in these lakes. Besides, no alligator—or any reptile of that size— could survive the winters here, where the lakes freeze over."

Denise looked doubtful, but she went swimming. I fear, however, that I do not have enough masochist in me really to enjoy that icy Adirondack water.

When we were dried and changed, we hiked out to Indian Point, partly to warm up and partly to see how the Scots were doing. Present were Farg, MacLachlan, and another man introduced to us as Professor Ballardie. Him I understood to be the big brain of the expedition. They were setting up a searchlight along with their other gear.

"There may be nought to it at all," said Ballardie, a cheerful little gray-haired man. "But this is the only way to find out."

"Aye," said Farg. "If we dinna try, we sanna learn."

I brought up the arguments of the M.I.T. professor of geology. As I expected, for every argument of mine they had ten counter-arguments. I thought it best to pipe down and listen; after all, I was not selling securities in their enterprise. When Ballardie ran out of breath, I asked:

"Where's Mr. Selkirk?"

"He's off this afternoon," said MacLachlan.

Farg added: "Forbye, he'll be makin' hissel braw for the ba'." At least that is what I think he said.

My aunt decided not to go to the "ba'." George Vreeland

49

came across the lake in his motorboat and carried Denise, Linda, and me back to the Lodge. Since this all happened before the era of youthful scruffiness in the sixties, both George and I had donned coat and tie. While we were trudging up the path from the Lodge dock, I could hear Lord Kintyre's booming laugh.

Inside, there was Joe Briggs, fat and red-faced, playing the genial host. I saw what Wallace Farg had meant by Selkirk's making himself "braw for the ba'." Selkirk had on a kilt, complete with sporran, dirk in the stocking, and one of those short little jackets with angular silver buttons—the works. Lord Kintyre was similarly clad, although the rest of the Scots made do with their weathered tweeds. We met Lady Kintyre, a mousey little gray-haired woman, and a couple more Scots whom I had not yet seen.

I was struggling through a rumba with Denise when Vreeland and Linda went by. Selkirk stepped up and tapped Vreeland on the arm. "May I cut in?" he said pleasantly.

I doubt if Vreeland even knew about the custom of cutting. While he gaped. Selkirk whisked Linda neatly out of his arms and danced off with her. When we passed them again, he had turned on the charm, whispering in Linda's ear and making her laugh.

After more dances and drinks, Lord Kintyre roared: "Now we'll show you a couple of Scottish dances. Ian, bring the young lady out here to demonstrate."

Selkirk led out Linda Colton. Having enough trouble with dances that I have practiced in advance, I was happy to steer Denise back to the bar. Since Lord Kintyre was paying, and since my Aunt Frances served nothing stronger than sherry, I was glad to wrap myself around some real booze.

There was George Vreeland, sopping up the sauce. His face was flushed, his speech was thick, and his manner was offensive. We avoided him.

We watched the Scottish dances from the sidelines. When it came time to go, Vreeland was not to be found. In the end, Selkirk drove us back to my aunt's camp in one of the expedition's cars. Linda had stars in her eyes when she bid us good-night.

About three in the morning came another outburst of

sound from Indian Point. From our windows, I saw nothing except the wavering beam of the searchlight. I was not fascinated enough by lake monsters to get up and go out, but the racket kept up for over an hour. We never did get back to sleep, although I would not say that the time till morning was wasted.

The Scots later said that they had seen Algy again and that he hung around so long that they launched a boat to get a closer look at him. Then, however, he dived.

Sunday was one of those rare fine days. Denise and I took a hike in the morning and in the afternoon went out on the lake. We had been rowing for maybe half an hour when Denise said:

"There is a canoe, Willy, which comes from your aunt's dock. I think I see the red beard of the Mr. Selkirk."

Sure enough, there came Ian Selkirk and Linda Colton out in one of Joe Briggs's rentable canoes. I waved, but they must have been so absorbed in each other that they never saw us.

When they got closer, I saw that they were in bathing suits. This is not a bad idea, if you want to paddle a canoe without previous experience. Linda, in the stern, was paddling and calling out instructions to Selkirk in the bow.

I rested on my oars, watching. After a while, they stopped paddling. I noticed something odd about their position. They had slid off their thwarts and were sitting on the bottom, so only their heads and shoulders showed. They were inching closer to each other, all the while talking and laughing at a great rate.

Denise said: "I think they are about to try *un petit peu de l'amour.*"

"It's an idea," I said, "if you remember to keep the weight well down in the boat." I wondered if I ought to try to save my cousin's virtue. This was before the sexual revolution, when many families still took their girls' virtue seriously. But then, I did not even know whether Linda had any virtue to save.

"Well," said Denise, misreading the look on my face, "don't you get any such ideas, my old. Me, I could not enjoy

51

it in a boat for fear of tipping over."

The two were now so close together that Selkirk was embracing Linda. I do not know what would have happened if Algy had not interfered.

Out of the water, on the lakeward side of the canoe and not ten feet from that craft, a reptilian head, as big as that of a horse, arose on a long, thick neck. The head had staring white eyeballs and long white fangs. It rose six feet out of the water and glared down upon the occupants of the canoe.

It took several seconds for the canoeists to realize that they were under observation. Then Linda shrieked.

Ian Selkirk looked around, jumped up, dove overboard, and struck out for shore at an Olympic speed. He left the rocking canoe and Linda behind.

"The dastard!" I said. "I'm going closer."

"Willy!" cried Denise. "It will devour us!"

"No it won't. Take a second look. It's just some sort of amusement-park dragon."

Disregarding Denise's plaints, I rowed towards the apparition. Algy proved a gaudily-painted structure of sponge rubber. I poked it with an oar to make sure and then rowed to the canoe.

Linda was in hysterics, but she calmed down when she saw me. Soon she was paddling the canoe back towards our dock. We followed in the rowboat.

Ashore, we met Mike Devlin. He said: "Mr. Newbury, what's all this about the monster? The young Scotchman is after asking—"

Then the two figures appeared running on the trail from Indian Point. First came George Vreeland with a bloody nose. After him pounded Ian Selkirk, in swimming trunks and sneakers, howling imprecations in some tongue I did not recognize. It may have been very braid Scots, or it may have been Gaelic. They vanished along the road to the Lodge.

"It's the pump shed," said Mike. "The Scotchman was asking me if there was any such place. I told him yes, and off he went like the banshee was after him."

"Let's go see," I said.

We had to push through heavy brush and second growth to get to the pump shed, for nobody had gone there in years.

A canoe was moored at the edge of the water below the shed.

Inside the shed, dust and drifted pine needles lay thick. The old hot-air engine and pump were covered with rust. But something new had been added.

"Mother of God, look at that!" said Mike. "So that's how the young felly had us fooled!"

On the inside wall of the shed were mounted a pair of windlasses. Each consisted of a drum, around which a number of turns of clothesline had been wrapped, and a crank handle for turning the drum. The ropes led out through holes in the wall. They extended to the water's edge and disappeared into the lake on divergent paths.

It was clear what Vreeland had done. He had laid a couple of stanchions—concrete blocks or the like—on the lake botton, with pulleys or rings stapled to them. The ropes, attached to Algy, led through these stanchions and back to the shed. By turning the cranks, one could make Algy, who was buoyant, rise or sink or, within limits, move horizontally along the surface.

Mike explained: "I heard the racket, and I seen the monster out in the water and the young Scotchman swimming for shore like the Devil was ahint of him. When he climbed out and got his breath, he says: 'It's after me!'

" 'Look, man' I says. 'Anybody can see 'tis not a real monster at all, with the boats paddling all around it, and it shtanding shtill in the water.'

"So he looks. 'By God, you're right!' he says. Now, this is a smart young Scotchman, and it don't take him ten seconds to figure out what's happened. 'Quick!' he says. 'Is there any sort of hut or cabin along the shore near here?' So I tell him about the old pump house. 'I'll show you,' I says. 'No, thanks,' he says. 'Just tell me where it is. I don't want any witnesses.' And off he goes. He must have caught Mr. Vreeland just coming out."

Denise went into a fit of giggles until I had to pound her back. "*Comme c'est rigolo donc!*"

Every boat on Lake Algonquin soon put out for a look at the monster. Selkirk did not succeed in annihilating Vreeland. The latter ducked into the woods and, knowing the terrain, soon lost his pursuer. Hours later, Selkirk, scratched and mosquito-bitten, staggered back to the Lodge. I suppose he felt his loss of face too keenly to show himself, for none of us saw him again.

My cousin Linda accepted neither of these dubious suitors. A year later, she married a rising-young-businessman type.

Next morning I got a telephone call. "Mr. Wilson Newbury, please...Oh, is that you, Willy? Alec Kintyre here. I say, Willy, could you do me a favor? My lads have packed up all our gear to leave, but I want to go over the ground once more with someone who knows it. Could you..."

Half an hour later, I was showing Lord Kintyre the shed in which Vreeland had set up his control mechanism.

"You know," said Lord Kintyre, "it was all Briggs's doing."

"How so?"

"When Vreeland came in this morning, he and Briggs got into a blazing quarrel, and Vreeland blew the gaff. Seems Briggs hired him last spring to set up this hoax, to draw more summer trade. It did, too.

"They might have got away with it, since Vreeland was supposed to surface the bloody monster only at night. He'd paddle over in that canoe so the noise of his motorboat wouldn't give him away. Everybody knew he was a damned stinkpot fanatic, so nobody suspected him of being a canoeist.

"Ian Selkirk spoilt the scheme. Vreeland was so eager to do Ian one in the eye that he brought up Algy in broad daylight. Then it took only a good second look to show it was a fake. The lads on the point realized that when they got their telescopes on it.

"Rum thing about Ian. He's not really a coward—he was in submarines with me during the war—but just this once he panicked. He didn't even wait to help with the packing but left last night. Trouble with Ian is, all he thinks of is dipping his wick. Now could we go out for a look at Algy?"

I took Lord Kintyre out in the Colton rowboat. We circled Algy, who was still sitting in the water as he had been left.

Algy consisted of head, six feet of neck, and an egg-shaped

body without limbs, save for a kind of rudder aft. This fin made the monster face forward when towed through the water, so that Vreeland could parade the thing back and forth, as far as his rope tackle allowed.

The last Scots had left Indian Point with their apparatus. We moved up close to Algy, and Lord Kintyre took out a pocket knife. "I'll cut a little piece off as a souvenir, if you don't mind," he said.

He got his piece of sponge rubber, and we started back. Then I said: "Hey, Alec! Look around!"

Something was happening to Algy. He was moving back and forth by jerks, stirring the water to foam. The jerks became wider and more violent. Have you ever seen a dog shake a squirrel or similar small prey to death? Algy was moving as if he had been seized from below and was being thus shaken. The boat rocked in the waves. Lord Kintyre's monocle fell out and dangled on its string. Algy was drawn down until he almost disappeared.

Then the water quieted. Algy bobbed up again—but in pieces. We sat quietly, afraid (at least I was) to move or speak, lest whatever had mangled Algy come for us.

When nothing more happened, I took a few cautious strokes towards the scene of the disturbance, backing water so that I could pull for shore in a hurry. I fished out a piece of blue-green sponge rubber, the size of my foot. I think it came from Algy's neck.

Lord Kintyre replaced his eyeglass and sighed. "Just my damned luck," he said, "to be without camera or other equipment."

"Are you going to call your boys back, to start watching again?"

"No. Some have already left for home, and the rest are all packed up. We've spend enough money and got enough material for our report to the Society. Someone else will have to chase the real Algy."

In the years since then, I have heard of no further mysterious phenomena on Lake Algonquin. But, although I have been back there several times, I have always found some excuse for not going swimming.

55

The
Menhir

Coming down the stairs after breakfast, I passed the beautiful Countess. She said: "*Bonjour*, Monsieur Newbury. Did you sleep well?"

"*Parfaitement, merci*," I said.

"Did you hear any sounds in the night?

"No, Madame. Should I have?"

She shrugged. "I just asked myself. This old château is full of strange knocks and creaks. Some of our guests are disturbed, although I am sure that the causes are natural."

"I shall watch for such phenomena, Madame. They will not intimidate me, I assure you, for I am not without experience in such matters."

"Good. Where did you and the little Denise go yesterday? You returned late."

"We walked around the city wall at Vannes and then took the boat ride around the Golfe du Morbihan."

"That is much for one day."

"It is the truth, Madame, but our time is limited. That is without doubt why we slept ourselves so profoundly."

"Where are you going today?" she asked. The Comtesse de la Carrière was a strikingly handsome woman in her early thirties. She forwent makeup, not needing it.

"We thought we should go to Hennebont. One says that there is a fine medieval gate and rampart."

The Comtesse made a slight grimace. "Certainly! But we, our memories of it are not of the most agreeable."

"*Ainsi donc?*"

"We were there, my sister and I, at the time of the massacre."

"Oh? I read of that in the guide."

"It is not exaggerated. Before the Germans left, on the seventh of August, 1944, they went to the houses, knocked on the doors, and shot the people as they came out. There were also many townspeople in the shelters, to avoid the

American bombardment; but the Germans went there, too, and shot them. Angèle—she was a little girl then, you know—would have been killed, but the young German lieutenant, who commanded the platoon that was shooting the others, whispered to her to run. Thus she survived. Have you made the tour of the megaliths?"

"We saw the *alignements* of Carnac the day before yesterday. We thought that this afternoon, if we get back in good time, we might continue on to Locmariaquer to see the big menhir and the dolmen."

"Well, if you do not have the time to go so far, you can see our private menhir, on a piece of our land one kilometer away on the Quiberon road. This Menhir of Locmelon is broken like that at Locmariaquer. It was complete until the war, when an explosion knocked it over. We say the Germans blew it up to show their Aryan superiority; they say it was a bomb from an American airplane, hunting for Lorient or St. Nazaire. The year past, the members of an English cult came here to march around the remains in long robes, carrying candles. They said they were Druids."

"If I understand my archaeology, these huge stones were erected long before the Celts and their Druid priests arrived."

"You have reason, Monsieur; but you know how people love to believe fairytales. Anyway, *bonne chance.*"

I have traveled enough not to be impressed by titles—especially French titles, since in that country any citizen may call himself by any title he pleases. If Jacques Leblanc wants to call himself the Grand Khan of Tatary, he may do so.

Still, it was nice to get on the good side of our titled landlord and landlady at the Château Kerzeriolet. Denise and I had seen only glimpses of them during the first few days of our stay. I suspect that a gaffe we pulled on our first day there had something to do with this.

We had arrived from Normandy with a suitcase full of dirty clothes. The first full day we spent washing up, and we had hung the garments on an elastic laundry cord across an open window. We did not realize that this festoon was plainly visible from the courtyard, until Jean-Pierre Tanguy, the professional *hôtelier* who handled the paying guests, telephoned in great embarrassment to ask us to take them down. We were even more embarrassed than the manager.

On the fourth day, however, we ran into the Comte and Comtesse de la Carriere long enough to exchange amenities. when they found that Denise was French and that I spoke the language, they thawed.

Denise had saved me from a couple of other blunders. On the first morning, for instance, I was all set to go down to breakfast, but she insisted that we stay in our room and wait for our coffee and rolls to be brought up. That was how it was done here, and we should merely gum up the works by trying to change the routine. To me, an eggless French breakfast has never seemed quite the real thing; but with all this talk of cholesterol, perhaps the French had the right idea all along.

The castellated wall at Hennebont can be seen in minutes. We could view only the outside of the great medieval gate, the Porte Broerec'h, because workmen were still repairing war damage. So we got back early and went on to Locmariaquer.

There we examined the Fairy Stone, the biggest menhir of all. When new, it must have stood sixty feet tall and have weighed over 350 tons. Archaeologists think it fell in ancient times, perhaps while being erected. The technology of those people was not quite up to handling so huge a piece.

Even so, I have always been impressed by the feats of those Neolithic peasants, in trimming, moving, and up-ending huge monumental stones, as at Stonehenge and Carnac. I was not, however, so awed as to think they had called in little green men from Venus to help them.

Anyway, the stone has been lying down as far back as recorded history goes. It had broken into five pieces, of which four still lie where they fell. We also examined the big dolmen called the Merchant's Table nearby. It was once a grave mound, with slabs of stone on the sides and top; but treasure-hunters and erosion had removed the dirt, leaving the slabs standing. A tunnel runs from beneath the dolmen under the Fairy Stone.

We had meant to take pictures of each other sitting on the

remains of the Fairy Stone, but the fickle weather was overcast and hazy, with an occasional drizzle. I took a few snaps without hope of getting first-class photographs. Then, on the way back to Kerzeriolet, the sky cleared just as we approached the field where, the Comtesse said, their private Menhir of Locmelon had stood.

Following her directions, we parked and hiked across the rolling, grassy countryside until we found the stone. It was not in the same class with the Fairy Stone, having been a mere ten or twelve feet tall. It, too, had been broken, into three large and several small pieces.

"It wouldn't be much of a job to glue it back together," I said.

"*Mon petit constructeur!*" said Denise. "Willy, you should have stayed with your engineering instead of becoming a banker. But you know, darling, in all these old countries, they have so many relics that it is all the governments can do to patch them up as fast as they fall apart. Besides, there would be a lot of rules by some Department of Archaeology to comply with. You would have to fill out forms in quadruplicate and file applications."

"God deliver me from European red tape!" I said. "Our own kind is bad enough. Anyway, I wasn't thinking of doing the job myself." I focused my camera on one of the fragments. "Looks as if this part had been carved into a face. Sinister-looking old coot, isn't he?"

"Have a care, my old. The spirit of the old coot might be offended."

"After some of the things I've seen, he doesn't scare me at all."

"Be careful anyway. Remember our poor children back home!"

Back at the château, we ran into the Comtesse in the lower hall. I told her of seeing the Menhir of Locmelon.

"He wants to put it back together, Madame," said Denise. "He is one of those who, on seeing anything broken, at once wishes to repair it."

"Such a man must be useful around the house," said the Comtesse. "That my Henri had more of that knack! He cannot drive a nail—ah, there you are, Henri. You know the Monsieur and Madame Newbury, is it not?"

The Comte was a slender, balding man of about my age—that is, a little past forty. If Hollywood had been looking for an actor and an actress to play a refined, ultra-gracious couple from the old European aristocracy, they could hardly have chosen better than these two.

The Comte bowed lightly and shook my hand. *"Enchanté de toute manière, mes amis.* Will you do me the honor to take an *apéritif* with us before dinner?"

We went into the Carrières' private parlor and sipped vermouth. The Comtesse's younger sister, Angèle de Kervadec, and another man joined us. Angèle looked like her sister but was even more beautiful. When she got older and put on a little weight, she would be a virtual double of Thérése, Comtesse de la Carrière.

Her companion was a burly fellow of my generation, with a close-cut black beard showing its first few threads of gray. He was introduced as Max Burgdorf, of Zürich. Although a German Swiss, his French had only the slightest trace of German accent. He said little, but when he did speak, it was in a stiff, abrupt manner. As he sat on the arm of Angèle's chair, she leaned against him. There was evidently some understanding between them.

The Comtesse brought up the matter of reassembling the Menhir of Locmelon. The Comte said: "Ah, Monsieur, that would cost money. Money is a problem here, with the franc in its present deplorable condition. One struggles to hold this place by every means. With taxes and inflation what they are, one must make every economy. Perhaps when De Gaulle comes to power...But meanwhile, one must be realistic. Perhaps you, as a man of finance, can advise us."

"I am desolated that I do not know enough about French laws and financial institutions," I said. "Otherwise I should be happy to do so."

The Comte's face fell just a trifle, although he was too well-bred to say anything. Having been through this sort of thing before, I knew that we were being cultivated not for our charm but for some sure-fire financial tips. I continued:

"But I do not think the reerection of the menhir would be

very costly. Monsieur Lebraz's garage in Vannes has a fine new wrecking truck with a crane in the back."

"The way those idiots drive," said the Comte, "Lebraz has plenty of business." To his wife he said: "Perhaps we should be in the garage business, *hein?* in lieu of trying to maintain this relic."

When the dinner bell chimed, Denise and I rose. The Comtesse said: "Some night soon, we shall have one of Angèle's seances. You must attend."

After we had gone to bed, I was jerked awake by the sound of footsteps in the hall. Not that there was anything unusual in that; there were a dozen other paying guests in the château. These footsteps, however, continued back and forth, back and forth. The sound brought Denise up, too.

"Now what?" I said. "Monsieur Burgdorf working up courage to visit the fair Angèle?"

"*Tais toi!*" she said, punching me in the ribs. "Nothing so vulgar here. These people are too careful of their blue blood, and you are just a dirty middle-aged man."

The footsteps stopped, and three raps sounded against our door. I sat up on the side of the bed. As a native of the crime-ridden United States, I did not rush to open the door. Instead, I called: "Who is there?"

For answer, the three raps sounded again.

"I think you can open," said Denise. "This French countryside is very law-abiding."

"Just a minute," I said. I got the family blackjack out of our luggage, stepped to the door, shot back the bolt, and jerked the door open. No one was there.

It took us over an hour to get to sleep after that. In any case, we heard no more odd noises.

Next day we left early, drove the Peugeot to Vannes, and continued on around the shores of the Golfe du Morbihan. This brought us out on the Rhuys Peninsula. Here, near Sarzeau and overlooking the Golfe, the guidebook said there was a ruined medieval castle.

We found the Château Morzon, a scruffy-looking pile rising amid the vinyards, and aroused the keeper. This was

61

a Monsieur Le Goff, a stocky, weather-beaten old gent with a huge gray mustache. When we had paid our twenty francs, he showed us around, explaining:

"...in that tower, Monsieur and Madame, one says that the wife of the Duc Jean was imprisoned. And on the wall east of the tower, where we are now going to mount, one says that, on moonlit nights, a ghost in armor walks. Me, I am not superstitious, but those legends are good for the tourism, eh? Some say it is the ghost of the Duc Alain Barbe-Torte; others, the ghost of our great Breton hero, Bertrand du Guesclin—*prenez garde!*"

We were climbing the stair that led up to the surviving curtain wall. I was on the outer side, abreast of the keeper, while Denise followed. At one step, the outermost stone of the tread gave way as I put my weight upon it. It skittered off the stair, leaving me with one foot on the staircase and the other over empty air.

Monsieur Le Goff caught the sleeve of my coat. Denise shrieked "Willy!" and seized the part of my garments nearest to her, which happened to be the seat of my pants. Between their pull and a desperate windmilling of my own arms, I barely avoided a thirty-foot fall to the grass-grown courtyard below. The errant stone hit with a crash.

"*Ah, quel malheur!*" cried the keeper. "But by the grace of the good God, Monsieur, you are still with us. I must have that stone cemented back into place. You know how it is. With an old ruin like this, it crumbles faster than one can repair it. Are you all right now?"

We continued our tour. At the end, I pressed upon Monsieur Le Goff a whole fistful that crummy paper the French then used for money. I figured it was the least I could do. On the way home, Denise said:

"I warned you about making fun of the sinister old coot. I am not altogether joking."

Back at the château, Denise took a nap while I prowled the grounds with my camera, taking advantage of one of our few periods of bright sunshine. I came upon the Comte, in old pants and rolled-up shirt sleeves, working on the flower gardens with trowel, watering pot, and insecticide spray. We passed the time of day, and I told of my visit to the Château Morzon.

"Have you a family ghost?" I asked, "as the keeper at Morzon said they have there, if one believes the stories?"

"No; not family, anyway. Why do you ask?"

I told about the knocks during the previous night. The Comte gave the ghost of a smile.

"There is no old tradition of a specter here," he said. "But then, this house is not really old. It is not medieval or even Renaissance. It is Napoleonic, as you have doubtless inferred. It was built around 1805, to replace the original castle, destroyed in the Revolution of 1789.

"On the other hand, I will confess that, since the last war, there have been certain—ah—psychic manifestations. My wife tells me that you know something of these matters."

"I have had some strange experiences, yes."

"Then, are you and the charming Madame Newbury free tonight?"

"Yes, Monsieur le Comte."

"*Bien,* would you do us the honor of attending our little séance? Perhaps you can explain certain things. We begin at twenty-one hours."

"Thank you; we shall be enchanted. But how do you proceed? With a planchette, or tipping a table, or trance mediumship?"

"Angèle is our psychic. She does automatic writing."

"Oh? That will be very interesting. Tell me, does she have an understanding with that man—Monsieur—ah—Burgdorf?"

"Yes, one might say so. Their formal engagement will be announced when Max has his French citizenship."

"He intends to become French?"

"If he wishes to attach himself to my family, he must. You see, Monsieur—how shall I explain? Madame Newbury and you, have you children?"

"Three. They are in America, with my parents."

"Ah, how fortunate you are! Thérèse and I, although we have been married for twelve years, have none. It is not for lack of desire, but the physicians tell us we never shall. I have no close relatives—or rather, those I had were killed in

63

the war. So, when I die, the title will become extinct, unless I make provision for passing it on."

"Can you do that legally?"

"Yes, if one is willing to go through enough administrative routine. Of course," he smiled, "I realize that you Americans are all staunch republicans, to whom any titles are medieval nonsense. But still, a title is a nice thing to have. Aside from its sentimental appeal, it lends a certain solidarity to the family. It is even good for business.

"So, I have determined to bequeath this title to Angèle's husband, when she has one, to be passed on to their heirs. But naturally, the husband must be French. Then Max, wishing to marry Angèle, must become French."

The seance assembled at nine. We—the Comte and Comtesse, Angèle, Max Burgdorf, Denise and I, and a younger man whom we had not met before—sat in a circle around a big table. The lights were turned down. Angèle held a pencil and a pad on a clip board.

The young man was introduced as Frédéric Dion, a family friend from Vannes. He was a blond youth of about Angèle's age, who watched Angèle with an intentness that did not seem to me called for.

After a while, Angèle leaned forward and began to write. She stared straight ahead without looking at the paper. When she stopped. the Comte got up and peered over her shoulder.

"The Old French again?" murmured the Comtesse.

"No; this time it is Breton. Do you read it, Frédéric?"

Dion shook his head. "They had not yet introduced classes in Breton when I attended school."

The Comtesse said: "Jean-Pierre would know. I will go for him."

While she was out, the Comte said to me: "Monsieur Tanguy is a fanatical Breton nationalist. He does not altogether approve of us, because our family in this area goes back only to the fifteenth century. Therefore we are, in his view, foreigners."

The Comtesse returned with the manager. Tanguy looked at Angèle's scribble, shook his head, and frowned. "This is a more archaic dialect than I am accustomed to. But let me

64

see—I think it says: 'Restore my house, if you know what is good for you. Restore my house. Restore my house.' Then it trails off into an illegible scrawl."

"My faith!" said the Comte. "Does he expect me to tear down this *baraque* and rebuild the original castle?"

"Even if we could afford it," added the Comtesse, "we do not have any accurate plan. There is nothing in existence to tell how it looked, save that engraving by Fragonard."

"Has this—ah—personality a name?" I asked.

"Sometimes he calls himself Ogmas; sometimes, Blaise," said the Comte.

"Could they be two separate entities?"

He shrugged. "Who knows? But he insists that both names belong to the same being."

"Perhaps one is a given name and the other a surname," said Dion.

"But," I said, "what species does this entity belong to? Is it the ghost of a mortal man, or is it some pagan godlet, left over from the Age of Bronze?"

"We have asked him," said the Comtesse, "but he gives only ambiguities or nonsense in response. Such inquiries seem to enrage him."

The Comte added: "The *curé* insists that it is a demon from Hell, and that we are in danger of damnation for having to do with it." He smiled indulgently. "The good Father Paré is, I fear, a little behind the times. He has never reconciled himself to the changes that are taking place in the Church."

We waited a while, but Angèle produced no more spirit writing.

That night, however, there were more ghostly footsteps in the halls and knockings on doors. In the morning, four of the Comte's paying guests left ahead of schedule. They had been kept awake all night, they said, and at their age they needed their sleep. Although they did not admit to being frightened, I have no doubt that they were.

The Carrières looked worried. The Comte said to me: "We are, as you would say, skating on the thin ice, financially speaking. A bad season could ruin us."

We spent most of that day in Auray, taking pictures of old

houses and streets. We saw the monument to the Comte de Chambord, the royalist pretender of the 1870s, and the house where Benjamin Franklin stayed in 1778. In the evening, we had another séance. The same group sat around the table.

When Angèle began to write, she first produced a medieval Breton scrawl that not even Jean-Pierre Tanguy could read. Then the writing broke into clear French. "*Vengeance!*" it said. "*Vengeance! Vengeance!*"

"Vengeance on whom?" asked the Comte to the empty air.

"On him who destroyed my house," said Angèle's writing.

"My dear spirit," said the Comte, "the castle was destroyed in 1795, at the time of the disaster of Quiberon. All those who took part in that vandalism are long dead. So how could one take vengeance on them?"

"Not this house. My house. My house of stone. My great stone."

"Stone?" said the Comtesse. "Do you by chance mean the Menhir of Locmelon?"

"Yes. Yes. Restore my house. Take vengeance on those who overthrew it. Vengeance! Vengeance!"

The Comte ran puzzled eyes around the circle, lingering for a fraction of a second on me and on Max Burgdorf. "Who, then, destroyed your stone?"

"Barbarians. Barbarians did it."

"Barbarians? My good phantom, the last barbarians we had here were the Vikings, chased out by Alain Barbe-Torte in the year 939."

"Not true. Barbarians here, now."

"Hm," said the Comte. "He must mean the destruction of the menhir in the late war. We French say the Germans did it, while the Germans say the Americans did it. We have no Germans here. Monsieur Newbury, were you by chance in the American Air Force?"

"No, Monsieur, I was not. I was in the army, but I had a desk job and never got near Brittany."

"You see, Monsieur revenant," said the Comte to the air, "nobody here could have had anything to do with the unfortunate overthrow of your megalith."

"Not so. Two barbarians here. One in army that did it. Vengeance on him. Vengeance coming. You shall see..."

Angèle broke into a frenzy of scribbling. The tension in the darkened room rose to a silent scream. The Comte said:

"But, my dear ghost, I have explained—"

"No," wrote Angèle. "One barbarian army missed my house; one hit it. I know which is which."

"Excuse me one moment," said Max Burgdorf. He got up and quietly left the room.

"Well, then," said the Comte, "which *is* which?"

The spirit writing went off into a sputter of illegible Dark Age Breton. Then the top sheet of Angèle's pad was used up. The Comte reached over her shoulder and tore off the sheet. Angèle began writing again.

"You have wrong," wrote Angèle. "Man with beard was in barbarian army. He shall die. Other barbarian warned. Warned yesterday. At Morzon. He shall help with [illegible]."

"But this—" began the Comte. He broke off, turned his head, and listened. There were footsteps outside in the hall. Saying "Pardon me one moment, please," the Comte rose, went to the door, and opened it. The rest of us, except Angèle, got up and followed him.

Max Burgdorf, suitcase in hand, was opening the huge, carved front door of the château. The Comte said sharply:

"Max! What are you doing? Where are you going so suddenly?"

"That is my affair," said Burgdorf.

"Oh, no, it is not! Are you leaving us, then?"

"I am."

"But why? Where are you going? What of Angèle?"

The Comte caught Burgdorf's arm just as the man was going out the door and turned him around. Burgdorf shook off the detaining hand.

"I warn you, do not try to stop me!" he said.

The Comte persisted: "Max! As a man of honor, I demand an explanation—"

"You will learn in due course," snapped Burgdorf over his shoulder, striding out towards his car.

Just then another car drove into the courtyard, and four

men piled out. Three wore the khaki of the local police and carried guns of various kinds. The fourth, in civilian clothes, shouted: "*Halte-là*, Monsieur von Zeitz!"

Burgdorf wheeled, drawing a revolver. Before he could shoot, a rifle cracked. The revolver spun away, and Burgdorf, dropping his suitcase, grasped his arm with a yelp of pain.

"Helmuth von Zeitz, alias Max Burgdorf," said the man in civilian clothes, "I arrest you in the name of the Republic!"

Burgdorf—or von Zeitz—offered no more resistance. The Comte said: "Monsieur the Commissionnaire, I pray you, have the goodness to explain!"

"Monsieur le Comte," said the official, "this man is wanted for war crimes. He was the officer commanding the S.S. detachment, assigned to the massacre of Hennebont. I cannot imagine why the fool returned to the scene of his crime, but that is the fact. His application for citizenship betrayed him, when the naturalization bureau investigated it."

Angèle, who had quietly appeared in the doorway, gave a shriek. "It is him! I know him now, in spite of the beard! He is the one who saved my life!"

"While depriving hundreds of our compatriots of theirs," said the Comte. In the light of the lamps flanking the entrance, the Comte looked suddenly older and grim.

Burgdorf-von Zeitz cried out: "I meant to make it up to you, Angèle! I did not mean to do it! I was only a junior officer, following orders! When you ran away, a little twelve-year-old girl, I told myself, I must come back some day and—" Tears on his cheeks shone in the lamplight.

"Come along, Monsieur," said the Commissionaire. "We must get you to the hospital, to repair that broken arm. It would not do to have you sneeze into the basket with your arm in a sling."

They hustled the suspect into the car and roared off. Angèle burst into tears. Frédéric Dion put his arms around her.

When the police car had gone, we straggled back into the château. Angèle disappeared with her sister. I asked the Comte:

68

"What will they do to him?"

The Comte looked at me with a slight smile and brought the edge of his palm sharply against his neck. The French are not a sentimental folk.

For the next half-hour, the Comte and Tanguy were busy reassuring the other guests, who had popped out of their rooms at the shot. At last we gathered again in the parlor— the Comte, Tanguy, Dion, Denise, and I. The Comte poured brandy all around. He said:

"Let us thank *le bon Dieu* that it was not worse and that it is now over."

"Oh," said Denise, "are you sure that it is, Monsieur le Comte? Your Blaise de Ogmas, or whatever he calls himself, still demands the restoration of his menhir. Otherwise...."

"I understand," said the Comte. "This calls for thought."

"Henri," said Frédéric Dion, "you are aware that Angèle and I are old friends, and that before this self-styled Swiss appeared, she was inclined to me. Have I your permission to pay my addresses to her again?"

"*Certainement*—but wait an instant. The specter wishes his menhir restored, or he will ruin us by driving away our guests with knocks and rattles. So, if you share equally with me the cost of reërecting the megalith, you may pay court to Angèle with my blessing. As for Monsieur Newbury, I am sure that you, Monsieur, will, for the sake of the ancient friendship between our countries, donate to the project your engineering skill. Are we in accord? *Bien.*"

The Comte might be a charming fellow, but that did not stop him from keeping a sharp French eye on his own interest.

I don't know how Frédéric Dion made out with his suit. He seemed a nice young man, so I hope he married Angèle and lived with her happily ever after.

But that is how, a week later, we were all standing in our rough clothes in the field of the Menhir of Locmelon, watching the crane on the back of Monsieur Lebraz's wrecking truck slowly hoist the last piece of the stone into the air. I had placed the cable around the fragment, hoping that nobody noticed my inexperience as a rigger.

When this piece was poised over the monument, I climbed the ladder. Denise handed me up a trowel and a bucket, and I slathered mortar on the broken surface of the stone. Then Lebraz lowered the topmost fragment, a centimeter at a time, until I could guide it into place. We pulled the cable out from between the stones. Surplus mortar was squeezed out of the join in gobs, which I scraped off with my trowel. At last, the sinister visage carved in the top of the monolith growered down upon us, as it had for forty centuries before its overthrow.

The next day, we packed our car to head for Cahors. Being behind schedule because of the work on the menhir, we got an early start. As we were saying good-bye to the Carrières in the courtyard, a car drove up and a little fat man got out.

"Monsieur le Comte de la Carrière?" he said.

"C'est moi," said the Comte.

"I am Gaston Lobideau, from the Office of Historical Monuments. I am reliably informed that you, Monsieur, without permission and without specialized archaeological knowledge, have restored the broken Menhir of Locmelon. I must warn you, sir, that this is a breach of the most serious of the laws of the Republic concerning the conservation of ancient monuments. You should have applied for permission through the appropriate channels. Then, in a few months, an expert would have come to check your qualifications for such an enterprise and to supervise the operation..."

Denise and I got into our Peugeot, waved, and drove off. When last seem, the Comte and Monsieur Lobideau were shouting and waving their arms. I never heard how it came out, but perhaps that is just as well. They might have hauled us into court, too.

Darius

The big black horse looked perfectly normal, except for his size. Denise said: "This great *rosse* looks too large for me, Willy. You will have to push me up by the behind."

The animal looked indifferently towards us and lowered its head to scratch behind its ear with its hoof.

"Don't worry none, Mr. Newbury," said Seymour Green, the horsemaster. "Darius is the tamest one we got. In fact, he's so lazy you can't hardly keep him moving."

"Sure, darling," I said to Denise. "Go on; I'll give you a boost."

With a vigorous push, I got Denise into the saddle. It did seem like a lot of horse for a small woman. Denise looked down apprehensively. "It is a long way to fall. Take care of our poor children, if anything should happen to me."

The horse gave a loud whinny, like an equine laugh. One of Green's helpers, Jim, was saddling a couple of other hacks. Green asked:

"Ain't I seen you around here before, Mr. Newbury?"

"Sure," I said. "I've been here off and on in the summer since I was a kid."

"I thought—" Green began, but then he yelped: "Watch out!"

I turned to see Denise's horse stalking me. As I turned, the animal shot out its huge head, with teeth bared.

I jumped like a startled bullfrog. Denise screamed and hauled on the reins. Green cursed, grabbed a length of strap, and whacked the horse across the muzzle. The animal backed up, gave its loud whinny, and became quiet.

"Ain't never seen him do nothing like that before," said Green. "Maybe I hadn't ought to send him out with you."

"Oh, I think we'll be all right once we're all mounted," I said. I swung into my own saddle, which I was glad to see was a Western. English saddles are all very pretty, but the Western gives more security. As you get on in years, your

71

bones don't knit so easily.

The ride went smoothly. Jim led Denise, two other summer visitors, and me on an hour's ride over the local paths, through the advanced second growth of maple, beech, and birch. The red squirrels chattered and the deer flies thrummed.

We had left the children with my Aunt Frances at her camp on Lake Algonquin. We were spending our vacation there. Since her daughter Linda had gotten married, Frances Colton had urged us to come and keep her company. Wanting at least one good ride, I had driven Denise down to Gahato, where Green maintained his stable in summer; in winter he trucked his animals down the line to Syracuse.

Denise's alarm became impatience as Darius stopped at every juncture to munch a fern or just to stand still. Hence she was always at the tail of the procession. When the rest of us cantered, Darius trotted. Bouncing on his back, Denise fell further behind. When she heeled him, he merely gave his braying whinny and refused to speed up.

When the ride was over, I swung off and stepped up to Darius to help Denise down. "He is too big for me," she said. "*Sacré nom!* I am like an ant trying to guide an elephant."

As she was sliding off, Darius suddenly moved and brought one big hoof down on the toe of my boot.

"Ouch!" I yelled, jerking the foot away. With Denise in my arms, I staggered and almost sat down in the mud and manure.

Green shouted and took another whack with a strap. The horse brayed again.

"Seems like he's got it in for you," he said. "How's that foot?"

"Nothing broken, I'm sure," I said. "The ground is soft, so he just pushed my toes down into it."

"When you coming back?"

"Tomorrow, weather permitting. We'll be stiff tomorrow, and the best way to get rid of it is to go right out for another ride."

"Ayuh. I'll put you down in the book."

Not having ridden for a couple of years, we were, as I

predicted, stiff as boards the next morning. Weather did not permit that day's scheduled ride. Instead, we had a two-day Adirondack downpour. We could only hobble about the Colton camp, read, and play games with the children. I got to telling Denise and my aunt about some of my boyhood experiences in these parts.

"When the Ten Eycks had that big place on the island between Upper and Lower Lakes—the one that sank in the earthquake—they used to run a regular free boarding house in summer. All their friends and relatives came in relays. My folks, with my sister and me, were regular guests.

"Alfred Ten Eyck and I used to go out in a rowboat to frog around the little bays and inlets, especially Porcupine Bay. I had a microscope, and we'd scoop up some of the muck from the swamp to look at the little wiggly things in the 'scope. Once Alfred got out into that patch of quicksand at the far end of Porcupine Bay, and I had to haul him back into the boat by his hair.

"Once, we caught one of the locals poaching deer out of season. He'd just shot the animal and was dressing it out on the shore of Porcupine Bay, when we came around the point and saw him. Nobody much ever went in there, so he wasn't expecting company.

"I knew who he was: Henri Michod, one of the lumber-jacks who worked in Pringle's sawmill. Larochelle, Pringle's forman, used to say Michod was strong enough to do two men's work but so lazy he did only half a man's. He had a couple of funny habits, too: always scratching behind his ear, and laughing so that one could hear him half a mile away. Some said he augmented his earnings by breaking into camps in the winter.

"Well, I've always been a wild-life enthusiast and a red-hot conservationist. At the time, I was around thirteen and full of self-righteous wrath. Anyway, I told the warden, old Roy Newcomb, about this kill, and he ran Henri Michod in. Henri had to pay a fine and lost his deer carcass.

"A week or so later, he passed me on the street in Gahato and said: 'I hear you tell the warden on me, *hein*? By damn, you better watch yourself, you little son of a bitch. I get even, you bet!'"

"I worried for a while, because Michod was a tall, powerful fellow with the reputation of being a bad man to cross. To me he looked as big as Goliath of Gath. But nothing happened, and the next couple of summers we went elsewhere. When we later visited the Adirondacks, I saw nothing of Henri Michod. In fact, I'd forgotten about him until that damned horse reminded me of him yesterday."

On the second rainy day, the treasurer of our bank, Malcolm McGill, showed up at Joe Briggs's Algonquin Lodge with his wife. (He was only assistant treasurer then.) I had recommended the place when he spoke of wanting to see the Great North Woods. While Denise, my Aunt Frances, and I were eating dinner with the McGills at the Lodge, Denise mentioned our recent ride.

"Oh, can you ride here?" said McGill, all enthusiasm. "Say, I'd like to try that!"

"Then come down the line to Gahato with us tomorrow, if the rain lets up," I said.

The rain did let up, so next morning found us at Seymour Green's stable. McGill and his wife were in jeans and sneakers, which are poor riding shoes because they lack heels. I wore the boots and breeches I had ridden in for twenty years, although Denise had let out the pants.

I am no cowboy or Cossack. Still, I have ridden a fair amount, starting at a fancy prep school my parents sent me to, before the Great Depression took us down several financial pegs. At that place, equitation was on the curriculum. I have even jumped a few times without falling off.

"Hey!" said McGill, "I want that one!" He pointed to the huge black that had stepped on my foot.

"Okay," said Green. "He won't give you no trouble; he's too lazy. Saddle him up, Jim."

Then McGill started to mount Darius from the wrong side. The horse shied away, and Jim corrected McGill.

"I never can remember which side is the right one," he said.

"Imagine you're wearing a sword on your left side," I said. "Then, if you tried to mount from the right, the scabbard would poke the horse in the rump and make him shy."

74

"But I'm left-handed, so I'd wear my sword on the right!"

I did not try to answer that one. Green handed McGill a switch cut from a tree branch to wake up Darius if the horse ignored its rider's heels. We started out along the trails.

Darius gave no trouble at first, but the McGills caused me apprehension. In conversation, they had given the impression of being old horsepersons. But the way they sat, and McGill's ideas of mounting, did not confirm that impression.

Furthermore, the deer flies bothered them, so that they were always slapping. They had come out bareheaded, not knowing that a deer fly goes for anything that looks hairy. Then you suddenly feel as if somebody had stabbed you in the scalp or neck with a hot needle. McGill rode with his knees sticking out, so that one could see greenery between them and the horse.

"Malcolm," I said, "how much riding have you actually done?"

"Oh, I've been on a horse maybe twice."

I gulped. "Well, if you want to stay on, press your knees hard against the animals's sides and keep them that way."

"Oh," he said. He tried to comply, but the knee grip is tiring when one is not used ot it. Soon his knees were sticking out again.

Still, he managed until we came to an open space, near the Gahato airstrip. Jim began a canter. McGill survived Darius's first few shambling bounds. Then McGill's saddle began to tip from side to side, going a little further each time as he swayed his body to compensate. Having no knee grip, he could not hold the saddle in place by main force.

I started to call: "Hey, Malcolm! Watch—"

Over he went. The saddle slid until it was under the horse's belly, and McGill landed on his back in a mass of raspberry bushes. Darius stopped to eat the vegetation.

The rest of us pulled up. Jim handed his reins to me, vaulted off, and helped McGill to his feet. McGill limped, and his hands and face were scratched by the raspberry thorns.

"Oh, boy!" he said. "I think I busted my big toe in pulling it out of the stirrup."

He was lucky at that. A fall from a horse may look funny but is no joke. If he had landed on his head on something

75

hard or had caught his foot in the stirrup, he could have been killed. In one of my few falls, I hurt my shoulder in a way that took a year completely to heal.

Examining Darius, Jim said: "He's pulled that goddam trick again. The smart ones learn to take a deep breath when you go to tighten the girth. Then, when they let it out, the girth gets loose. Damn your hide, hold still!" This was to the horse, whose girth Jim was ferociously tightening. "Now it won't come loose. This critter's lazy, but he's the smartest damn horse I ever seen. Seems almost like he's got a man's brain. Can you get back up, Mr. McGill?"

When McGill was again mounted, the rest of the ride was made in a subdued and cautious spirit.

Wisely, the McGills elected to go boating on their second day, so Denise and I did not ride again until they had left. This time, I took Darius.

"Sure you want to?" said Seymour Green. "He don't like you."

"We'll see about that," I said. "I think I can handle him."

"Oh, Willy!" said Denise. "You have one of your *têtu*— your stubborn streaks on again."

"Yep," I said. "Saddle him up."

When the black was ready, I stepped towards him. Darius bared his teeth.

"None of that," I said. Then, not so loudly as to be overheard: "Tell me, are you really Henri Michod?"

Darius threw up his head and gave his thunderous whinny.

"And you've been laying for me for the last quarter-century, eh?"

He whinnied again.

"How'd you know me? By hearing Green say my name?"

The horse nodded.

"Well, you'll have to behave yourself."

I walked to the animal's nigh side and put my foot in the stirrup. Darius reached down and back and tried to bite my foot, but I got up without damage.

I watched Darius, lest he lie down and roll or try to buck me off. Luckily, he was too lazy to lie down, because that

76

meant that he had to get up again. With his weight, that was a job. As for bucking, perhaps he did not know how.

"Be careful, darling!" called Denise. She was up on a docile little mare.

We rode with four other summer people. Jim led us. It was one of those beautiful summer days that you get now and then in the Adirondacks, if you don't mind waiting through a week or two of cold, overcast, fog, and rain.

Then the Gahato fire-house siren went off, out of sight but plainly audible. All the horses danced and fidgeted. I leaned forward to pat Darius on the neck to gentle him down. I did not quite know whether to deal with the creature as a man or as a beast.

Darius chose that moment to throw up his head, so that his great skull hit me in the face. I heard my sun glasses go crunch. A little dazed, I lost a stirrup but got it back before Darius could take advantage of me.

"Are you hurt, Willy?" said Denise.

"Don't think so," I said, "except for having these glasses pushed into my face. Probably have a black eye tomorrow."

I took off the glasses and exmained them. The frame was cracked, so the glasses would have to be replaced. I put them in my pocket, resolving never to wear glasses of any kind on horseback again.

For a while, all was peaceful. We walked, trotted, and cantered. None of the other riders was such a tyro as the McGills had proved.

"All right there, Henri Michod," I said to my horse. "You see, it's not so bad when you do what you ought—"

We were trotting along one of the dirt back roads and came to a fork. One way led to Gahato; the other, to the Lower and Upper Lakes. As Jim pulled up to collect his riders, the whole Gahato high-school track team—a score of youths in fluttery running gear—came racing towards us along the road from the village.

"Yippee!" yelled one of the youths. "Ride 'em, cowboy!"

That was all we needed. The horses spooked. Denise's mare whirled and started back for Green's stable at a dead run; so did those of the other riders.

Darius headed into the other fork of the road, towards the

lakes. I leaned back and hauled on the reins, but the accursed beast had clamped the bit in his big yellow teeth. There was no holding him.

On he went. I heard yells behind me but was too busy keeping my saddle and stirrups to pay heed.

The dirt road petered out into an old logging road, partly overgrown with saplings. Darius pounded on through the saplings, which lashed my legs. I grabbed the horn of the Western saddle and hung on, glad there was nobody to see me commit such an unhorsemanlike gaffe.

"God damn it, Michod, use some sense!" I yelled. Darius merely whinnied and thundered on.

The logging road in turn began to peter out. Trails, on which we had ridden before, branched off. Darius raced along one of these, up and down and then, leaving the trail, cross-country. We came to a place where no trees had been cut for many decades, so that the area was almost like a virgin forest. Darius aimed at a big beech, whence a massive horizontal branch stuck out at just the right height to scrape me off.

I flattened myself out on the horse's back. The branch grazed my head and carried away my cap but left me otherwise unharmed.

Twice again, Darius tried the same stunt. Each time, I avoided disaster by a hairbreadth. Then he ran down a slope, beyond which I glimpsed water through the trees.

We burst out of the woods on the swampy shore of one of the lakes. As Darius plunged into the water, I recognized Porcupine Bay, on Upper Lake.

"You idiot, you'll get us mired!" I shouted.

Darius careened on, up to his knees in water. The toes of my boots threw up little bow waves.

He scrambled out on a shallower place. I saw yellow, sandy bottom an inch or two below the surface—and then, suddenly, his legs sank in again. He had blundered into the quicksand.

The next thing I knew, Darius was in up to his belly. My feet were dragging in the quicksand. Darius snorted and plunged, but his struggles only got him in deeper. The quicksand rose halfway up his barrel, almost to the tops of my boots.

"Serves you right, you son of a mule!" I told him.

I remember that, while a man cannot walk on quicksand, he can in effect swim in it. The trick is to keep yourself spread out.

I gathered my legs up until I got my right foot on the saddle. Then I heaved myself erect, standing on the saddle, and threw myself backwards, away from the horse. I came down with a splash on my back on the thin film of water over the sand. Not trying to raise myself, I went through the motions of swimming a backstroke, digging my elbows into the yielding quicksand.

After a few strokes, I found myself on firmer ground. I reached up, caught a branch of an overhanging hemlock, and hauled myself out of the muck. Darius was still struggling and sinking. He snorted and rolled his eyes.

"Yah!" I yelled. "See what you got yourself into, Henri?"

He made a strange noise—not exactly a whinny; more like a whine, if you can imagine a horse's making such a sound.

"Oh, you'd like me to haul you out, eh?"

He whinnied.

"Serve you right if I left you to sink," I said.

Again the piteous whine.

I heard a faint halloo from the woods and shouted back. Presently Seymour Green, Jim, Denise, and one of the other summer people appeared on horses, pushing through the undergrowth. Denise said:

"My God, darling, have you been swimming in the swamp? You are mud all over, from the head to the foot."

"Exactly," I said, and told my tale.

Green said: "How d'you reckon we can get that horse out, Mr. Newbury? I'd sure hate to lose him."

"Somebody ride back to the village and fetch me a hundred feet of half-inch rope from Tate's Hardware store," I said. "If you hurry, maybe you can get back before Darius goes under."

Jim galloped away. The others dismounted, tied their nags, and squatted on the bank. Denise tried to dab the mud off me, but the task was hopeless.

79

Out in the quicksand, Darius till gave an occasional heave. He seemed, however, to have become either exhausted by his struggles or resigned to his fate. His head, neck, and saddle were still above the surface.

I asked Green: "Seymour, how old is that horse?"

Green thought. "Eight and a half or nine year, I guess. Why?"

"Ever know a French-Canadian lumberjack named Henri Michod?"

"I don't—ayup, there was a guy by that name, I think. He was working somewheres else for a few years, and then after the war he came back. Worked as a guide in the hunting season."

"What became of him?"

"Dead. One of them tenderfoot hunters mistook him for a deer, for all his red shirt and cap, and shot him."

"When was that?"

Green scratched his head. "Let me see—forty-six? Forty-seven? About nine year ago, anyways. Why do you want to know, Mr. Newbury?"

"Oh, just a crazy idea. Here comes Jim, with the rope. Now, I'm going out into the swamp. You fellows hold on to my shirt tail, so I can't sink in."

I tied a bowline on a bight in the end of the rope and felt my way out through the shallows towards the horse. The water squilched in my boots. When I felt the bottom begin to give beneath my foot, I stopped advancing. While I am no lariat artist, I got the loop over the horn of the saddle on the third cast.

"Do we haul him in, now?" said Jim.

"Not yet."

I carried the rope back to shore, looped it around the trunk of the hemlock, and went back into the water. I threw another loop around the saddle horn. My purpose was to get a mechanical advantage, as you do with a compound pulley.

Then, with five people on the free end of the rope, foot by foot we hauled Darius shoreward. In another ten minutes, he stood in the shallows with drooping head, shivering, with mud and water running off him.

"All right, Henri," I said to him, "will you behave yourself now?"

Green and Jim stared at me. They stared even harder when Darius took a shambling step forward, stuck out a tongue the size of one of my boots, and sloshed it against my face.

"By God, I never seen *that* before?" said Green.

I sputtered, wiping my face with a paper handkerchief that Denise handed me. The incident proved, as far as I was concerned, that Darius was either possessed by the spirit of Henri Michod or was a reincarnation of Henri Michod. No mere horse ever had the intelligence to know when somebody had saved its life or to demonstrate its gratitude afterwards.

Darius was a perfect gentleman, as horses go, on the way back. When we got in the car, however, he broke loose from Green's men and bounded up to us, whinnying.

"Hey!" I said. "He wants to adopt us! If—blub—"

Darius had stuck his muzzle in the window of the car and licked my face again. I pushed his nose out and cranked up the glass. Green's men came running up to collar their horse. I started the car, backed, turned, and headed for Lake Algonquin.

"He is coming after!" cried Denise. "Could we maybe buy him?"

A glance in the rear-view mirror showed Darius, still saddled, galloping in our wake, with his empty stirrups flopping. I stepped on the gas and left him behind.

"No," I said. "We don't have a place to keep him, and it would be too expensive to board him at a stable. Don't forget that we have three children to put through college some day.

"Besides, you know how people are. They can ooze gratitude today. Then, tomorrow, they say: 'But what have you done for me lately?' and turn against you. I'm sure it would work out the same way with Darius."

"But," she said, "Darius is just a horse!"

"Oh, yeah? Maybe so, but I for one don't intend to find out!"

81

United Imp

There is nothing like a brush with the unknown to knock the self-conceit out of one.

I had just been promoted to vice-president of the Harrison Trust Company and was feeling pretty pleased with myself. Looking back, I suspect that my promotion owed less to my financial expertise than to the fact that, in my late thirties, my hair had turned prematurely gray. This gave me the sober, reliable look that people approve in their bankers. So, when the then vice-president retired, Esau Drexel moved me into that slot.

At first, Denise fussed about my hair, saying she did not want to seem married to an old man just yet. I tried some dye but found it more trouble than it was worth; you have to repeat the treatment every week or two. So I put on my stubborn face and refused to dye any more. Denise complained of my hair for years; but, when I got promoted, the salary reconciled her. She takes the realistic French view of money.

I had not been long at this job when Drexel called me into the president's office.

"Willy," he said, "here's a puzzle. Fellow in Atlanta wants to borrow five hundred grand. Claims he has enough commercial orders to support the loan; but I can't find him in Dun and Bradstreet, or anywhere. Besides, what does he want to come to us for? There are plenty of banks in Georgia."

"Maybe they've all turned him down," I said. "What's his line?"

Drexel tossed a letter across his desk. The letterhead said UNITED IMP, with a Post Office box number in Atlanta. A sheaf of photostats of orders for the company's products was stapled to the letter.

The letter explained that the company manufactured wrought-iron grillwork. They had been swamped with orders; hence they needed the loan to expand. The letter went on:

> You are doubtless aware of the current vogue for nostalgic restoration. All over the South, decrepit mansions are being refurbished as tourist attractions. In many of these houses, the original grillwork has rusted away and must be replaced. Since we command the services of a labor force, on one hand highly skilled and on the other not unionized, we hope to capture a substantial part of the market for our products.

"Of course," said Drexel, "we don't want to get involved in a fight with the goddam unions. If that man in the White house—but never mind; what's done is done. What do you think, Willy?"

I frowned at the letter. "I see some funny things here. What does 'United Imp' mean? What's the 'Imp'?"

"Imperial? Imports? Or maybe impostors?"

"Perhaps it doesn't stand for anything. There's no period after the *p*."

"You mean 'imp' as in gnomes or elves?"

"Or kobolds or knockers. Then, look how the man signs his name: 'Colin Owens, Magiarch.' "

"Some kind of cult leader, I suppose." Drexel buzzed his secretary. "Miss Carnero, please get your dictionary."

The dictionary did not list "magiarch," but the meaning was plain. Drexel said:

"If he's one of these fakers, telling his suckers they're reincarnations of George Washington, or promising to make supermen of them in one easy lesson, no wonder the Georgia banks turned him down. I think we'd better give him the brush-off."

"Oh, I don't know," I said. "A man can be a nut in one way and a shrewd businessman in another. We ought at least to look into his proposition. Besides, business has been slow around here, and we've got too much cash lying idle. We could charge him the prime plus one-half."

"Prime plus two, more like. But at such a high-risk rate, we'd have to send someone to Atlanta to watch him."

"Well, let's say prime plus one or one and a half."

"It won't be any rate at all unless we know more about the fellow. Tell you what, Willy: You fly down to Atlanta and look over his plant. How soon can you go?"

"Early next week, I guess."

"Fine. I'll write this Colin Owens, telling him you're coming. Think you can handle the job?"

"Oh, sure. Don't worry about me, boss." Famous last words.

At the Hartsfield Airport, two men met me. Colin Owens turned out to be small, slight, and elderly, with silver hair and an English accent. His blue eyes beamed benignly through steel-rimmed spectacles as he introduced his assistant, Forrest Bellamy. This was a tall, lean, dark man in his thirties, with Southern Mountain twang. While Bellamy was polite enough, there was something uncomfortably tense about him.

"I am delighted you've come, Mr. Newbury," said Owens. "Have you been in Atlanta before?"

"No; this is my first visit."

"Then we shall be pleased to show you the sights of the new queen of the South."

"Where are you putting me?"

"We have reserved a good motel room in Decatur. That's on the side of town near our plant."

"Fine. When can I see your plant?"

"There's no hurry about that. First, we shall give you a general orientation tour. Take Mr. Newbury's bag, Forrest."

I was not so naïve as to expect an Atlanta of Southern belles in crinolines and parasols. I was, however, surprised by its bustling, up-to-date air, with skyscrapers and freeways sprouting here and there. As I was being whirled through the Memorial Arts Center, the Cyclorama, and other sights, I kept trying to pin down my hosts on their operations.

"Why," I asked, "did you come to us, instead of to a local bank?" Owens and I were sitting in back while Bellamy drove.

"I thought you might ask that," said Owens. After a pause, he answered: "I might as well confess that we tried the local

84

sources but were refused—not, however, for reasons germane to our finances."

"How do you mean?"

"Well—ah—"

"What he means," said Bellamy, "is, we reckon like there's a certain prejudice against us, irregardless of how sound the business is."

"How so?"

"Well, for one thing, Mr. Owens ain't a Georgian. He's not even a native-born American, but a naturalized Englishman."

"Excuse me, Forrest," said Owens. "I am a Briton but not an Englishman. I am Welsh." He turned to me. "I never can get Americans to make the distinction. Go on, Forrest."

"For another, United Imp is, in a kind of a way, a sideline with us. Some folks are ignorant about our main business, so they get funny ideas."

"And what's your main business, if I may ask?"

Owens's faded blue eyes took on a faraway look. "Merely endeavoring to dissuade our fellow men from inflicting needless 'wounds and sore defeat' upon one another, by the application of the ancient wisdom."

"You mean you head a religious sect or cult?"

"What's in a name? The Anthropophili are a benevolent society devoted to the pursuit of truth, peace, and beauty..."

Owens gripped my forearm, while his guileless blue eyes stared into mine as he launched into a sermon—lofty, earnest, and cloudy. It did not greatly differ from what you can hear every week in a church or a temple—or for that matter at a Vedanta meeting. He spangled his talk with tags from Aeschylus, Shakespeare, and Milton.

My reaction to Owens's preaching was mixed. On one hand, I rather liked this learned old occultist. On the other, I shuddered at the thought of entrusting our depositors' money to him. Still, I tried to view his project objectively.

When we were fifteen miles or so east of Atlanta, Bellamy turned his head to say: "Here's Stone Mountain." On the plain ahead, a huge granite dome loomed up for nearly a thousand feet, like the half-buried skull of some mythical monster. "We got time to take him up before dinner,

Master?"

Owens looked at his watch. "I fear not, Forrest. 'The dragon wing of night o'erspreads the earth.' Continue on to the Oecus; Maggie can be quite difficult if we are late for meals."

Bellamy made a couple of turns and drew up in a small graveled parking lot, near a large house shaded by longleaf pines.

The Oecus was a rambling structure, which seemed to have been built by a committee, each member of which had designed one part to suit himself, without reference to his colleagues' plans. No two rooms appeared to be set on the same level. There were spiral stairs in odd places, decorative mosaics of colored glass set in cement, and a couple of amateurish mural paintings of winged beings flapping around a cloudy sky. Sounds of hammering came from one end of the building, and I glimpsed a small group of young men and women in work clothes, nailing and plastering.

"What's the origin of this house?" I asked.

Owens explained: "It was built before the First World War by an eccentric architect. The property was subsequently abandoned and had fallen into disrepair before the Anthropophili obtained the title and restored the building. As you see, the repairs are not quite complete. Would you like a drink before dinner?"

"Why, yes indeed," I said.

Owen disappeared and returned with three small glasses and a bottle of sherry. "Ordinarily we do not indulge in alcoholic beverages in the Anthropophili, but we make exceptions for eminent visitors. 'Moderation is the noblest gift of heaven.' "

He poured me, Bellamy, and himself each a thimbleful. It was good stuff as far as it went. While we sipped, Owens talked a monologue about the ideals of his organization. I was ready for a second when the dinner gong sounded and Owens put his bottle away.

There were about thirty members of the cult at the long table. The members, including those who had been working on the house, were mostly young and casually dressed. Several were black. Since this was in the early days of civil rights agitation in the South, I wondered if the racial integration of Owens's cult had barred him from local financing. That subject, however, never came up.

The food was plain but excellent. The conversation was mostly over my head, dealing with local politics and personalities. When dinner was over, Owens said:

"Mr. Newbury, I should like to show you our products."

He led me to one end of the house, down steps, and into a storage room. There were heaps of wrought-iron grilles, railings, gates, wall brackets, planters, outdoor furniture, and other examples of the modern blacksmith's art. While I am no judge of such matters, these artifacts seemed well-made.

"It's a matter of price," said Owens. "With the unusual personnel of my crew, I can undersell any other maker of such products. If I can expand, there won't be the slightest difficulty about repaying the loan, with a handsome profit to our organization. This profit will be used to further the aims of our movement."

"Do you use the members of your society as workers?"

"Oh, dear, no! They are seekers of truth, fully occupied with our crusade to bring peace and prosperity to the world. My workers are persons of quite a different sort."

He steered me gently to the door. Then he and Bellamy whisked me off to my motel.

"We'll see you first thing in the morning," said Bellamy. "What time do y'all like to get up?"

In the morning, they drove me to Stone Mountain. We parked and took one of the new cable cars to the top. The car soared up over the colossal statues of Davis, Lee, and Jackson on horseback, which were carved in the west face. I understand that the sculptors meant, when the project began, to add a mile-long parade of Confederate soldiers as well. They ran out of money, however, before the project got that far.

Holding a stanchion in the crowded cable car, Bellamy said: "Every year, some young numbskull tries to show off to his girl by climbing all the way down one of the steep sides. Then he gets to where it's too steep to hold on, and that's the end of him."

87

On top, we strolled about admiring the view. Bellamy told me of their further plans for my entertainment—the river-boat ride, the restored ante-bellum plantation—until I said:

"I certainly appreciate your hospitality, gentlemen. But, before we do business, I simply must see your plant and these extraordinary workers."

Owens said: "Well—ah—you saw the quality of our ironwork last night. I can show you lists of the prevailing prices for such products and what we sell ours for. I can explain our system of advertising and distribution—"

"Please. I am merely a trustee for our depositors' money; I have to know what I'm putting it into. So I must see your facilities with my own eyes."

Owens coughed. "There are—ah—some practical difficulties to that. You see, sir, there is some question of the title to the site of our factory. If the precise location should become generally known, it might cause us great inconvenience. We might have to relocate. Furthermore, our personnel are averse to letting outsiders see them at their tasks."

I shook my head. "Sorry, fellows. No factory tour, no money."

Owens and Bellamy exchanged looks. Bellamy scowled, glared, and took a step towards me, as if his temper were about to explode in violence. A slight movement from Owens caused Bellamy to step back and make his face blank. Owens said:

"Put your ear down against the granite, Mr. Newbury, and tell me what you hear."

The prospect did not look promising for my pants; but, I thought, I could bill the bank for a new pair. I got down and put my ear to the elephant-gray rock. A couple of other tourists, fifty feet away, stared at me.

"I hear a faint rumble," I said. "A vibration almost below the lower limit of audibility. I suppose it's the machinery that runs the cable cars."

Owens shook his head. "We are too far from that machinery, as you can ascertain by repeating the test in other parts of the rock."

"What then?" I said, getting up and dusting off my clothes.

"Are you familiar with the lines from Spenser:

'...such ghastly noise of iron chains
And brazen cauldrons thou shalt rumbling hear,
Which thousand sprites with long enduring pains
Do toss, that it will stun thy feeble brains...'?"

"'Fraid not," I said. "*The Faerie Queene* is one of those things I'm always promising myself to read but never getting around to. What's the point?"

"The story, as Spenser tells it, is that Merlin once summoned up a host of spirits and compelled them to set about prefabricating a brazen wall for his native city of Carmarthen. Then he went off and got himself entombed by Vivien, or whatever her name was. But nobody told the poor devils to stop, so they are still at work. Or at least, they were before I got in touch with them."

"Yes?" I said. "You mean you've got Spenser's spirits hammering out wrought-iron grilles in a cave beneath Stone Mountain?"

"Quite. Some might question the propriety of the term 'spirits' for my workers, who are very solid, substantial creatures."

"You mean gnomes or dwarves?"

"They are called by various names. I shan't try to explain how I secured their service, because that would take us into the complexities of magical theory."

"But how did you get them to this country? Did you smuggle them aboard a ship, or did they tunnel under the Atlantic?"

Owens smiled. "Such beings have their own resources, their own—ah—mysterious ways."

"If the demons of Carmarthen were brass workers, did they have to learn how to handle iron?"

"Be assured, they can handle any metal. Now, since you insist, we shall descend the mountain and visit our manufactory—at least, to the extent that it is safe to show it to you."

We drove back to the Oecus. Owens and Bellamy took

me around the house to the rear. Here I found a curious structure: a large sunken area bounded by stone walls, which rose to waist height above the outer ground surface but extended down fifteen or twenty feet below ground level on the inner side. It was as if someone had begun to build a big house but had gotten no further than the cellar. A couple of honeylocust trees shaded the area with their feathery leaves.

A ramp between two curving stone walls provided access to the lower level. There were also a couple of other down-sloping passageways, but these came to blind ends. The thing conveyed the impression of being the product of a very strange mind.

In the middle of the lower level was another, narrower depression, perhaps six feet deep, ten wide, and thirty long, and brick-paved. Owens and Bellamy led me down steps to this sub-basement. At one end, I saw a heavy iron door, which Owens unlocked and opened with a screech of hinges.

"Watch your head," he said.

I ducked under the lintel and followed the little magus, while Bellamy brought up the rear. The down-sloping tunnel was lined with planks and dimly lit by an occasional electric light bulb. We hiked for some minutes in silence. The planks gave way to solid granite, and the passageway became level. Owens paused to indicate a series of side chambers.

"Storage for our products," he said.

A glimpse showed piles of wrought-iron artifacts, like those I had seen in the Oecus. We plodded on.

Early in the descent, I had become aware of a sound like the rumble I had heard atop Stone Mountain. As we went onward, the sound waxed louder.

We came to a dimly-lit vestibule, containing stacks of wrought-iron objects and several chairs. The noise was now so loud that we had to raise our voices. I could feel the vibration through the soles of my shoes.

There was a great metallic banging and clanging, mixed with guttural shouts. The speech was too much mingled with the clangor to make anything of. I could not even guess the language.

"This is as far as we shall go," said Owens. "As I have

90

explained, our workers are extremely shy. They allow nobody but Forrest and me into their workshop. In any event, you can now report that we do have a production work force, can't you?"

"I guess so," I said. "If you don't mind, I'd like to get the hell out of here." I was finding the noise and the confinement oppressive.

"Surely," said Owens.

We hiked back up the long slope in silence. When to my relief we reached the surface, it was lunch time. I ate one of the Oecus's simple but sumptuous meals and spent the afternoon with Owens, going over his books and learning the economics of the wrought-iron business.

They invited me to dinner, but I begged off. I had to get back to the motel to organize my thoughts, write up my notes, and telephone Drexel.

When I called Esau Drexel that evening, I told my story, saying: "I still don't know what he's got in that cave, but it must be something. I can't imagine that all that wrought-iron stuff and correspondence that he showed me is some elaborate charade. His business seems to be thriving."

"Then why is he so hell-bent to expand? Why can't he be satisfied with his current profits?"

"He's an idealist who wants to save the world from blowing itself up. Maybe he's got something there. He figures to earn enough from this expansion, while the vogue lasts, to make his Anthropophili a force in world public opinion."

"As if any dictator ever cared a hoot for world public opinion! You didn't see these gnomes or whatever the hell they're supposed to be?"

"No, but I heard them. Nearly busted my eardrums. I'd say to go ahead with the loan."

"Willy," growled my boss, "you've got a thing or two to learn about the lengths to which people will go to get their hands on the other guy's money. How do you know all that racket wasn't a recording, played over a loudspeaker?"

"Unh," I said. "I hadn't thought of that. Maybe you're just being too suspicious."

"Any time somebody wants to borrow half a million bucks on the pretext that he has spooks or fairies working for him, you're damned right I'm suspicious. What's the name of Owens's cult again?"

"The Anthropophili."

"Doesn't that mean 'man-eaters' or 'cannibals'?"

"No; you're thinking of 'Anthropophagi.' I think this name means 'lovers of man.'"

"Maybe they love man the way I love a good steak. Now, you go back and tell 'em: if you don't see their alleged gnomes, it's no deal."

"They say their workers—whatever they are—are touchy about letting people see them."

"That's their problem. You do as I say."

Next morning, when Owens and Bellamy came to the motel, I delivered Drexel's ultimatum. Again, Bellamy seemed about to burst with suppressed rage. Owens soothed him:

"Never mind, Forrest. 'Even the gods cannot strive against necessity.'" To me he said: "You understand, Mr. Newbury, that there may be certain—ah—difficulties in dealing with these beings? There might even be some risk."

"I'm not worried," I said.

Overnight, I had become half converted to Drexel's suggestions that the noise was from a recording. In any case, I was ninety-eight per cent certain that the workers, if any, would prove to be ordinary mortal men.

Back at the Oecus, Owens again unlocked the iron door in the pit. Down we went.

As we descended, I noticed a difference. The metallic clangor, instead of starting faintly as we entered the tunnel and slowly rising to an earsplitting din, was missing. There was a faint susurration, which grew to the sound of a multitude of bass voices, all talking at once. But this time, there was no anvil chorus.

My companions noticed it, too. Owens and Bellamy stopped to confer in low tones.

"Are they taking a coffee break?" I asked.

"Dunno," said Bellamy. "They sure ain't doing what they're supposed to."

"Some emergency must have arisen," said Owens.

"Perhaps an accident. We shall know when we get there."

We entered the vestibule. The noise was loud, although nothing compared to the previous uproar. Owens said:

"You and I shall wait here, Mr. Newbury, while Forrest goes ahead to make the arrangements."

"You mean to get these trolls' permission to bring me in?"

"Quite. Sit down and relax; this may require some time."

Owens and I sat. Bellamy disappeared into a passage at the far end of the chamber. This passage was angled so that one could not, from the vestibule, look into the working space beyond.

The rumble of voices died to near-silence. I heard Forrest Bellamy's voice, too muffled to tell what he was saying. Then the bass voices rose again. I still could not identify the language.

Owens and I sat and sat. Owens spoke of his ideals and his grandiose plans for the Anthropophili. At last he took out his watch.

"There must be more difficulty than I anticipated," he said. "I'll give Forrest another quarter-hour."

We sat for fifteen minutes more. Then, with another look at his watch, Owens rose.

"I shall have to take a look myself," he said. "Please remain where you are, Mr. Newbury. You must *not* attempt to follow me without instructions. Do you understand?"

"Yes," I said.

Owens disappeared into the same passage that had swallowed Bellamy. The vocal noises died down briefly and then rose again.

I waited another quarter-hour. The temptation to sneak a look into the cave was strong, but I withstood it. I have the normal quota of curiosity and perhaps a bit more; but with a wife and three children at home, I did not care to let curiosity kill this particular cat.

Then the noises rose sharply. I thought I recognized the sound of an angry mob.

Colin Owens popped out of the passageway. His hair was awry, he had lost his glasses, he bled from a scratch on his face, and his coat lacked one sleeve.

"Run for your life!" he cried as he scampered past me.

I leaped from the chair and caught up with him in a few strides. Being much bigger than he, twenty years his junior, and in good physical trim for a man of my middling years, I could have left him far behind. Instead, I grabbed his arm and boosted him along. Even so, he had to stop now and then to catch his breath.

Behind us, the sound of voices mingled with the slap and tramp of many feet, running through the tunnel.

"Keep on!" gasped Owens. "They'll pound us—sledge hammers—"

I doubled my efforts to manhandle the little man along. The next time he stopped for breath, he gasped: "That idiot—should have gone in sooner myself—serves him bloody right..."

Then the lights went out. Owens uttered a shrill cry: "Oh, my God!"

"Put your hand out and feel the wall," I said. "Pick up your feet!"

The footsteps and the rumbling cries intensified. I could see nothing. When we came to the place where the passage sloped up, I stumbled and almost fell. I thought: this is it. With a desperate effort, I got my feet under me again and ran on.

Brushing the wall, we jogged up the slope, while the sounds of pursuit came ever louder. Something whirled through the air behind us, to strike the stony wall and rebound to the floor with a clatter. While I could not see the missile, a thrown sledge hammer would have made such a sound.

"I'm—I'm done," wheezed Owens. "Go on, Mr. Newbury. Save yourself."

"Nonsense!" I said. I scooped up Owens and carried him like a child. Luckily he did not weight much over a hundred.

In my imagination, I could almost feel the breath of our pursuers. Any minute, I expected a hammer to come down on my skull.

As my eyes adjusted to the darkness, a little dot of gray appeared ahead. I recognized it as a bend in the tunnel, near the exit. The short leg between the door and this bend was lit by the sunlight outside.

The gray spot grew larger and took rectangular shape. Then we were around the bend and through the door, blinking in the sunshine. I put Owens down and collapsed on the bricks. Owens shut the door, locked it, and stood over me.

"It's all right," he said. "They are allergic to sunlight and hate to expose themselves to it. You saved my life."

When I got my breath back and my racing heart slowed down, I asked: "What happened?"

"Forrest came in on a union organization meeting. He got into an argument with the would-be leader, and he has—had—a violent temper. He was foolish enough to strike the—the organizer. My workers, also, are rather short-tempered, and the next I knew, they were all over him with hammers and other implements. When I saw his brains spattered, I jolly well ran for it."

"What now? Whom do you notify?"

"I shall take care of that, never fear. Your business is finished here, Mr. Newbury. Obviously, my great dream will have to await a more propitious occasion. Let me drive you back to the motel."

Although usually loquacious, Owens was silent on the return trip. While I was curious about his plans, he answered my questions evasively until I stopped asking.

That evening, I reported to Drexel. Next day, I heard nothing from the Oecus. Their telephone did not answer. I finally made an airplane reservation and called a taxi. On a whim, I told the driver to detour to the Oecus on the way to the airport.

The house had overnight become a deserted ruin. Of Colin Owens and his followers there was no sign. The place looked as if a gang of vandals had gone through it with crowbars and hammers.

Every window was broken. Furniture was thrown about and smashed. Wall fittings had been ripped out and floor boards pried up. Some of the plaster had been battered from the walls. Rugs had been ripped or fouled. Such a wreck was the building that it was dangerous even to walk about it, for fear of falling through the floor or having something collapse on one.

I went out back and looked into the pit. The iron door had been broken open and torn from its hinges. It lay on the bricks, crumpled like a piece of tinfoil.

I remembered Owens's saying that his workers avoided sunlight, but that would not hve stopped them from coming out at night to raid the Oecus. Whether they had caught any members of the Anthropophili, I could not tell. I saw no bloodstains in the ruin, but there was nobody about to answer questions. Could the cult members have inflicted this destruction themselves, before abandoning their head-quarters?

I even wondered if the whole thing had been a hallucination or a dream. But there had been nothing imaginary about the application for his loan, with supporting documents, which Owens had sent in, or about my visit to Atlanta. The only way to straighten things out would have been to invade the tunnel again, but I was neither brave nor determined enough to embark upon such an adventure. Besides, I had a 'plane to catch.

I suppose I ought to have reported to the State Police. But I could not imagine explaining to a trooper that I had been chased through a tunnel under Stone Mountain by a mob of infuriated gnomes.

Besides, there was the bank's reputation to consider. Nobody wants to leave his money with an institution run by *hallucinés*. Although my inaction has nipped my conscience since, it is one of the things one must learn to live with, along with the memory of the other follies and blunders of a normally active life.

When I reported back to Esau Drexel, he said: "Well, Willy, you know I'm no goddam pink liberal. But I've got to admit that labor unions are here to stay. Even the elves, gnomes, and other hobgoblins have 'em!"

Tiki

The giant spider crab of the North Pacific, the largest living crustacean, is said to be a sluggish, harmless creature.

I first heard of Esau Drexel's giant crabs at a party at the Museum of Natural Science. As a faithful member, I had taken Denise to a meeting. We stand around among elephants, dinosaurs, and Eskimo artifacts and booze up. When the noise rises to where you have to scream to be heard, the lights are blinked to summon the members to dinner. Afterwards, we listen to somebody like the late Dr. Louis Leakey or the late Sir Julian Huxley, or perhaps see a movie on the life of the Bakhtiari tribesman or of the common flea. As one whose boyhood ambition was to be a naturalist-explorer, I get a great kick out of these events.

Before the movie began, Dr. Esther Farsace, the Curator of Invertebrates, announced a donation to finance a hall in the new wing. This would be the Drexel Hall of Crustaceans Everybody clapped. Looking, with his dark, three-piece suit and white mustache, every bit the prosperous, conservative old banker, Esau Drexel rose and bowed.

Everybody thinks of bankers as rich. I am not, but Esau Drexel was. When not presiding over the Harrison Trust Company and a junior banker named W. Wilson Newbury, he was off in his yacht, recording the songs of the finback whale or counting the elephant seals of Antarctica. He had fitted out this ship as a marine laboratory. The Japanese Emperor had been his guest on board, because of their common interest in marine biology.

After the lecture, we congratulated Drexel on his gift. Denise said: "Whatever gave you the idea, Esau?"

"When I was up in Bering Sea last summer," he said, "the dredge brought up one of those giant spider crabs. It struck me that this poor old museum had no proper place to put it. We have some fine collections of Arthropoda, but far too many to display in one hall. So, being a director of the

97

Museum but never having given it anything much, I thought it was time I did, while I was still around to see how the money was spent.

"Tell you what," he continued, "when the new wing is further along, I'll give you and your kids a guided tour of it!"

Denise wrinkled her nose. "Willy will bring the children. Me, I like the animals with fur and feathers better than those like great bugs."

"Just a mammalian prejudice," said Drexel. "Where will you find a more gorgeous creature than *Odontodactylus scyllarus*?"

"*Zut!*" she said. "I still prefer my crabs in a can, ready to eat."

Drexel turned to me. "Willy, are you playing golf Saturday? You don't mind a little snow on the greens, do you?" For all that he was twenty years older than I, he had the constitution of a polar bear.

During the next summer, Drexel was off on his ship, collecting rare isopods and other sea creatures with lots of jointed legs. When he got back, I saw him (outside of working hours, that is) at the first fall members' meeting. We were drinking our cocktails in the Hall of Oceanic Anthropology, and Denise was reading the caption on a big statue of dark, mahoganylike wood.

"Tiki of Atea," she read. "Hiva Oa, Marquesas Islands. *Que veut dire* 'Tiki of Atea,' darling?"

"A tiki is a Polynesian statue or idol," I said. "*Indubitablement*, Atea is the god the statue is of." Since Denise is French, we run a bilingual menage.

This statue was one of the oldest exhibits in the Museum. It had been there since the nineteenth century. When Christian missionaries in the South Seas were exhorting their converts to burn up all the relics of 'idolatry,' some enterprising scientist had salvaged this eidolon.

That must have been a job, for the statue is seven feet tall and massive. It is just as ugly as those stone images on Easter Island, of which it reminded one, although better-proportioned. It was a highly stylized piece of folk art, squat and blocky, with a snarling, thick-lipped mouth and round

98

bug eyes. I daresay it had seen plenty of human sacrifices in its day.

Esau Drexel barged up with martini in hand and wife in tow. "Willy!" he roared. "Remember my saying I'd give you a guided tour of my new hall? Well, how about next week end?"

"I never see him by daylight any more," said Mrs. Drexel to Denise. "He spends all his week ends here, supervising. I wonder the Museum people haven't gone on strike, to get him out of their hair."

I said I should be delighted to bring such of my children as I could catch. I can take my crustaceans or leave them, but an invitation from the big boss is a command performance.

Our girls begged off. Stephen said he would go if he could bring his friend Hank. I hesitated at this.

Stephen was a sweet, docile twelve-year-old, who never needed to be punished. He was also a natural follower, and his leader was his friend Henry Schnell. Hank was a young hellion; but a parent should think carefully before trying to pry a boy loose from his best friend. So I said that Hank might come.

Knowing Hank's tendency to dash wildly off towards anything that caught his interest, I warned the boys to stay close to me. We met Esau Drexel at the information desk and started towards the new wing. Then we stopped to talk to David Goldman. Professor Goldman was full of the argument, whether therapsid reptiles evolved into birds by developing feathers to fly with, or developed feathers first to keep warm and then adapted them to flying. Goldman was excited by what he said was new evidence on the question.

While we were listening, the boys disappeared. I guessed that Hank, typically, had dashed on ahead, through the Oceanic Hall towards the new wing, and Stephen had followed. I did not worry about the boys. But, knowing Henry Schnell, I did worry about the Museum.

When we got to the Hall of Oceanic Anthropology, the first thing that caught my eye was the Tiki of Atea. On the statue, someone had painted, with one of those thick, felt-tipped pens that kids use to make grafitti on subway cars, a big, crude mustache.

While I stammered humble apologies for my young savages, Drexel said: "Never mind, Willy. I'm sure it'll wash off, even if it's the indelible kind. The statue's varnished. Some idiot put a coat of varnish on at the time of the First World War, and we've never taken it off. Now it's a good thing."

Then I heard another sentence. It said clearly: "You shall rue your insolence, mortal!"

I jumped and stared at Drexel. My boss was looking at the statue, with his hands in his pockets and his mouth closed. Anyway, I could hardly imagine Esau Drexel's telling anyone he should rue his insolence. That was not his style. In one of his more pompous moods, he might have said: "My good man, you'll be sorry for this!"

While I was staring, the same voice added: "You and your seed, both!"

Drexel had not opened his mouth, nor had he given any sign of hearing the voice. Nobody else was nearby. I must, I thought, be getting auditory hallucinations. Naturally, I did not want to say anything to Drexel to cause him to suspect that such was the case. I wondered whether I should consult a neurologist or a psychiatrist. I knew a couple of nice, gentle shrinks...

"Well," growled Drexel, "let's catch your little bums before they do something else."

On we went. At the end of the Oceanic Hall is a small, square hall housing, on this floor, a mineral exhibition. It has no logical place there; but then, museum halls seldom do. As fast as one director begins to get things in what he thinks is a logical order, another director takes his place and starts moving them around again.

It is like one of those puzzles in which you move little wooden blocks in a box, this way and that to bring them into some desired array. In a museum, nobody lives long enough to complete one solution of the problem. The minerals had been left over from some previous arrangement.

The mineral hall opens on the new wing. This is not really a wing but a fourth side to a hollow square. On the far end of the new wing was another side of the square, housing some of the Museum's working and storage spaces. Visitors seldom realize that more space is devoted to these purposes than to exhibition halls. Any mature museum has far more specimens than it can show at any one time. Besides the fourth side of the square, a huge maze of cellars also contains storage and preparation rooms.

In Mineral Hall, we caught up with the boys. They tried to look casual and innocent but could not help smirking and snickering.

They vigorously denied putting a mustache on Atea. When I searched them, I did not find any felt-tipped pen or similar instrument. I supposed that they had ditched it. While I might be morally certain that they had done this vandalism, I could not prove it. One of them must have stood on the other's back or shoulders to reach the statue's bug-eyed face.

"Come on," said Drexel, opening the locked door with a key. Beyond lay the second story of the new wing, the incomplete Crustacean Hall.

There were the usual wall cases and central cases, most of them with their cover glasses still off. The central cases formed a continuous row down the middle of the hall.

Crustaceans of all sizes and shapes were mounted, but only half the spaces in the cases had been filled. There was a lobster that must have weighed thirty pounds alive. There was a Pacific coconut crab almost as big as that lobster. There were gaudily-colored stomatopods and other scuttly creatures.

There were signs of work in progress: a stepladder standing in the fairway, pails, a fire extinguisher, stacks of panes of glass, tools, a box of fasteners to hold the glass of the cases in place. Muttering something about "slobs," Drexel began moving these things into the corners to give the hall a tidier look. I helped him.

Drexel pointed to a blank wall space. "A giant spider crab would go well there, I think."

The boys were getting restless. Few of them can maintain interest for very long in static exhibits. Drexel was spouting his enthusiasm. I gently suggested:

"How about the hall in which these things are being prepared, Esau? I think they'd like that."

"Sure thing!" said Drexel.

He unlocked another door, at the far end of the Crustacean Hall, and led us into one of the preparation halls, which smelled of formaldehyde. There were workbenches, on which the preparators had been painstakingly cleaning the meat out of crabs, shrimps, and other denizens of the deep before wiring them up for mounting. There were racks with dried specimens, and jars and tanks with others floating in preservative. None of the scientists or technicians was at work that day.

The biggest object was a huge metal tank, nearly full of liquid. In it lay what looked at first like a disorganized tangle of the limbs of some fictional super-spider—Tolkien's Shelob, for instance.

"We just got these in," said Drexel. "I didn't catch these beauties. The *Lemuria* got 'em off the Aleutians."

"What are they?" asked Stephen. "They look horrible."

"They," said Drexel, "are the so-called Japanese spider crab, *Macrocheira kampferi*. I don't see what call the Japs have to claim them when they're found all over the Pacific north of latitude forty. And they're not horrible. They're beautiful—at least, to another spider crab."

"How many are there? They're all tangled up so I can't tell."

"There are four," said Drexel. "We figure on mounting the biggest and keeping the rest in storage."

"Are they man-eaters?" asked Henry.

"They're harmless, although I suppose if you went scuba-diving and bothered one, it would defend itself...Yes, Angela?"

A young woman had come in, through the door at the far end of the hall. "Mr. Drexel, Mrs. Drexel wants you on the telephone. You can use the one in my office."

"Excuse me, Willy," said Drexel. "I'll be right back. You and the kids look at the stuff here. Don't let 'em touch anything."

Angela's heels went click, click as the two marched out the door at the far end. The door slammed shut.

I bent over the tank with the spider crabs. They were tremendous creatures, the biggest with legs four to six feet long and chelae of eight or ten feet. One of those nippers, I thought, could easily take off a human hand or foot.

"What's that stuff? Water?" asked Stephen.

"Formaldehyde, I suppose," I said. "Don't stick your finger in it and then in your mouth to find out."

"Yech!" said Hank. "Putting the stuff those things have been lying dead in, in your mouth!"

"Well, you eat crab out of a can, don't you?" said Stephen. "And it's dead, isn't it?"

"Not me," said Hank. "I don't eat no dead monsters. Say!"

"What?" I asked.

"Did Mister—you know—the old guy—your friend—"

"Mr. Drexel," said Stephen.

"Mr. Drexel—did he say they were dead?"

"Of course he did," I said. He had not, but I was not about to make a point of it.

"Well, they ain't. They're moving."

"You're crazy, Hank," said Stephen.

"Look there!" said Hank. "His legs are wriggling, like he was waking up."

"Just your imag——Hey, Dad, take a look!"

I did. As I looked, all four crabs stirred, gathered their tangled limbs under them, and stood up. They rose from the liquid like Venus from the sea foam, only it would take a more avid seafood lover than I to see any resemblance to Venus. They were a pale, bonelike gray, with bits of olive-green sponge and other marine growths adhering to them.

The boys and I jumped back from the tank. The boys shrieked.

Stepping deliberately, the four crabs climbed dripping out of the tank. Led by the biggest of all, they started towards us, chelae extended and open.

"Run!" I yelled. "This way! Don't let 'em lay a claw on you! They'll take your heads off!"

I started for the Crustacean Hall. The boys dashed past me. Behind us, in single file, came the four spider crabs, their clawed feet going clickety-click on the tiles.

The crabs did not move faster than a brisk walk. Amazed and horrified though I was, I did not, being in good shape for a man past forty, expect any trouble in outrunning them.

When the boys got to the far end of the Crustacean Hall ahead of me, they tried the door. It would not open.

I caught up with them and heaved on the knob. The door was shut on a snap lock, to keep out the unauthorized. It could only be opened with a key, and the key was in Esau Drexel's pocket.

The four crabs came clattering down the Crustacean Hall, along one side of the row of central cases. I yelled and banged the door, to no avail.

"Boys!" I said. "They're on one side of the cases. We'll run back on the other and try the other door."

The crabs were now a mere nine feet from us. We dashed back up the hall on the other side of the central cases. The crabs continued their course. They came to the end of the row of central cases, rounded it like Roman racing chariots rounding the end of the *spina*, and continued their pursuit.

We went back through the Crustacean Hall, through the Mineral Hall, and through the preparation hall. After us came the crabs.

The door at the far end of the preparation hall was also locked. I fruitlessly yelled and banged some more.

As the crabs clicked past the big tank on one side, the boys and I ran the other way on the other side. We made the Crustacean Hall all right. Then, when I looked back, my heart sank. The crabs, or the spirit of Atea, or whatever motivated the monsters, had done the obvious thing. The crabs had split up into two pairs. One pair approached on either side of the row of central cases. Now there was no way to get past them, so we could not continue to play ring-around-the-rosy with them. They had us.

I kicked the door and nearly burst my lungs screaming. I looked around for something to use as a club. Since the crabs were slow and clumsy, I thought I might have a change of bashing in a carapace or two before they got me. At least, I thought, I might save the boys.

When the crabs were over halfway down the hall, I saw something in a corner. It was the fire extinguisher that

Drexel had moved out of the way. This was of the big cylindrical type that you turn upside down.

I grabbed that extinguisher, inverted it, and pointed the nozzle on the end of the hose at the nearest crab. I had no time to read the directions and only hoped I was following proper procedure.

The extinguisher made a great fizzing. Liquid shot from the nozzle, spraying all over the crab. The creature halted, waving its chelae in a disorganized way.

I sprayed another, and another, and another, and then back to the first one. I don't know what chemicals were in the extinguisher, but the crabs teetered on their spindly legs. They waved their chelae wildly, banged into the cases, and fell over. One lay on its back with twitching egs. Another collpased against a case....

When Esau Drexel came in a few minutes later, he found four motionless crabs and one motionless banker. The last-mentioned leaned breathlessly against a case and held an empty fire extinguisher.

"But—but that's impossible!" said Drexel when he heard the story.

I shrugged. I have had too many funny things happen to me to be very free with the word "impossible."

When the door to the Crustacean Hall was unlocked, others came in. Drexel told a guard to admit only Museum personnel. The boys and I repeated our story.

Doctor Einarson, the assistant curator of Pacific anthropology, spoke up. He talked with a funny little smile, as if hinting that we were not to take him seriously.

"Put a mustache on Atea?" he said. "No wonder. She's a goddess, you know. No mustaches for her!"

The following Monday, when the whole Museum was closed, you would have seen one junior banker and his wife, with a stepladder, a bucket, a sponge, a scrubbing brush, and soap. They were painstakingly erasing the mustache on Atea's tiki.

It must have worked, because nothing more like that has happened to me in the Museum in all the years since.

Far
Babylon

Under the lucent moon, a man in a black cowboy hat was
squatting by the stream, making a castle of sand.

I had given up trying to sleep. No matter how I squirmed
and turned, there was always some stick or stone poking
into me through the sleeping bag. At last I crawled out of the
bag, pulled on my pants and shoes, and wandered off.
Somewhere a coyote howled.

I marveled at the soundness with which Denise and the
children managed to sleep. I thought: Wilson Newbury, you
were a fool to yield to their pleas to go camping. You are
past the age when sleeping out of doors is fun; you should
have left such Tarzanism to scoutmasters and camp
counsellors. But that's the hell of trying to be a good father.

The stream near which I had parked the station wagon
was some obscure affluent of the Pecan. One difficulty with
camping in a mixed party in that flat, open country is to find
a place where the campers can perform their natural
functions with decent privacy. We had finally found this
place, where the little dry ravines and the screen of scrubby
vegetation bordering the stream provided cover.

The weather was fair, even though, during the afternoon,
a couple of distant puff-balls of cumulus cloud built up into
thunderheads. The weather down there is deceptive.
Because of the clearness of the air and the openness and
flatness of the country, you often see little local thunderstorms twenty or thirty miles away and think it is going to
rain. Actually, there is only a tiny chance that any rain will
reach you.

I sauntered down the slope in the brilliant moonlight,
pushed through the screen of brush, and stopped at the
sight of this man in the broad-brimmed hat. I took a few
steps towards him, to see what he was doing. He did not
look up or seem aware of my approach.

By pinching and patting the damp sand, the man had built

a square wall, about an inch high and a yard on a side. With his fingers, he had scooped a trench diagonally across the square, going through the wall on both sides and meandering like a stream bed. Along each bank of this depression, he had continued the wall from the break on one side to that on the other.

Inside the square, he had drawn a number of lines in the sand with his finger, dividing the area into polygons. Inside one of these figures, he was working on a couple of structures. One, completed, was an L-shaped block, a couple of inches on a side. Nearby, the man was building a pyramidal structure, several inches high.

"Howdy, mister," I said, trying to copy the local speech.

I have always moved warily in that part of the country. Many years ago, my father warned me to be careful. When he was young, early in this century, he and a friend were traveling through there. They stopped where a dance was in progress. The friend asked a girl to dance; she accepted. Then her boy friend appeared and shot my father's friend dead. The stiff was removed and the dance went on. This made a strong impression on my old man.

"Good evening, sir," said the man in a deep, soft voice like distant thunder. He turned towards me, but the moonlight on his sombrero cast his face into deep shadow. I could see nothing of his features but a blur. I had bought a similar hat in order to look more like a local, but I had not put in on to walk about on this balmy night.

"Nice weather," I said.

"Yes, sir, if the drouth doesn't spoil the crops." He added another story to the pyramid.

"It's none of my business," I said, "but would you mind telling me what you're doing?"

The shadowed face turned towards me again. "This is a model of Babylon."

"You mean Babylon, Iraq, not Babylon, New York?"

"Yes, sir. I hadn't even heard there was a Babylon, New York. This that I'm building is the great zikkurat of Marduk. That's what the Bible called the Tower of Babel."

His accent was local, but his grammar and vocabulary were those of an educated man. This did not astonish me. I

107

have come upon too many cases of unexpected knowledge in unlikely places, like the Iraqi shaykh who could recognize most of Mozart's six hundred-plus tunes. I asked:

"Isn't it a little—ah—unusual for somebody around here to be interested in ancient Babylon?"

He shrugged. "The sons of bitches around here always thought I was crazy. But that's a place I always wanted to see. I used to dream about it and write about it. I can imagine it to this day." Softly, the rumbling voice began to chant:

"At Babylon, far Babylon, the brown Euphrates crawls
Where once arose the city's blue and gold and scarlet halls,
And silver spires loomed behind its frowning, lofty walls.

In Babylon, old Babylon, the river, wide and slow,
Meandered through the city's heart, where on its turbid flow
There swam a swarm of rafts and barges, wherries and bateaux.

In Babylon, vast Babylon, with folk of every hue,
The streets were filled: with Scyth and Mede, Egyptian, Arab, Jew;
With workman, soldier, strumpet, slave; with lord and retinue.

At Babylon, dead Babylon, a boundless plain of clay
Lies flat beneath a dusty sky and stretches far away,
And dust are holy Babylon and all her people gay."

"Whose poetry?" I asked.

"Mine. I used to make up these jingles. There wasn't any money in it, though, so I quit. But I still wish I could have seen Babylon."

"I saw it a couple of years ago."

"You did? Tell me about it, sir."

"It's just a big, flat area beside the Euphrates," I said, "with a few tufts of grass here and there. It looks like the plain in your poem, except where they've excavated the remains of the ancient buildings. These seem to have been all made of plain brown mud brick. Must have been a pretty monotonous-looking place when it was alive."

Even in the shadow of the sombrero, I saw a flash of teeth bared in a grin. "Reckon I'd prefer my dream Babylon to the real thing. But that's life. Still, I wish I could have seen it. I thought, when the change came, that at last I'd be able to go. It didn't seem much to ask."

"I don't quite follow you. What happened?"

"Turned out I'd violated some damn-fool regulation. Now they won't let me leave the county. So I've got to make my own. Every full moon, I come here to build my little Babylon." The hatted head turned away to glance up at the moon. "Well, sir, I've got to get back. Hope you have a good time, and don't worry about the people hereabouts. Some of you Northerners come down here with funny ideas about us."

"Is it as obvious as that? I thought I talked pretty good Southwestern."

"You do, but I saw your license plate. They think they're going to see cowboys shooting each other in the streets. Nowadays, the crime is all in the big cities; the little towns and the countryside are so peaceful, it's disgusting. What brings you down here, if I may ask?"

"I'm a banker, and we're thinking of opening a branch in Fort Worth. Since I had to stay here a couple of months, I brought the family along to make a vacation of it. We have to start back soon because of school."

"Well, have yourself a nice time. Good night, sir; nice talking to you."

"Good night," I said.

The man rose, big and bulky, and headed up the stream. The low water caused by the dry spell left a wide expanse of sand on either side, between the water and the screen of trees and shrubs. He walked up this strip and was almost at once out of sight.

The sun was breaking the horizon when Stephen and Héloise poked me awake. "Hey, Dad!" said the former.

"When you gonna get us some breakfast? I could eat a whole steer."

"I want to see Daddy make toast without a toaster," added little Priscille.

As I wriggled out of my sleeping bag again, I remembered the talk with the man in the black cowboy hat. I also remembered something else. This, strangely, seemed to have slipped my mind altogether during that nocturnal conversation.

In a small town through which we had driven the day before, I had gotten into talk with the garage mechanic, a garrulous oldster, while having an oil change. He corrected my pronunciation of the name of the Pecan Valley, saying:

"Mister, like we say here, a pe-CAHN is a nut; a PEE-can is something you keep under the bed."

He doubled over laughing; this was evidently his favorite joke. When he got over his guffaws, he told me about some of the local characters he had known. One in particular, he said, had wanted to be a writer. They said he sold a lot of stuff to the magazines, but my informant had not seen any of it.

"He didn't look like my idea of a writer," said the mechanic. "Writers ain't nothing but skinny little characters who couldn't punch their way out of a paper bag. This was a big, two-fisted guy. I think he was a little touched, always talking about old ruins and fooling around with stories instead of getting a regular job."

"What happened to him?" I asked.

"Dead. Shot hisself."

When I recalled this conversation, I told the family: "Excuse me a minute." I hastened back to the side of the stream, where the night's colloquy had taken place. There was, however, no sign of the model of Babylon or its zikkurat, nor yet of the stranger's footprints. I did see my own prints from an earlier passage that way.

I also remembered something I had long forgotten. Years before, when I was an undergraduate at M.I.T., I used to visit a fellow in Providence, who wrote for the pulp magazines. Once this friend told me about a pen pal of his, another pulp writer, who lived in the Southwest and wrote gory stories about heroes with muscles of steel and heads of oak. I did not rememer the pen pal's name, but the description fitted.

When I returned and started to gather the makings for breakfast, Denise said:

"Willy darling, what is the matter? You look as if you had seen a ghost."

"Maybe I have," I said, fanning the fire with my cowboy hat.

The
Yellow Man

The yellow man said: "And what, Monsieur, are you doing, moving into my house?"

I had rented the station wagon in Fort-de-France and driven out to the place I had taken. I, my wife, and three children were carrying suitcases, dress bags, cameras, and other gear into the house when this man appeared in the driveway.

Something told me at once that he spelled trouble. He was about of my height, but slender, with a yellow-tan skin and curly rather than kinky hair. Before such people became hypersensitive about the term, we used to call them mulattoes.

"Your house?" I said, putting down the two suitcases. "Excuse me, Monsieur, but is this not the house of Marcel Argenton?"

"Technically, it is," he replied. My family, also, had put down their burdens to listen. "But Monsieur Argenton has rented it to me for the summer."

"There must be some mistake," I said. "Monsieur Argeton has rented the house to me for the next three weeks. I can show you the lease."

"Me also, I could show you the lease if I had it with me. I rented the house only the past week, through the agent Privas, in Fort-de-France."

"Ah," I said, "that explains it. I met Monsieur Argenton in the United States, three months past. I rented the house from him directly, and I suppose he forgot to cancel his listing with the local agent. I regret to cause you of the trouble."

"You will not cause me of the trouble, Monsieur. On the contrary, it is I who must excuse myself for dispossessing you."

This was going to be sticky. Luckily, I outweighed the man by twenty pounds and was in good condition for a man

112

of sedentary occupation. I put on my fighting face.

"You will not dispossess me, Monsieur," I said. "I am here; my lease antedates yours; and here I stay."

The man started to say something, then jerked his head around as another appeared. This was a stocky, muscular, black Martiniquais in shabby shirt, pants, sandals, and a big straw hat with a wide, unbound brim. He parked his bicycle, looked from one to the other, and said:

"Which of you gentlemen is the Monsieur Nevuree?"

"I think that you mean me, Wilson Newbury," I said. "Are you Jacques Lecouvreur, from Schoelcher?"

"Yes, Monsieur. Monsieur Argenton arranged that I should work for you."

"That's good, Jacques. Please, help the family to carry this baggage into the house."

"Lecouvreur!" said the yellow man sharply. "Knowest thou who I am?" He used the familiar form.

Jacques Lecouvreur looked puzzled. "Are you—are you that Haitian gentleman, Monsieur Duchamps?"

"C'est moi, donc. Now tell Monsieur Newbury that, when I demand that he retire and leave the house to me, who has a valid lease on it, he would do better to comply."

Jacques's eyes grew large. "Oh, Monsieur Newbury, this is a bad business! He can make of the trouble for you."

"I have known of the trouble before," I said. "Carry that baggage into the house, Jacques. Go on, Denise; go on, kids. Take the stuff in."

Duchamp's lips tightened; he took a step toward me, with a malevolent look in his eyes. I stood my ground. After a silent minute of confrontation, Duchamps said: "You will regret this, Monsieur." He turned and walked away down the drive.

As soon as we were settled, I called Jacques Lecouvreur aside. I had met Marcel Argenton, a white Martiniquais, at a banker's convention in New York. Learning that he was from Martinque, I expressed a wish to spend a vacation there. He explained that he planned to go to France for the month of June—something to do with exports of sugar — and that I might rent his house, near the shore between Fort-de-France and Schoelcher, during that time.

Argenton had also arranged for Jacques Lecouvreur to work for me. Jacques was a fisherman of Schoelcher, but he wanted the job to get money for an outboard motor. I asked Jacques:

"What's all this about Duchamps? Who or what is he?"

Jacques gave a little shiver. "I do not know, Monsieur. I know nothing at all."

"Oh yes, you know! *Allons*, open up."

With a little gentle arm-twisting, I got it out of him: "He is Oreste Duchamps, a big *quimboiseur* from Haiti."

"A *what?*" the word was strange to me.

"You know, Monsieur, a *houngan*; a *bocor*. What you would call a *sorcier*."

"Oh, a sorcerer! A priest of voodoo, *hein?*"

"Ah, no, Monsieur. Respectable followers of *vodun* will have nothing to do with him. Me, I am good Catholic; but not all partisans of *vodun* are so wicked as the priests would like us to think. But Monsieur Duchamps has his own following. He is trying to bring all the *bourhousses* of the island under his control. He is a bad one to mock oneself of."

I sighed. Although I am no more psychic than Paddy's pig, I seem to draw such people as garbage draws flies.

We spent the rest of the day at moving in and setting up. During this time, we drove Jacques to the village of Schoelcher, named for a man instrumental in freeing the slaves in 1848. Denise laid in a stock of food.

While she shopped, Jacques showed me his boat, the *St. Timothée*, drawn up on the beach with a score of others. They were narrow, sharp-ended craft, with the peculiar projectng keel found in Caribbean fishing boats. This keel sticks out beyond the stem like the ram of a battleship of 1900. Nearly all the boats had good Catholic names—*St. Pierre, St. Jean, Sainte Famille*—but one fisherman, evidently a Muslim, defiantly called his boat the *Inchallah*.

Jacques explained how he meant to attach the motor. He spoke volubly but mostly in such strong Créole that the meaning passed me by. Denise claims to understand it, but she is a Frenchwoman born and thus familiar with at least some French dialects. Still, Jacques had given much thought to the motor, comparing models and taking measurements.

Having promised us a cook, he went away and came back with a huge, shapeless, scowling mass of black fat, with her belongings tied up in a flour sack. She wore one of those turbans they make by folding a bandana around a cap of newspaper, with the points sticking up. Jacques introduced her as Mme. Claudine Boussac. We squeezed her into the station wagon and drove back to Argenton's house.

I was not prepossessed by Claudine's looks. Nonetheless, after our servantless life in the land of the free, it seemed like an almost indecent luxury to have people to fetch and carry for very modest wages. I felt a little guilty about such economic imperialism. It was made possible by the fact that, despite some progress, most of the folk of these isles of the Spanish Main were still dirt poor. But then, if I did not hire Jacques and did the fetching and carrying myself, poor Jacques could not buy the outboard motor on which his heart was set.

When evening came, Claudine was rattling about the kitchen. Denise and I were enjoying daiquiris on the verandah; any liquor but rum is sky-high in Martinique. We were admiring the blaze of the hibiscus and bouganvillia, sniffing the aroma of a million blossoms, and watching the lizards scuttle, when the drumming began.

It was a dry, metallic tap-tap-tappety-tap, as if someone were hitting an empty kerosene can. It did not seem to come from any particular direction. I wondered if some of the locals had gotten up a steel band, on the Trinidadian model, and were practicing on their tuned oil drums.

Jacques came out on the porch to tell us that dinner was ready. The he froze, bug-eyed and slack-mouthed. If he could have turned pale, I am sure he would have.

"Come on, Jacques!" I said.

"Those drums," he said, almost in a whisper. "That is the deed of Monsieur Duchamps."

"*Eh bien?* No one has ever died of a little drumming."

"If that were all—" he said, and finished with a Créole sentence that I missed.

We had seen something of Fort-de-France; besides, that city, lying in a bowl of surrounding hills, gets uncomfortably hot in summer. So next day we drove in the other direction, to St. Pierre and Mt. Pelée. You cannot appreciate what a huge thing this mile-high "Bald Mountain" is until you have seen it looming, its summit hidden in condensation clouds.

We stopped at St. Pierre, a narrow, crescent-shaped town built on a slope arising from the shore. Clumps of pale-green banana trees grew on the adjacent slopes. Once the island's main city, St. Pierre is now hardly more than a village. There are still Pompeii-like ruins left over from the great eruption of 1902. We poked around these and went through the museum, viewing the samples of glassware and metallic objects fused into lumps by the heat of the death cloud.

"But," said daughter Héloïse, "if the volcano was erupting for a week before the disaster, why didn't the people get away?"

"It was the governor, Louis Mouttet," I said. "Although he was appointed by Paris, they had a local legislature, and an election was coming up. The Liberals represented the white planter class, who had all the money; the Radicals were mostly Negroes, who had the numbers. The governor, who backed the Liberals, feared that any public disturbance might lose the election for them."

"You sound like a Communist," said little Priscille. "Bankers aren't supposed to talk that way."

"Never mind how bankers are supposed to talk. That's what happened. Anyway, those caste distinctions have pretty well broken down by now."

"So Mouttet opposed any plan for evacuation. He even posted soldiers on the road to Fort-de-France to turn back fugitives. Then, at eight o'clock on the morning of May eighth, 1902, off she went. Wiped out thirty-odd thousand people in a few minutes. The only survivor in the main part of town was a condemned murderer in an underground cell. Men didn't beat that record until they got the atomic bomb."

"What happened to the governor?" asked Stephen.

"Nobody knows. He was in St. Pierre at the time, but

116

they never found his body."

We returned in the late afternoon. The roads were fairly good as to surface, having little heavy truck traffic and no freezing winters to tear them up. They are, however, the most hair-raising roads I have ever driven.

On the way back from St. Pierre, the road goes down a slope that calls for low gear to avoid burning your brakes. Then it turns sharply to the left. If you miss the turn, you go right on down into the blue Caribbean, hundreds of feet below. A heavy steel guard rail at the turn had been pushed over and squashed flat; somebody had not made it. I see why they have no roller coasters in Fort-de-France. With the local roads, who needs them?

At cocktail time, the drumming began again. Jacques came out in even greater agitation.

"Monsieur Newbury!" he said. "Look what I have found under the house!"

He held out the separated parts of a little bird: the head, the wings, and the legs.

"That's a lugubrious thing to show at meal time," I said. "What in the name of God is it?"

"It is a *wanga,* Monsieur."

"You mean some sort of bad-luck charm? What about it?"

"It appeared under the house. I do not know how it arrived there; I have been working around the place all day. But there it was."

"*Eh bien,* put it in the garbage can."

Jacques sighted. "I wish you well, Monsieur, but I do not know if—" The rest was Créole.

That night, I dreamed I was walking a street in St. Pierre as it was before the eruption. The sun had risen some time before, but the town was so blanketed with black smoke that it was almost as dark as night.

A few others were up and about. Their footsteps made no sound, because of a layer of dark-gray, powdery volcanic ash, several centimeters deep, which covered the streets. I doubt if I could have heard them anyway, over the roar of the volcano. It was eight kilometers away but loomed

117

huge—such of it as could be seen through the murk—even at that distance. The roaring was punctuated by explosions; boulder-sized lava bombs crashed down on the houses.

Then the people in the street were crying out and pointing towards Pelée. An enormous cloud, distinct from the general pall of smoke, had appeared on the side of the mountain. It was a bright, incandescent red, and black around the edges. That is, the interior was red-hot and the surface black. One could see the redness, mottled and shifting, through this black integument.

This ameboid, fiery blob moved swiftly down the mountainside towards the city, flowing over intervening ridges and growing ever larger. I knew what it was: a mixture of incandescent gas and volcanic dust. The high temperature kept it churning, so that the dust could not settle out. At the same time, the dust gave the mass a specific gravity higher than that of air, so the cloud slid down the slope at turnpike speed.

In a few minutes, the red cloud reached the upper parts of the city. The heat became blistering. Buildings in the path of the cloud burst into flame, as if they were paper houses doused with gasoline and ignited.

The cloud slowed up as it reached the lower town, where the slope was less steep. All of a sudden, the streets were full of people running and screaming with their clothes afire. Some fell and lay writhing. Some, left naked by the burning of their garments, burst open. Can you imagine the sight of hundreds running and being burned alive at the same time? Their shrieks merged into a continuous ululation, audible even over the roar from the mountain. My own clothes smoldered and started to burn...

"Wake up, Willy!" cried Denise, shaking me. "What is it?"

I groggily rubbed the sleep from my eyes and told her.

"No wonder you screamed!" she said. "Now go back to sleep, darling. You are safe here."

The appalling sight I had seen, however, kept me awake for an hour. When I did get to sleep, there I was, back in St. Pierre a few minutes before the eruption. Again the great red cloud of death oozed out of the mountain. While one part of me realized that this was a dream, the rest of me went

118

through all the emotions of a victim, until my shrieks again led Denise to awaken me. I got no more sleep that night.

We spent the next day on Argenton's private little stretch of beach of black volcanic sand. I brought along a pocket timer to make sure that nobody stayed too long in one position in the bright Caribbean sun. But I got drowsy myself, went to sleep on my belly without setting the timer, and woke an hour later with a burned back.

That evening, the drums were at it again. I asked Jacques: "Any more wangas today?"

"No, Monsieur. But do you do well? I heard you call out in the night."

"Just a bad dream, from reading too much about Mt. Pelée."

Jacques looked sorrowful. "I tell you, Monsieur, that Duchamps is a bad man to cross."

"That's his problem."

"If you say it, Monsieur."

That night, I dreamed I was back in St. Pierre again, on that fatal morning in 1902.

"Willy," said Denise, "we must do something about this. A middle-aged man cannot go without sleeping, night after night."

"Okay; I'll see a doctor. We were going to Fort-de-France anyway."

We had one minor set-to with our undergraduate older daughter. She wanted to visit the city in what was then the new uniform of rebellious youth: ragged blue jeans and a man's shirt tied up to expose the midriff. (The youth revolt had just come to a boil in the United States.) Denise and I stood firm, insisting that such scruffy garb was unbecoming to foreigners in a French city.

"Even if they're black," I said, "these people are just as French as the white Frenchmen of France. Same virtues, same faults. One thing they don't like is for outsiders to come in and throw their weight around."

Héloise gave in, put on a dress, and sulked for a couple of hours.

Fort-de-France is a bustling, businesslike place, with little tropical languor. We took one another's pictures standing before the statue of the Empress Josephine; having been born there, she is the leading ikon of Martinique. We toured through the Museum of Fort St. Louis, ate a huge but delicious French restaurant lunch, and shopped. At least, the girls shopped. Stephen and I wearily stood or sat, save when Stephen bought one of those strange, cartwheel-shaped straw hats they wear on Guadeloupe.

After Denise had, with a few well-chosen French words, verbally beheaded a snippy black salesgirl in M. Alfred Reynard's perfumery shop, we hunted up a physician listed in the international medical directory. He gave me a phial of sleeping pills.

"If it marches not," he said, "come back and we will try something else."

We had a fine dinner at *The Hippopotamus.* I said: "If I eat here very often, I'll begin to look like a hippo myself."

Back at the Argenton house, Jacques had left, to bike back to Schoelcher and his family. The next day, Sunday, he had off.

Jacques Lecouvreur seemed a good man and not unintelligent, but Claudine left much to be desired. She was a sullen slattern, who drank a lot and cooked badly. When Denise, with the proper French reverence for food, gave her instructions, she listened dumbly and then went on doing exactly as before. Héloise, full of what she thought were advanced ideas, explained Claudine's behavior as a case of colonial neurosis, brought on by capitalistic exploitation. I, however, think Claudine would have been the same anywhere.

We had drums that evening, but, thanks to the pills of *Monsieur le médecin,* no more dreams. Nor did I suffer any Sunday night, either.

Monday morning, we were loading the car for an expedition to the church of Sacré Coeur de Montmartre de Balata and to Morne Rouge, when Oreste Duchamps again materialized in our driveway. He gave a strained little smile and polite greeting.

"Does all go well with you, Monsieur?" he said.

"Very well, thank you."

"Have you decided to leave?"

"At the end of my three weeks, Monsieur; not before."

"You have not been incommoded by any—ah—psychic manifestations?"

"No, Monsieur, I have not. To what do you refer? Do you know something special?"

He shrugged. "There are rumors, such as the recent one of the phantom of Louis Mouttet. But we, as civilized men, dismiss them as the idle superstition. Still, I asked myself."

"Well, you may cease to concern yourself, Monsieur. All marches well."

He growled something about *"bâtards blancs"* and walked off.

That evening, Claudine came out on the porch with another wanga, made of parts of a rat.

"Bad place," she said. "I think you better go."

At least, that is what I think she said. Jacques could speak *français ordinaire* when he put his mind to it, but Claudine had only Créole.

That night, Denise and I were just going into our bedroom, when she said: "What is that on the floor? A piece of old rope—"

Her words were cut off as I grabbed her and swung her around behind me. In the gloom of Argenton's inadequate electric lighting, I saw the rope move. It whipped into a spiral coil and drew back its head to strike.

"Snake!" I said. "Get me a broom, quick!"

Then it was simply a matter of whacking the reptile with the broom handle until it was dead, despite its efforts to strike.

The snake was a fer-de-lance about a meter long, brown with black diamond-shaped markings like those of a rattlesnake. It had the wide, heart-shaped head of the rattlesnakes and all the other pit vipers.

"Monsieur Duchamps doesn't give up easily," I said. "I'll try the cops."

Next morning, I drove into Fort-de-France and stopped at the nearest police station. I brought the battered carcass of the fer-de-lance in a paper bag. The man on the desk referred me to a *brigadier* or sergeant of police, Hippolyte Frot.

Sergeant Frot was a big black man, as tall as I, younger, and heavier, with the beginnings of a paunch. I told him my tale, and he examined the snake in a relaxed and genial manner.

"They have become rare since the introduction of the mongoose," he said. "The only time we see them is when some peasant brings one down from the hills, to stage a snake-and-mongoose fight. Some like them better than cockfights."

That is not what my biologist friends at the Museum of Natural Science tell me. They say the mongoose generally avoids the pit vipers, whose strike is much faster than a cobra's. Instead, the mongoose have wrought such havoc among the West Indian birds, lizards, and other small game, not to mention the farmers' chickens, that on some islands the bounty has been taken off the snakes and put on the mongoose instead. Still, I was not going to argue the matter with Frot.

"About this Duchamps," he went on, "you understand, Monsieur Newbury, that we have the freedom of religion here. If Duchamps wants to proselyte his primitive polytheism, that is his affair, so long as he behaves himself. Such superstitions are all but extinct on this island, anyway."

West Indians like to deny that there is any voodoo left, at least on whatever island the speaker belongs to. Other islands may still have it, he says; but not *his*, which is much too advanced and cultured.

"On the other hand," continued Frot, "we must not forget the *mission civilizatrice* of France. This demands that things be done in an orderly, civilized manner. If the cult of Duchamps creates disturbances or introduces serpents into houses, we shall have to take stern action. But please remember that, from what you have told me, we have no evidence that the serpent did not crawl into your house on its own initiative. We could not arrest Duchamps on any such accusation.

"Permit me to suggest that you leave the remains of the

122

serpent with me. I shall assign men to look in on the house of Monsieur Argenton from time to time. If there are any further manifestations, be sure to let me know. What is your telephone number?"

"There is no telephone. I came here to get away from such trammels of civilization."

Frot chuckled. "But now it seems a less admirable idea, *hein*? I have seen it before. We find that the oars of civilization raise blisters on our hands and cause our back muscles to ache. So we cast them away. Then we find that the current carries our little boat towards the cascade. So we try to snatch the oars back, if they nave not drifted out of reach. Anyway, you have an automobile, so keep me informed."

For several days, there were no more manifestations, save for the nightly serenades of the drummers. The children caught on, as children will, despite Denise's and my efforts not to discuss the matter before them. Stephen, who had been writing notes for a high-school paper on Martinque, which he meant to present next fall, said:

"If this Duchamps gives any more trouble, Dad, why don't you shoot him and claim self-defense?"

"First," I said, "because I don't have a gun; and second, because the law wouldn't recognize an attack by witchcraft as a legitimate excuse for killing anybody."

Héloise said: "They'd convict him of murder, stupid, and cut off his head with a guillotine."

"Gee!" cried Priscille. "Wouldn't that be something to see? Of course, we'd miss you, Dad."

"Thanks," I said. "Actually, they don't use the guillotine here. They hang miscreants."

"Why?" asked Stephen.

"They tried a guillotine during the French Revolution, but it didn't work. The dampness warped the wooden uprights, so the slicer tended to stick on the way down. Sometimes the poor fellow's head would be cut only half off."

"Nowadays you could use a steel or aluminum frame—" began Stephen.

"What a conversation for breakfast!" said Denise.

"Oh," said Priscille, "I like a little blood and gore with my meals."

At cocktail time, Denise said: "Willy, we must get rid of that Claudine. She does nothing right, and I cannot teach her. I had a hundred times rather cook myself than to spend hours trying to beat sense into her thick head."

Jacques Lecouvreur overheard. He said: "Pardon me, Monsieur and Madame. Please do not do that."

"And why not, if we choose?" said Denise with hauteur.

"She would put a curse on the house. She is in with the *bourhousses*."

"Oh?" said I. "Then why did you hire her for us, Jacques?"

"Please, Monsieur, I did not know then. I am very sorry. I found out later that she has the power. If she cursed the house, not even a good Catholic exorcism could lift it. You would have to hire a team of *chango* dancers to drive out the evil spirits, and all the troupes hereabouts are under the control of Monsieur Duchamps."

"She is hardly the species of person we want for our cook," I said. "She might poison us. In fact, I sometimes suspect that she has been trying to do just that."

"I know, Monsieur, I know. But, if you dismiss her, I must go, too."

"Why? We don't want to lose you, Jacques."

"You do not understand, Monsieur. If she put a curse on this house, the misfortunes of those who stayed would descend on me, also. I must consider my family."

"We'll think it over," I said.

As often happens, we thought it over so long that we finally decided, tacitly, that with only a week more to stay, there was no use in stirring up unpleasantness. Besides, we had taken to driving in to Fort-de-France for dinner at *The Hippopotamus*, the *Chez Étienne*, and other establishments.

The drumming continued, becoming ever louder and more insistent. One morning, Jacques said:

"Monsieur, I have a message from Monsieur Duchamps. It was circulated to me through Claudine."

"Well?"

"He says that this is your last chance. If you have not departed by the fall of the night, he will not be responsible for your safety."

"Kind of him," I said. "Tell him that, while I regret the withdrawal of his protection, I shall have to manage the best possible."

"He also spoke a Créole proverb: '*Fer couper fer.*' Do you understand, Monsieur?"

"I think he meant: 'Iron to cut iron,' or 'Extreme cases demand extreme remedies.' Right?"

"*Oui.* And, oh, there is one more thing." Jacques fidgeted, then brought out the hand he had held behind him. It gripped a human skull, minus the mandible and most of the teeth. "I found this on the sill of the door this morning."

I examined the skull. "Another wanga?"

Jacques frowned thoughtfully. "Not exactly, Monsieur. A veritable wanga is made of the parts of a bird or an animal, according to a formula. It is sung and danced over in a certain way, to reduce the spirits to one's service. This is more a simple warning gesture. I think I know where it came from."

"Where?"

"There is a beach on Guadeloupe where, they say, long ago the English and French soldiers killed in fighting the Caribs are buried. Now the sea is eroding it, and one can find all the bones and skulls one wants."

"Put it on the matelpiece," I said. "I may take it home with me."

Jacques departed, shaking his head at the whims of these crazy Americans.

I drove into Fort-de-France to see my philosophical sergeant. Frot said: "We still have nothing to go on. This obeah man has been careful not to utter legally actionable threats—"

"Obeah man?" I said. "I thought Obeah was the Jamaican variety of *vodun.*"

Frot smiled. "You do not know that there has been an ecumenical movement among the Afro-Caribbean supernaturalists. The obeah men, the *houngans,* and the *quimboiseurs* assemble in councils, to debate whether Obboney or Damballah shall be considered the number one god, or whether they are but different names for the same being. They have the same trouble in finding common ground that Christians have had under similar circumstances. But, despite some fierce theological disputes, they seem to be hammering out some species of unity. So the old distinctions no longer apply.

"We will, however, try to keep your section under closer surveillance. Be sure to report to me anything that could form the ground of a formal complaint."

"Thank you, Sergeant," I said. "You're very kind."

"It's nothing. It is just that I am enchanted to meet an American who speaks the good French. You know, your compatriots come here, counting on everyone to know their own language; and when people do not, they shout at them in an uncivilized manner. *Bonne chance,* Monsieur."

We put in a strenuous day on the beach, swimming and playing games. When it was over, we ate one of Claudine's indifferent dinners. The kids were tired enough to go to bed early, but I felt full of life. The drumming had died away, so the only sound was the chirp of a million crickets. I said to Denise:

"Let's take a walk on the beach. The moon is full."

So we did. Our stroll ended in an impromptu swim, and then we made love on the sand.

We dressed and, hand in hand, started back for the house. We had climbed halfway up the steep path when a man stepped out of the shadow of a banana tree. The moon threw silvery spots on him, so that I could not clearly make him out. I had an impression that he was white of skin and stout, with curly hair and a little beard.

Without a word, the man came towards us, down the slope of the path.

"Who are you?" I said.

The man continued his silent advance. The moon gleamed upon a machete blade.

"Run, Denise!" I said in English. "I'll hold this guy off. Get the cops!"

When I glanced around, Denise had vanished. I heard faint, receding footfalls. Although she, like me, was no longer so young as once, she still could run like a deer.

The man with the knife came on. My thought was to get around him to the house to telephone. Then I remembered we had no 'phone. Perhaps, if I could get to the station wagon, I could lock myself in. I might even use it as a weapon, if I could catch him on the roadway in front of the vehicle. But that would leave our sleeping children...

While these thoughts ran through my head, the man kept coming. Another step, and he would be within slashing distance. If I ran back to the beach, I should lead him on Denise's trail.

Instead, I cut off at right angles to the path, into the wild growth. I blundered into shrubs and trees, sounding like a herd of stampeding elephants. I felt like one of those characters in Fenimore Cooper who, whenever there is the utmost need for silence, always steps on a dry twig.

A glance back showed the man coming after me. When he encountered thick shrubbery, a slash sent it tumbling. The man was no insubstantial wraith or illusion. While I moved faster than he in the open, he got through the heavy stuff at least as fast as I did.

I tried to circle around him to get to the house, but he kept angling off to keep himself between me and it. I worried about getting lost. That would be no matter in daylight, when one could always tell direction by sun and sea. Night was something else.

The man got closer, herding me away from the Argenton house. Thinking that such a tubby fellow would get winded sooner than I, I led him straight up the slope. He plodded after, now losing a meter, now gaining one.

The distance to the Fort-de-France road seemed much farther than I remembered it. But then, I had not made the climb before on foot, at night, through tropical vegetation. After me came the man with the machete.

When I came out on the road, I was bushed. My pounding heart and laboring lungs reminded me that I was, after all, pushing fifty. My pursuer, too, emerged on the road. He did not seem to pant or labor at all.

As the man came out into full moonlight, I saw that his face bore a blank, unwinking stare. Tales of zombis ran through my head. Without a word or a cry, he trotted towards me, swinging the machete.

I thought that, even with my longer legs, I could not escape him along the road, since he did not seem to tire like normal mortals. On the other side was a stand of banana trees, once cultivated but now growing wild. Their huge, ragged leaves afforded easy cover, in which I might be able to lose him.

I plunged into the bananas. At first I thought I was gaining. I tried to throw him off by changing direction, but my woodcraft was not up to moving silently. Every time I looked back, there he was, plodding along. If I could only find a club, now, I could parry that slash and then clout him over the head or ram it into his belly...

There were no clubs. I passed a clump of bamboo. A length of bamboo would do fine, but I needed time and my own machete to cut a stalk and shape it. I blundered on.

Then I could go no further. I had no idea where I was, and the man was still coming. I thought of lunging at him, head down in a football tackle. If I could duck beneath the swing of the cutlass...

Panting, I crouched and spread my arms. On he came, the machete before him. Up it went.

Someone shouted: *"Halte-là!"*

When my pursuer kept on, a flash and explosion deafened and blinded me. The man was whirled around. He fell, and I saw that one of his legs had been hit. The trouser leg was torn and darkening, and the leg had a bend where none should be.

Still, the fellow recovered and began hopping grotesquely towards me, dragging the wounded leg. A second report brought him down again. Still he crawled nearer, using his arms alone, with both shattered legs trailing. He still gripped his machete.

A third shot spattered brains. The man lay still.

A man in uniform stepped into the moonlight, replacing the spent cartridges in a revolver. Although the peak of the kepi shadowed his shiny black face, I knew Hippolyte Frot.

"Well, Monsieur!" he said. "If you had not fled so fast and

drawn this species of camel after you, the affair would have been finished long ago. My faith, I have never seen a man with gray hair run through the woods like you! Are you a retired Olympic champion?"

When I could get my breath, I said: "It is like the tale of the rabbit who escaped the fox: the rabbit ran faster for his life than the fox for his dinner. Where did you come from so *à propos?*"

"I told you we were going to watch this section more closely."

Frot holstered his pistol. I recognized it as one of those .44 magnums, which have almost the punch of an elephant gun and a recoil to match. I used to be a pretty good pistol shot, but if I had to shoot one of those things, I'd grip it in both hands to keep it from getting away from me.

Sergeant Frot shone a flashlight on the body. He said: "*O mon Dieu!*"

"What is it?"

He turned a face on which, even in shadow, I could see bewilderment. In a man as well-integrated and self-possessed as Hippolyte Frot, that was alarming. He said:

"Do you know who this is?"

"No. Who is it?"

"This is Louis Mouttet, the rascally governor who perished in the great eruption—or else someone made up to resemble him. I have seen photographs of the original Mouttet, and there is no error. *Formidable!*"

"That was over sixty years ago!"

"Exactly. But, you know, the body of Mouttet was never found, although the government made strenuous efforts to identify the victims."

"You mean some gang of *bourhousses* has been keeping Mouttet as a zombi all this time? And Duchamps borrowed the body to send against me?"

"Monsieur," said Frot heavily, "you may indulge in such speculations if you like. We have the freedom of opinion. But we also have the *mission civilizatrice* of France. For that reason, I cannot permit this explanation to enter the official records. It is undoubtedly a man, the mind of whom has been turned by the preachings of Duchamps and his like

129

and who was chosen to accentuate a natural resemblance to the real Mouttet. Back, if you please!"

Frot drew the big revolver and fired one more shot into the corpse's head, at such an angle that the bullet came out the face. That face was instantly reduced to a gory ruin, which nobody could have identified.

"Now," he said, "there will be no more cause to spread these rumors that lend themselves to primitive superstition. As you know, Monsieur Newbury, the civilization is but a thin crust over our savage interiors, no matter if our skins be white or black. We must try to keep this shell of egg intact."

I heard a thrashing in the banana grove and a halloo.

"*Oui, nous y sommes,*" called Frot. "*Tout va bien.*"

It was Denise and two policemen from Frot's station, drawn by the shots. She had circled around to the house. After the zombi and I had plunged into the banana grove, she got into the car and drove like mad to Fort-de-France. There they told her that Frot was out patrolling our area himself; but, in view of the seriousness of the situation, two of the *flics* had returned with her.

Jacques Lecouvreur got his motor. Having had engineering training in my youth, I helped him install it. Stephen and I lent a hand to the villagers of Schoelcher at hauling in the net on one of their seining operations. We incidentally learned that barracuda are good eating, although some are prejudiced against them.

The next time I saw Frot, I asked about Oreste Duchamps.

"Deported to his native Haiti," said the sergeant. "We cannot permit such primitive buffooneries to trouble the course of our civilization. And what of you, Monsieur?"

"All is tranquil, thank you, save that our cook has disappeared. I think she was in league with Duchamps. She was a terrible cook, anyhow; and we leave a few days hence."

"In that case, Monsieur, I think you need fear no further disturbances. Perhaps you would care to extend your sojourn? Really, you should give Martinique a chance to show how charming she can be, when she is not vexed by barbarous intriguers."

"I am tempted, but my job calls me back."

"Till next time, then."

"À coup sûr, Monsieur Frot. But you may be certain that, if ever again I rent a house in a foreign land, I will make sure that I am the only one with a lease!"

A Sending
Of Serpents

I was not thinking of snakes. I was thinking of the loan that we—that is, the Harrison Trust—had made to the shaky Gliozzi Construction Company, when Malcolm McGill, our treasurer, came in.

"Willy," he said, "you know old Mrs. Dalton?"

"Sure. What about her?"

"She wants to close out her account and give everything away."

"I suppose that's her privilege. But why?"

"I think you'd better talk to her."

"Oh, lord! She'll talk my ear off," I said. "But I suppose I'd better."

McGill brought Mrs. Dalton into my office. She was one of a number of rich oldsters who had custodian accounts with us. We kept them in sound high-yield stocks and tax-free municipals, clipped their coupons, looked over their accounts a couple of times a year to see if some trading was indicated, and sent the owners their monthly checks.

I pulled out a chair for her. "Well, Mrs. Dalton," I said, "I hear you're leaving us."

She smiled sweetly. "Oh, not really *leaving* you, Mr. Newbury. Not in spirit, that is. But I've found a better use for that material stuff you call money than just sitting there in the bank."

"Yes?" I said, hoisting an eyebrow. "Tell me, please. We try to protect your interests."

"The money will be given to the Master to carry forward his great work."

"The Master?"

"You know. Surely you've heard of the wonderful work Mr. Bergius is doing?"

"Oh. I've heard something, but tell me more about it."

"The Master's organization is called Hagnophilia, meaning 'love of purity.' You see, he's the earthly representative of the Interstellar Ruling Council. They chose him for his *purity* and *vision* and took him up in a flying saucer to the planet Zikkarf, where the Council meets. After they'd tested him, they decided he was *worthy* of becoming an associate member. By helping his great work, we can assure his promotion to *full* membership. That means that the earth will have a voice in interstellar affairs."

"Indeed. And what do you get out of this, Mrs. Dalton?"

"Oh, his teachings will enable us to retain our full health and vigor until the time comes for us to pass. When that time comes, we'll pass directly into our next bodies without this messy business of dying. And, he says, we'll retain the *full* memory of our previous life, so we can take advantage of the lessons we've learned. The way things are nowadays, we forget our previous existences, so the lessons we learned in them have to be learned all over again."

"Very interesting. How has Mr. Bergius' scheme worked?"

"It hasn't been in operation long enough to tell, really. But when old Mr. White passed, it was with such a *peaceful* smile on his face. that showed that he had gone directly to his next incarnation, just as the Master promised."

"Well, Mrs. Dalton, your Master has made some pretty big claims. Hadn't you better wait a while, to see how they pan out? He wouldn't be the first to arouse large expectations and fail to fulfill them."

Her mouth became firm. "No, Mr. Newbury, I have decided what I want to do, and that I shall do. Will you please make out the papers?"

Later, Mrs. Dalton went out of the bank with a large cardboard envelope, containing all her securities and a check for the cash balance, under her arm. Her chauffeur helped her into her car, and off they went. McGill, glumly watching, asked me:

"What's this all about, Willy?"

I told him. He said: "Hagnophilia sounds like a blood disease. What does it mean: 'love of hags'?"

"No; 'love of purity.' Greek."

During the next month, two more of our custodian

accounts were terminated likewise. My boss Esau Drexel called me into his presidential office to ask me about it.

"It would take more than the loss of a few custodian accounts to rock us, even though we're a small bank," he said, "but it sets a bad precedent. When these people are broke, we'll be blamed for letting them blow their wads on this mountebank."

"True," I said, "but the world is full of suckers. Always has been. Short of starting a rival cult, I don't see what we can do."

"Might start one to Plutus, the god of wealth," said Drexel. "Damn it, the only way to get anything done nowadays is to start some goddam cult. Did I tell you, my grandson had dropped out of college to join one?"

"No. What's this? I'm sorry."

"Some guy named the Reverend Sung—Chinese or something—has what he calls Scientific Sorcery, and he filled poor George's head with his nonsense. He's convinced the kid that his family are all possessed by evil spirits, so George won't have anything to do with us. If half of what George says is true, they can do things to curl your hair."

"Can't you get the law on this Reverend Sung?"

"No. We tried, but he's protected by the First Amendment. My lawyer says, if we tried force on George, we'd end up in jail for kidnapping."

Then old John Sturdevant decided to close out his account and give the funds to the Master. His account, however, was an irrevocable trust, which we could not have released even if we had wished.

Sturdevant was a nasty old man. Of few can it be truthfully said that they snarl their words, but Sturdevant snarled his.

"Young man," he said (I was just past fifty), "I've lived long enough to know a good thing when I see it. You're standing in the way of progress and enlightenment, damn it. You're condemning me to a lingering, painful death from something or other. I've got sixteen things the matter with me now, and with the Master's help I could grow a new set of teeth, get my prostate back to normal size, and everything. Then I could pass, zip, into my next body without a hitch. Besides, with

134

this money the Master could end war, control the population explosion, and distribute the world's wealth equitably. You're a butcher, a sadist, a Hitler. Good-day, sir!"

He stamped out, banging his walking stick with each step.

The next dust-up occurred when Bascom Goetz wanted to withdraw all the money from the trust fund of his twelve-year-old nephew and ward, to enroll the boy in one of Bergius's educational institutes. These far-out schools promised to turn their pupils into superbeings who could do everything short of walking on water. The trust allowed the spending of principal for the boy's education and necessities, but we did not consider the Master's schools as coming under either head. Since Goetz had to have our consent for this withdrawal, we had a thundering row with Goetz. He stamped off to consult his lawyer.

My next contact with Hagnophilia occurred when our freshman son Stephen brought home a friend for a week end. The friend, Chet Carpenter, wore blue jeans and had hair hanging halfway down his back—a male coiffure that has always made me wince.

During dinner, Carpenter said he planned to drop out of college and devote his life to Hagnophilia. With a little prodding, he launched into a harangue about the sect:

"You see, Mr. Newbury, it's all a matter of bringing your *purusha* up to full acromatics. Your purusha is the immaterial nexus of energy-processing between the seven planes of existence. It manifests for billions of years, until its psychionic charge is exhausted. The Interstellar Council is working on a project for recharging exhausted purushas, so we won't just terminate after a mere trillion years or so.

"Well, you see, as one envelope unwinds, the purusha hovers in interspace until another issues for it to inform. But that time of hovering is out of the seven-dimensional time stream, so the memory of previous informings is laniated.

"You see, as the human population has ramped, there's gotten to be more envelopes than purushas to inform them. So the purushas of lower organisms—apes, tigers, even centipedes—have filled the vacancies. That's why so many humans act so beastly. Their purushas haven't fruited in accordance with the akashic plan but have shunted the intermediate rungs. So, you see, they're not yet qualified for human somatism.

"The Hindus and the Druids had some inkling of this, you see, but the Interstellar Council has decided it's time to put religion on a scientific basis. So they've sent the Master back to Zamarath—that's what you folks call the earth—with the true doctrine. You see, up to now the human soma, with all its limitations, has been the most etheric envelope that a purusha could inform. But with our science, we are ready for the next rung, when we can mold our envelopes as easily as you can model clay. Do you follow me?"

"I'm afraid not," I said. "To be frank, it sounds to me like gibberish."

"That's because I've given you some of the advanced doctrine without the elementary introduction. After all, a textbook on nuclear physics would sound like gibberish, too, it you didn't know any physics. I could arrange for you to take our elementary course—"

"I'm afraid I have my hands more than full. I'm supposed to lecture the Bankers' Association on the fallacy of the Keynesian theories, and I have to read up for it. But tell me: how does your cult—"

"Please, Mr. Newbury! We don't like the word 'cult.' It's a religio-scientific association and qualifies as a church for purposes of taxation. You were saying?"

"I mean to ask how your—ah—religio-scientific association gets along with the other—with the cults, such as that of the Reverend Sung."

Carpenter bounced in his chair with excitement. "He's terrible! Most of the cults, as you call them, are deluded but harmless. A few even have glimpses of the truth. But the Sungites are an evil, dangerous gang, conspiring against the human world.

"You see, there are a lot of abnormal purushas drifting around, which have been so distorted by the stresses of the last ten billion years that they won't fit into any envelope. So they watch for chances to inform a human soma when its own purusha isn't watching and run off with it."

"Like stealing somebody's car?" Privately, I thought that

anybody so hated by the Hagnosophists could not be all bad.

"Exactly. You see, these homeless purushas are what they used to call 'demons' or 'devils.' Sung claims he can control them, but actually they control him and all his suckers. They hope sooner or later to take over Zamarath this way. The Master is going to expose this plot the next time he is translated to Zikkarf. Meanwhile, we have to watch the Sungites and try to stop their evil plans."

"Zikkarf," I repeated. "How do you spell it?"

Carpenter spelled the word. I said: "I thought that rang a bell the first time I heard it. Now I know. There was a pulp writer back in the thirties, who wrote about life on an imaginary planet of that name. He spelled it differently."

"He must have had an inkling of the truth," said Carpenter.

"What does your Master propose to do with all those poor lost souls?"

Carpenter told me of the cult's program for capturing these errant spooks and, by some sort of ghostly psychoanalysis, beating them back into normal shape. At least, that was how I understood it, albeit his explanation was couched in such cultic gobbledygook that it was hard to be sure. I said:

"Do you ever have services—I mean, general meetings, open to the public?"

"Oh, yes. We're not a secret organization in any way." Carpenter's eyes glowed with zeal. "Matter of fact, we're having one near here in a couple of weeks. The Master himself will be here. Would you like to come?"

"Yes," I said. If I was going to do anything about the racket that was siphoning off the funds of my gullible old depositors, I ought to see what the enemy looked like.

The meeting, in an auditorium a few miles from my home, was a fine piece of dramaturgy. There were candles and incense. I was made uneasy by the sight of the Master's henchmen—burly fellows in white uniforms, with their pants tucked into shiny black boots. Some assisted in seating people, while others stood at attention with grim, don't-start-anything expressions. Several at the entrances collected "free-will offerings" in baskets.

There were songs and announcements and the reading of some creed or manifesto. Then, with a flourish of trumpets, the Master appeared, white-robed, with spotlights on him.

Ludwig Bergius was a tall, spare, blond, blue-eyed man, who wore his hair down to his shoulders. The hair was so brassy that I suspected either dye or a wig. He startlingly resembled those self-portraits that Albrecht Dürer painted as pictures of Jesus Christ, which have been followed by Western religious art ever since. Bergius had a splendid voice, deep and resonant, which could easily have filled the auditorium without the public-address system.

Bergius spoke for an hour, making vast if nebulous promises and denouncing countless enemies. He especially berated the Reverent Sung's cult by name as a Mafia of demons in human guise. His voice had a hypnotic quality, which lulled one into a kind of passive daze. One ended with the impression that one had had a wonderful revelation but without remembering much of what the Master had actually said. Some of his assertions seemed to contradict what others had told me of his doctrines; but I understood that he brought out a new doctrine every month or two, keeping his suckers too confused to think.

When Bergius had finished, his white-clad storm-troopers bustled into the aisles with long-handled collection baskets to take up another offering. There were more songs, announcements, and the other routines of religious services, and the show was over. On the way out, the storm troopers were active at the exits, collecting more offerings. They were politely aggressive about it. I paid up, not being prepared to fight a whole gang of husky thugs half my age.

One of our depositors is the Temple Beth-El. The next time Rabbi Harris was in, I spoke of the Hagnophilists. With a sigh, he said:

"Yes, we've lost several members of our congregation to these ganifs. Naturally, we're stronger for religious freedom than anybody, but still—Mr. Newbury, you gave a talk last year on financial rackets, didn't you?"

"Yes, at the YMCA."

"Well, why don't you give one, with accent on these cults, at the YMHA? Turn about's fair play."

"Okay," I said.

That was how I came to give my celebrated exposé at the YMHA. I presented grim examples of elderly suckers who had blown their all on Hagnophilia, been reduced to nervous wrecks by their 'treatments,' and then had been cast into outer darkness. I ended:

"...of course, any of you is free to take up any of these forms of the higher nonsense—Homosophy, Hagnophilia, Cosmonetics, and the rest—that you like. It's still a free country. Personally, I'd rather pick up a rattlesnake with my bare hand and trust it not to bite me. Thank you."

I had to go out of town for a few days on business. When I got back, I found a new piece of furniture in the living room. It was a small terrarium, with pebbles, moss, and a little pool. Coiled up at one end lay a garter snake.

"Denise!" I said. "What's this?"

"A boy came around with the serpent," she explained. "He said you had advertised for snakes, at a dollar a snake. Why did you do that, *mon cher*?"

"Huh? I never did. Somebody's made a mistake. What then?" I reached into the terrarium and ran a finger along the scales of the snake, who wriggled away in alarm. It had not yet gotten used to captivity. "I do like them, though."

"Priscille has always wanted a pet, ever since our old dog died. So she got this glass case from one of her friends and fixed it up."

"What do you feed it?"

"Priscille buys little goldfishes and puts them in the pond. When Damballah gets hungry, he grabs them and swallows them."

"Hm. How much do these fish cost?"

"Forty cents each, at the pet shop."

"That won't do, especially when we've got a perfectly good garden full of worms."

That night, our younger daughter and I were out hunting earthworms with a flashlight. The trick, I told her, was to grab them when they had extended their front halves out of their burrows to browse on the surface. Then you shouldn't pull on them, or they would break in half. Instead, wait for them to relax and stop trying to pull back into their holes, and they would come out easily.

Priscille was not pleased with the idea of grabbing a slimy worm with her bare hands. Instead, she used paper handkerchiefs. We had caught several when a youth appeared in our driveway with a carton in his arms.

"Mr. Newbury?" he said. "I got a snake here, like you advertised for."

"Who says I advertised for a snake?" I demanded.

"Why, uh, that sign. The sign in the railroad station."

I learned that a notice had appeared on the bulletin board of the suburban station, reading: SNAKES WANTED FOR SCIENTIFIC PURPOSES. WILL PAY ONE DOLLAR FOR EACH, ANY SPECIES, followed by my name and address.

"This is a hoax," I told the youth. "I never put up such a notice, and the one snake we have is plenty."

During the next week, we were offered six garter snakes, two pine snakes, one ring-necked brown snake, and one black snake. All were declined.

I also learned that our unknown ill-wisher had planted twenty or thirty of these posters in the windows of shops in the neighborhood. I visited some of the shopkeepers, who were glad to remove the signs. I asked for descriptions of the prankster but got contradictory accounts. This led me to believe that several persons were involved. I asked the president of the local chamber of commerce to spread the word of this hoax and to watch for any more attempts.

Next, I began receiving letters reading somewhat as follows: "Dear Mr. Newbury: I have read your ad in *Natural History Magazine* for July, in which you say you will pay for snakes. Do you want them alive or dead, and how much are you offering? Very truly yours..."

I called up the magazine. Yes, somebody had placed the advertisement in the classified section. They did not know who, but the check had been signed with my name and had not bounced. So for some time I was busy writing post cards, saying no snakes, thank you.

So far, this harassment had been a minor nuisance. We

were sorrier for the people taken in by these hoaxes than for ourselves.

"I think," I told Denise, "that it must be the Hagnophilists. Somebody reported to them what I said in that YMHA speech about picking up a rattlesnake in my bare hands. They jumped to the conclusion that I have a morbid phobia or horror of snakes and are trying to drive me out of my gourd."

"My poor Willy! If they only knew that you were a secret snake-lover at heart!"

The campaign then took a nasty turn. A neighbor told me that, a month before, he had received an anonymous poison-pen letter, aimed at me. He had turned it in to the local police. Other neighbors had received them, too.

"For God's sake!" I said. "Why didn't you tell me about it then?"

He shuffled his feet. "I was too embarrassed. We know you and Denise are all right—best neighbors we have, in fact—and we didn't want to upset you. Anyway, we couldn't imagine that they really meant a sober, conventional person like you."

I located some of the others who had received the letters, but none had kept them. Some had given them to the police, while others had discarded them.

I went to the police station, where Sergeant Day dug the letters out of their file. They all read:

Dear Neighbor:

Recently my young son was outside watering the lawn, when a man jumped out of his car and attacked the boy. He seized the hose and began chopping it up with a hatchet, screaming "Snake! Snake! Damned snake! I'll teach you to send snakes to torment me!" He abused my son so that he came home terrified.

For obvious reasons, I wish to remain anonymous in dealing with this matter. No father wants his children frightened by insane persons like this, who is probably still in the neighborhood.

I am circulating this letter in the hope that anyone who knows of somebody who has a psychotic problem about snakes will report it to the proper authorities, so that the victim of these delusions can be treated before he harms someone. He is described as a man in his late forties, tall and powerful, with graying hair cut short, a close-cut mustache, and driving a green foreign sports car. If you know any such person, try to convince him to turn himself in to the authorities so that he can be cured of his madness.

Sargeant Day said: "We had the boys watching for this guy for weeks without results. I guess if any of 'em saw you, they just said: 'Oh, that's Mr. Newbury the banker. *He* couldn't be the one.' Some kook, of course."

"Anyway," I said, "the kook gave me a flattering description. Can you trace the author of this letter?"

Day shook his head. "The envelopes were postmarked from the center-city post office. If you've had any crank letters, you could compare the typing with that of this letter. It was typed on a manual typewriter with standard elite type. Notice that the capital *N* is battered, the lower-case *a* has lost its tail, and the *p* hits above the line. But we can't examine every typewriter in the county."

Day made me a photocopy of the letter. At home, I went through my correspondence for comparison, but no letter that I had received in the past year had been typed on the troublemaker's machine.

While all this bothered me to some extent, it drove Denise frantic. She said: "When we were married, Willy darling, you should have come to France to live instead of taking me to America. We French are more logical; we do not commit such *bêtises*."

The following week, the parcel service delivered a carton, securely bound with heavy staples and adhesive tape, but with several small holes punched in it. Foreseeing a struggle to get it open, Denise left that job for me when I got home. I got a screwdriver, a knife, and a pair of pliers out of the tool box, set the carton on the kitchen stepladder, and got to work. In a few minutes I lifted the top of the carton.

Up popped a mouse-colored, serpentine head, and a forked tongue flicked out at me. As I stood there stupidly, movable ribs on the sides of the neck spread themselves, disclosing a cobra's hood.

I jumped back, yelling: "Denise! Get the hell out of here!"

"Why, Willy?" came Denise's voice from the next room. "Is something the matter?"

The cobra poured out of the carton to the floor. There seemed to be no end to it. I guessed it to be at least ten feet long. (It was twelve.) It was not even the ordinary Indian cobra, but the hamadryad or king cobra, the biggest and meanest of all.

"Never mind!" I screamed. "Just run like hell! It's a cobra!"

The cobra reared up until the first yard of its length was vertical and lunged at me. Luckily, the cobra's lunge is slower than the strike of an American pit viper, such as a rattlesnake. I jumped back, so that its stroke fell short.

The snake then tried to crawl towards me, but the slick vinyl floor gave it no purchase. It thrashed from side to side, fluttering like a flag in the breeze but making only slight forward progress.

Backing away, I passed the broom closet. I opened the door in hope of finding a weapon. There were a broom and a mop, but their handles were too long for that limited space. Then I spotted the plumber's friend, with a stout thirty-inch wooden handle.

As the cobra, still skidding, inched towards me, I faced it, gripping the end with a rubber plunger. When the snake began again to rear up, I stepped forward and made a two-handed slash at its neck, like a golf stroke. The stick connected with a crack, hurling the cobra sideways.

The creature went into convulsions, thrashing and writhing, knotting and unknotting. I struck at the head again and again, but this was not really necessary. My first blow had broken its neck. Its skin now decorates my den.

Esau Drexel said: "Willy, we've got to do something. Some day I'll have to retire, and the Harrison Trust will need at least one man with his head screwed on right."

I said: "True enough, Esau, but what? The return address on that package was a phony. The cobra was stolen from the zoo—by a pretty brave thief, I'd say. The cops say they're up against a dead end. That private detective didn't do a thing but send in a whopping bill."

"Maybe if you gave your story to the newspapers, it would flush out the Hagnophilists."

"All that would get me would be litigation. I have nothing but an inference to connect them with this sending of serpents. My lawyer warns me that those characters are both crazy and dangerous. If anybody writes something they don't like, they sue him for ten megabucks. The suits never come to trial, but the threats and harassment keep most of their critics quiet."

"Well," said Drexel, "when all the natural means have been exhausted, we must try the unnatural ones. I told you about my grandson George and the Scientific Sorcerers, didn't I?"

"Yes. Set a thief to catch a thief, so to speak?"

"What have we got to lose?"

"Will it cost more dough?"

"The bank will pick up the tab. We'll charge it to 'security,' which won't be any lie."

"'Public relations' might be better. Anyway, better not let the stockholders or the Federal Reserve boys know."

"I won't. But I'll get in touch with the Reverend Sung's cult."

The Reverend Sung Li-pei, late of Taiwan, was a short, round-faced man with an air of intense sincerity. I did not assume that this air truthfully reflected the inner Sung. Having come across many con men, I have found that all of them radiated bluff honesty and sterling worth. Otherwise, how could they make their livings as crooks?

Sung began: "Mr. Newbury, you wish to have this persecution by the minions of Mr. Bergius stopped, is that light?"

"That's light—I mean right."

"That is what I said, light. Now the spell of the Red Dragon is very expensive, as its lesults are often fatal—"

"I don't want to kill the guy," I said, "just make him harmless, so he'll let me alone. Better yet, make him stop conning my depositors into giving him all their worldly

144

goods."

Sung put his fingertips together and thought. Then he said: "In that case, the spell of the Gleen—ah—Green Dlagon would be more suitable. Some of the entities I control can, I believe, lender our Mr. Bergius as harmless as a new-hatched chick, ha-ha." He gave a little forced smile.

"You won't hurt him physically?"

"No, nothing like that. You will have to attend the Sabbat. It will be held in my house this evening, beginning at eleven p.m. Now may I have your check for one thousand dollars, prease?"

"I prefer to pay in cash," I said, handing him an envelope containing ten hundreds.

He counted the bills, held them up to the light, and finally grunted satisfaction. "Good-day, then, Mr. Newbury. I shall see you tonight, yes?"

Sung held out, not in some spooky, crumbling old mansion, but in a neat, prosaic modern suburban home a few miles from my own house. The lights on the front terrace were lit to show the house number. Inside, a couple of white-clad fellows in turbans, evidently Sung's servants, flitted about.

"Ah, right on time, Mr. Newbury," said the Reverend Sung, shaking hands. "Light this way, prease...You understand that you will not be introduced to the other members of the coven. They might incur unfortunate plejudices if their scientific activity were known. Here is the dressing room. Please put your valuables in this box, lock it, and hang the key around your neck."

"Why?"

"Because you will next lemove all your clothing and leave it here. The box is to make sure that nothing will turn up missing, ha-ha."

"You mean, I've got to strip to the buff?"

"Yes. That is necessary for the spell."

I sighed. "Well, my wife and I have gone nuding in France, but this is the first time for me in this country."

I started to unbutton and unzip, wishing that I did not have that slight middle-aged bulge below the equator. It is nothing

145

like Drexel's real paunch; but, despite exercise and calorie-counting, I am no longer so flat in the belly as in my youth.

Sung donned a black robe. He led me, feeling very naked and a little chilly despite the summer warmth, down the cellar stairs.

The place was lit by black candles, burning with a greenish light. On the concrete floor had been drawn or painted a pentacle or magical diagram. Around this sat twelve naked men and women.

"You will take that vacant space, Mr. Newbelly," said Sung, pointing.

I lowered myself between two of the women. The concrete felt cold on my rump. I glanced at my neighbors.

The one on the left was elderly and not well preserved; she sagged and bulged in all the wrong places. The one on my right, on the other hand, was young and well-stacked. Her face was not pretty, at least in the crepuscular light; but she more than made up for it elsewhere. She whispered:

"Hello—ah?"

"Call me Bill," I whispered back. Nobody calls me "Bill," but "Willy," short for "Wilson." Still, this seemed the best way to handle the situation. "Good-evening—ah?"

"Marcella."

"Good-evening, Marcella."

Somebody shushed us, and the Reverend Sung stepped into the diagram. He raised his arms and said something in Chinese; then to the circle:

"Tonight, fliends, we shall invoke the spell of the Green Dragon for our friend here, to protect him from the unjust persecution to which he have been subjected by that gang of pseudo-scientific, pseudo-magical fakers, of whose abominations we are all aware. We shall start by singing the *Li Piao Erh*. Are you ready?"

The gang went into some Chinese chant. I am told that Chinese music, like that of the bagpipes, can be enjoyed as much as that of Beethoven and Tchaikovsky, when one has been educated to it. I, alas, never have had this opportunity, so to me Chinese music still sounds like a cat fight.

The song over, Sung stepped outside the circle and said: "Now join hands, prease. You, too, Mr. Newbury."

146

I joined hands with those two women. There followed endless chants, invocations, and responses, some by Sung and some by the circle. It went on and on. Since most of it was in Chinese, it meant nothing to me.

I began to find this spate of meaningless chatter tedious. My mind wandered to my right-hand companion. Now, I am no swinger; but still, the sight of well-turned female flesh still arouses my normal male reactions.

In fact, it aroused them in an all-too-visible way. My God, I thought, what shall I do about this? I'm sure it's not on the program. What will they do to me if they see me here with a totem pole sticking up from my lap?

By doubling up my legs, I managed to hide the offending organ. I tried mentally reciting the multiplication table. But the devil would not down.

Then something drove lustful thoughts from my head. In the center, a dim luminescence took form. It looked like a patch of luminous fog, glowing a faint, soft green. It brightened and became more substantial but did not take any definite shape.

Sung shouted in shrill Chinese. The circle repeated his phrases in unison. Sung's voice rose to a shriek. The green light faded. Sung staggered and collapsed.

A couple of sitters caught him as he fell and eased him down. Someone else flipped the light switch. The light showed thirteen naked people including myself, some sitting, some standing, and some scrambling ungracefully to their feet. They were of various ages, displaying a variety of bushes of pubic hair.

While I wondered whether to call an ambulance, Sung's voice came weakly out of the group around him: "I all light, please. Just give me minute."

Presently he got up, seeming none the worse. He said: "This incident shows that these evil cultists have strong magical defenses. Let us hope that the influences we have sent to counteract their malignant plots will not recoil upon us or upon Mr. Newbury. This is all we can do for the present, so let us adjourn upstairs."

I straggled up the stairs with the rest and joined them in the dressing room. In that crowded space, I tried to don my

147

clothes without poking anyone in the eye.

I recovered my wallet from the lock box and followed the rest out into the living room. Sung's servants had prepared ice cream, cake, and coffee. Now the coven looked like any gathering of American suburban bourgeoisie.

They chattered among themselves. Most of their talk was about people I did not know. There were several of these covens, all apparently full of intriguing and scheming for power, just as in any corporation or governmental department.

Marcella came up, with a coffee cup in one hand and a slice of cake in the other. "Bill," she said, "wasn't it a thrill? It's my first Green Dragon. We ought to get together again, since you're such a fine, upstanding man." She giggled.

I admit that, for once in my otherwise happy married life, I was tempted, but only for a moment. Besides my family feelings, I have my image as a banker, sober and staid to the point of stuffiness, to maintain. I am not really so stodgy (I have even been known to vote Democratic), but it's good for business. I said:

"Yes, I guess we ought, but I've got to run along. Good-night, Marcella."

The next day, I tried to concentrate on my business, but my mind kept wandering to the Reverend Sung's ominous remark about his spell's recoiling back on me. Of course I did not really believe it could; but still...

The day after that, I left the Harrison Trust at noon to drive home for lunch. I saw a crowd in the street and walked towards it, wondering if there had been an accident.

It was the Master in his white robe, strolling along and talking, while peeling bills from an enormous wad and handing them to his nearest hearers. His deep voice intoned:

"...whosoever believes in me shall not perish but shall have eternal life. For I am no longer Ludwig Bergius, but the true son of God, whose spirit has taken possession of the body of that misguided mortal Bergius. I that speak unto you am he. Labor not for the food that perishes, but for the food that gives eternal life. I am the light of the world; he that follows me shall not walk in darkness..."

148

The police struggled with the crowd, but the sight of money being given away was driving the people frantic. They surged and pushed. They began to shout and to claw one another to reach the Master.

A siren gave a low, tentative growl, and an ambulance nosed into the throng. Three men in white coats jumped out and, with help from the cops, pushed their way to Bergius. They took him by the arms, spoke soothingly into his ears, and led him unresisting away to the ambulance. The vehicle backed out of the crush, turned, and purred away.

Somebody tugged my sleeve. It was McGill, the treasurer. "Willy! I've been looking for you. Know what's happened? Mrs. Dalton and the rest have been coming in to reinstate their accounts. They say the Master gave them back their stuff. What do you make of it?"

"I'd have to think," I said. "Right now my mind is on lunch."

Later, Esau Drexel said: "Well, Willy, I guess your Taiwanese shaman earned his grand. No more sendings of snakes?"

"No."

"Luckily we've got a good county mental hospital. Might even cure this so-called Master."

"Do you want that?" I asked.

"Oh, I see. You think he might go back to culting." He sighed. "I don't know. We can assume that Sung is a faker like the rest. In that case, Bergius' mind just cracked under the strain of messiahship, so he succumbed to delusions of divinity, irrespective of Sung's spells.

"Or we can assume that Sung's treatment really worked the change in the man. In that case, was Bergius a real representative of some Interstellar Council, before the spell drove him nuts? Or was he a faker before and—and—"

"And a genuine incarnation of Jesus afterwards, you're saying?"

"Jeepers! I hadn't thought that far. Well, it's been said that, if Jesus did come again, he'd be locked up as a lunatic." Drexel gave a little shudder. "I don't like to think about it. Let's tackle something easy, like the relation between the rediscount rate and the rate of inflation."

The
Huns

On one of our vacations at Lake Algonquin, my Aunt Frances said: "Willy, Phyllis wants you to come over to Panther Falls to help her sell Wilderfarm."

"Oh?" I said. "I didn't know Aunt Phyllis was planning to sell."

"Well, she is. Will you go?"

"Look, Aunt Frances, I'm a banker, not a real-estate broker; and I don't practice in New York State anyway—"

"You still know more about mortgages and things than poor Phyllis ever will."

"Why is she selling?"

"She says it's too much place to keep up by herself, now that her children have moved away. Says she's too old to manage. The fact is, she's just too fat. If she'd control her appetite....Besides, she said something about peculiar things happening lately."

"Eh? What? If she's got spooks, let her get an exorcist. I've bumped into enough of that stuff to last me—"

"I didn't say spooks, Willy."

"Then what?"

"Some sort of terror gang, I take it."

"That's a job for the troopers."

Frances Colton sighed. "Willy, you are deliberately being evasive. I'm not asking you to cast out devils or fight a gang of juvenile delinquents. I'm only asking you to give poor Phyllis some advice on selling the place. Some developer wants to take it over. Will you go?"

I sighed in turn. "I was going to take Stevie trolling for bass tomorrow."

"If the weather's good, take him; but the first rainy day, you can go over to the Falls. It's only an hour."

Two days later, leaving Denise to cope with our three restless adolescents, I drove to Gahato. I stopped at Bugby's Garage for gas and an oil change. While this was being done, I stood in the drizzle in my slicker, watching the locals walk past. I said howdy to a few whom I knew.

Then I sighted Virgil Hathaway, with his hair in two long black braids. Virgil has been friendly ever since I arranged a small bank loan for him when he was hard up in the fifties. Nowadays, with all the publicity about the poor Indian, Virgil does all right; but he still remembers a favor.

"Hello, Virgil," I said. "How's Chief Soaring Turtle these days?"

Hathaway's copper-hued visage wringled into a grin. "Can't rightly complain, leastaways not as far as the old lady and me be concerned."

"Then what?"

He shrugged. "Oh, I dunno. The kids are grown up, and they've quit the Indian business."

"You mean they're assimilating?"

"Ayuh. The girl's working for the telephone company, and Calvin's got a job as an engineer. Makes more money in a week than I ever did in a month, selling my toy canoes and moccasins and things. Worst of it is, he's planning to marry some white girl."

"Ts, ts, Virgil; don't tell me you've got racial prejudices!"

"Yep, I guess I do. At this rate, there wunt be no more Indians left at all. All mixed into the mass."

"Well, you Penobscots acquired a good deal of white blood over the centuries."

Hathaway grinned. "Sure. In the old days, when we entertained a visiting white man, we sure *entertained* him. If he left a few half-breeds behind, that was more warriors for the tribe. But that's all over and done with. How be you?"

I brought Hathaway up to date on the Newbury family, adding: "I'm on my way to Panther Falls to help my aunt on a real-estate deal. Seems she's in trouble with some local group"

"Ayuh? What kind of trouble?"

"I don't know. Sore sort of terror, I hear."

"Jeepers! What you need, Willy, is some good old Indian medicine man to put a hex on 'em. Like that guy on the Tonawanda Reservation, who came through here nineteen years ago. He'd fix your terrorists."

"Thanks," I said. "I'll bear it in mind."

Wilderfarm, which Phyllis Wilder was planning to sell, adjoined another tract in the patrimony of my great-grandfather. This other lot contained Floreando, the Victorian-rustic mansion that Abraham Newbury built in the eighties. One passed this house on the way to the farm. After my great-aunt and great-uncle died, none of the heirs wanted the place, which needed a platoon of servitors to make it livable. Where, nowadays, would anyone but an oil billionaire retain a platoon of servitors?

First came a grand share-out of movables. A swarm of Abraham Newbury's descendants carried off furniture, pictures, chinaware, and so on in cars, trucks, and station wagons. Then, just before the War, the property was sold. It passed through several hands; but I had not kept up with its vicissitudes.

With a sudden attack of nostalgia, I turned in between the two big stone pillars that flanked the graveled driveway. I wanted one more look, to revive my childhood memories of rollicking parties, with swarms of cousins riding, swimming, picnicking, and horsing around. My cousin Hereward—the one who became a playwright—used to put us through abridgments of Shakespere's plays; I once played Hamlet's father's ghost.

The big old three-story stone house was still there; so was the iron deer on the lawn. A porch ran three-quarters of the way around the building, ending on one side in a shingled porte-cochère. An upstairs porch, surmounted by a conical roof like those on castle towers, jutted out from the second story. If Floreando did not have a resident ghost, it ought to have had.

I took the branch of the driveway leading back to the highway, instead of continuing on the loop, which went around the house and under the porte-cochère. I stopped the car and sat, remembering.

The fountain on the spacious lawn played no more. The grass was so long that it needed a scythe or a reaper instead of a mower. Something else, too, had changed.

On the strip of lawn, between the porte-cochère and the

152

trees, stood half a dozen shiny motorcycles in a row. These were no little one-lung gas-savers, but big, heavy, two and four-cylinder road bikes.

"You looking for somebody, mister?" said a voice.

A burly fellow in his twenties slouched up to my car. He put one hand of the roof and leaned forward, thrusting his face within a foot of mine. He had a mane of blond hair, hanging over his shoulders, chest, and back, and a full blond beard. He wore a suit of blue denim, with the pants tucked into heavy boots. These boots had half a dozen straps and buckles down the side, metal toes, and curved metal shin plates, rather like an ancient warrior's greaves.

"No," I said. "I just drove in to take a look. I used to play here when I was a kid."

"Oh," he said.

When the young man continued to stand beside the car, blocking my view to the right, I glanced the opposite way. The land across the Black River still rose, dim in the drizzle, in green tiers towards Tug Hill.

"Seen all you want to, mister?" the young man said at last.

"I think so," I said.

Having no intention of getting into a fight, I forbore to remark on his opacity. This youth was half my age and at least as big as I—and I am above average. He looked quite able to take a middle-aged banker apart.

"Who owns the place now?" I asked.

"The—the Lewis County Motorcycle Association."

"Oh." When the young man still stood, with beady blue eyes boring into me from under shaggy blond brows, I started up and drove back to the highway.

At the Farm, on the porch of the old white clapboard house, my aunt welcomed me with her usual extravagance. She hugged me to what they used to call her ample bosom. I said:

"Aunt Phyllis, you didn't use to have lightning rods on the farm, did you?"

"No, but so many places have been struck lately that I thought it wise."

"That's funny. I haven't heard of a change in the local

climate."

"Neither have I," she wheezed. "I can't quote figures, but there have been a strange lot of local strikes. That's what set the Reverend Grier's house on fire. Some superstitious people think it was meant that way."

"How do you mean? Unless it's one of those climate-control experiments, I hadn't heard that anybody could govern the direction of lightning."

She shrugged, making her fat quiver. "I shouldn't say anything about anybody..."

She broke off, listening. A snorelike, sawmillish noise was heard from the west. We looked in that direction, where the sun had begun to break through the rain clouds. A parade of motorcycle riders went past on the highway. A ray of the afternoon sun sparkled on their handlebars.

Aunt Phyllis jerked a thumb. "Especially them."

"The Lewis County Motorcycle Association?"

"Or the Huns, as they call themselves."

"What *is* all this? Are they staging a reign of terror?"

Aunt Phyllis made fluttery motions. "I oughtn't to talk about them—but so many queer things—you know, they say they make members of the gang do things that would turn a normal person's stomach, to show their manhood. And now, when somebody gets in their bad graces, his house gets hit by lightning or something. I called up the troopers to complain about one of their wild parties—they bring in their girls, and you can hear them clear to Boonville—so I got hit. It only knocked off a couple of shingles, praise be, but then I had the lightning rods put up. So now they just wheel in and out of the driveway, throwing beer cans and shouting vulgar things at me."

"Why doesn't somebody lower the boom of them?"

"It's hard to prove anything, because they all look alike in those helmets. Besides, their head man, young Nick, is the son of Jack Nicholson, the richest man in the county. Jack is getting a little senile now; but he's still a power in local politics, so nobody dares to touch his son. Jack's money bought Floreando."

"Trouble is," I said, "you've got a one-party system here. By the way, I drove in to Floreando to look it over."

154

"Run down, isn't it? But we have to expect it. Our family has come down in the world since Abraham's day. Only you, Willy, had the sense to get where the real money is, praise be."

"More by accident than design. I only hope I'm as able a banker as I might have been as an engineer." I told her about the Wagnerian character in blue denim.

"That would be Truman Vogel, Marshall Nicholson's second in command. Watch out for him. He kicked Bob Hawley with those iron boots and sent him to the hospital. They burned a cross on Doctor Rosen's lawn. They're talking about making this a white man's country."

I sighed. "The nuttier the program, the more nuts you'll find to join it. How about that sale of yours?"

I briefed Phyllis Wilder on the intricacies of mortgages, settlements, titles, agents, and lawyers. At the end, I promised to come back three or four days later, when the developer would have made a firm offer. Then I set out for Lake Algonquin, hoping to reach the Colton camp for dinner.

Passing through Panther Falls, I spied a name plate, saying "Isaiah Rosen, M.D.," on a lawn. I glanced at my car clock and drew up.

I had known Rosen slightly before the War, when I was an undergraduate and he a young physician who had taken over old Doc Prescott's practice. I remembered mentioning Rosen at one of the gatherings of cousins. My cousin Winthrop Colton—the one who was killed in the War— looked down his nose and said, with a kind of sniff: "Oh. You mean the Jew."

Such attitudes were common upstate in those days. Happily, things have changed, although you can still find pockets of such views among the old timers.

Now a balding Rosen greeted me. "I remember you, Mr. Newbury. What can I do for you?"

"Not a medical problem," I said. "I've been seeing my aunt, Mrs. Wilder."

Rosen shook his head. "I keep telling her to cut back on carbohydrates."

155

I told Rosen about the Huns. "I hear you've had a brush with them, too?"

Rosen stared. "You might say so. The whole thing has an unpleasantly familiar sound. Not that I was in Europe during the Holocaust—I was right here, building up a practice—but naturally I take an interest in such things. This campaign has already cut into my practice."

"What did you do to antagonize them?"

He shrugged. "With my background, I didn't need to do anything. When I heard that Marshall Nicholson was turning the motorcycle club into some kind of neo-pagan cult, complete with blood sacrifices, I told Jack Nicholson that his son needed psychiatric care. Old Jack scoffed, saying Nick had a right to freedom of religion like everyone else. Presumably the story got back, and that's what touched it off."

"The First Amendment doesn't let anyone sacrifice unbelievers to Mumbo Jumbo—at least, not unless the Supreme Court gets even goofier. What about these alleged supernatural feats? The lightning business."

Rosen snorted. "The usual moonshine. When lightning hits twice within a radius of half a mile, some folks suspect that God or a local witch has it in for someone in the target area. As a man of scientific training, I take no stock in such talk."

"I hope you're right," I said. "but I've had a scientific training, too, and I've seen enough oddities to be skeptical even of my own skepticism."

The next time I went to visit Aunt Phyllis, I drove down the line to Gahato. I stopped at Virgil Hathaway's curio shop, the sign before which read:

CHIEF SOARING TURTLE
INDIAN BEAD WORK—POTTERY

Hathaway was selling a customer a Navaho blanket made in Connecticut. When he had finished, I said:

"Virgil, those eyeglasses somehow don't fit the Amerind decor."

156

"I got to be able to read my own price tags," he said. "Anyway, it dunt matter nowadays. When I started the business, I used to play up to the kids, talking funny English and saying *ugh* and *how*. But kids are smarter'n they was."

"You still have your braids."

"Ayuh, but that's what-you-call-it functional. Saves me three or four bucks a month getting haircuts. What can I do for you?"

"You told me about some medicine man out at Tonawanda. How could I get in touch with him?"

"You mean Charlie Catfish. Ain't seen Charlie in two-three years, but we send Christmas cards." Hathaway consulted an address book and gave me a telephone number.

At the farm, Phyllis Wilder threw herself upon me, nearly knocking me flat. "Oh, Willy! Do you know what those wretched young thugs have done?"

"What now, Aunt Phyllis?" said I, staggering back in her embrace.

"They spoiled the deal with Mr. Fife, at least for now." Fife was the developer. "He came over with his surveyor to look the place over. While he was here, the Huns rode up the driveway on their motorcycles and circled the house yelling, like a tribe of Indians riding around a water hole. It scared Mr. Fife so he went away, saying he couldn't consider buying the place while the neighborhood was so disturbed."

"Did you call the troupers?"

"Yes, but by the time they got here the Huns were gone. Trooper Talbot told me afterwards they went to Floreando and talked to the Huns, but they just denied everything. I'd have to file a formal complaint, and I'm afraid of what they'd do. They'd be out on bail, delaying the case for months or years...You'll stay the night, won't you, Willy? I'm so scared."

"Sure, I'll stay. Speaking of Indians, there's one I want to call. He might be able to help."

"An Indian? How do you mean? To get up a war party, the way they did two hundred years ago—but no, Willy, you wouldn't do anything so silly. You were always the sensible one, praise be. What then?"

"You'll see when he gets here—if he does. I thought—no,

157

wait. I'll meet him in the village. If I like his looks, could you put him up here along with me?"

"I guess so. At my age, nobody'll suspect me of entertaining a redskin lover." She gave a girlish giggle.

I called the number that Hathaway had given me and asked for Charles H. Catfish. When a man answered, I gave Hathaway's name and sketched my aunt's difficulties. I ended:

"Hathaway suggested that you might be able to help out, by means of your—uh—your special powers."

"Mought," said Catfish, "If it was made worth my while. Means I got to take time off from my job."

"What do you do, Mr. Catfish?"

"I sell Chevrolets in Kenmore. What was you thinking of paying?"

After consultation with Phyllis Wilder, I went back to the telephone and agreed with Catfish on a daily retainer. He promised to meet me in Panther Falls the next day.

"What time?" I asked.

"How about lunch time?"

"You'd have to get up pretty early. It's a four or five-hour drive, even with the Thruway."

The voice chuckled. "I know. Getting up early don't bother me none. It's an old Indian habit."

That night nobody came near Wilderfarm. There were, however, ominous sounds from the direction of Floreando: drumming and chanting. I suppose it was cowardly of me not have gotten dressed and gone skulking over there to see what the Huns were up to.

Charles H. Catfish kept me waiting in Panther Falls for over an hour. I do not want to generalize, but I fear that punctuality is not an outstanding American Indian virtue. At last a new, shiny Chevrolet sedan drove up.

My medicine man was a roly-poly fellow, about my age, in a handsome sports jacket, a necktie bearing Amerind motifs, and big black horn-rims. He wore his stiff black hair in a crew-cut brush. One had to look twice at his copper complexion and Mongoloid features to realize that he was an Indian and not just a middle-aged, sun-tanned fat man.

158

"Hello, Mr. Newbury," he said. "What's your problem? When the palefaces get stuck, they come around to sons of bitches like me for help."

Over lunch at the Panther Falls Diner, I told Catfish about my aunt's troubles.

"Have to think," he said. "Maybe old Eitsinoha can help us out. She ain't what she used to be, on account of having so few followers; but still, a great spirit is a great spirit."

Catfish proved a garrulous joker and storyteller, al- though my aunts would not have approved of many of his jokes.

"A few years ago," he said, "a damn funny thing happened to me. There was an assembly of professors from all over the world, at Ithaca—some learned society. Well, the guys at Cornell wanted to show these frogs and squareheads and dagoes some Indian stuff. Now, I got friends who try to keep up the old dances and ceremonies, and sometimes we put 'em on for pay. So I says, what the hell.

"I got Brant Johnson and Joe Ganogeh, and Joe's two boys, and we went to Ithaca with our feathers and junk. Of course, I know no real old-time Iroquois ever wore a Plains Indian war bonnet. Joe's older boy was the only one with anything like a proper Seneca hair crest and leggings. But these foreigners would never know the difference.

"So we did the corn dance and the war dance and the rest, beside Lake Cayuga, where all these wise guys were having a picnic. They gave us a good hand—all but one frog, a Catholic priest in a long gown and a berry hat. He stood with his back to us.

"When somebody asked why he wasn't watching, he said: 'Je démontre contre les injustices infligés sur les peaux-rouges!' You know French? This guy didn't know I knew it, on account of I've worked in Quebec. Then one of the Russkies snarled at him: 'Oui, et maintenant par les français dans l'Algérie!' This was when the Algerians were giving the French such a hard time that the frogs pulled out a little later.

"It was nice to have somebody sympathize with the injustices inflicted on the redskins; but I'd rather he'd watched us dancing and trying to earn an honest dollar."

We left the diner and stood on the sidewalk while Catfish finished one of his stories. As he spoke, I saw two men marching in step towards us. One was the big, burly youth with long blond hair, with whom I had spoken the time I drove in to Floreando.

The other, also young, was smaller and slighter—about average in size—and clean-shaven. Instead of blue denim, he wore whipcord riding breeches and real riding boots. I wear similar breeches and boots when I ride a horse; but I am of an older generation. Among young riders today, one doesn't often see such an outfit except on formal occasions, like a horse show. Otherwise it is blue jeans, often with high-heeled cowboy boots.

As the pair approached, I saw them check their stride. While they hesitated, the Siegfried type in blue denim said something to the other. Then they walked straight towards us. The smaller, he of the peg-topped breeches, looked me in the eye and said:

"Excuse me, but aren't you Mrs. Wilder's nephew, Wilson Newbury?"

"Yes."

"Well, I'm Marshall Nicholson. I'm pleased to know people of the old families." He stuck out a hand, which I shook without enthusiasm. "and—uh—" He looked a question at Catfish, who said:

"Charlie Catfish."

"Glad to meet you, Mr. Catfish. This is Truman Vogel." Nicholson looked sharply at Catfish. "Indian?"

"Yes, sir. Seneca."

"Mr. Newbury," said Nicholson, "Truman told me how you dropped in on us last week. I'm sorry I wasn't there to meet you. I also understand you've been hearing things about our little club."

"Well?"

"People will insist on misunderstanding us, you know. They tell all sorts of silly stories, just because we like to ride the hogs. I thought you might drop over to Floreando to talk it over. That's kind of an ancestral home of yours, isn't it? You, too, Mr. Catfish, If you'd like to come."

The young man had a good deal of charm, although experience had made me wary of charmers. Catfish and I exchanged looks.

"Please!" said Nicholson. "We're really harmless."

"Okay," I said. "When?"

"Right now, if you've got nothing else on."

Catfish and I formed a motorcade behind the two motorcycles. We wheeled into the driveway between the pillars and up to the porte-cochère. This time, no other motorcycles were parked beside the building.

The huge living room had changed since my boyhood. The floor was bare and much scratched. Gone were the ancestral pictures of men in wreath beards and high collars and women in poke bonnets. The bookshelves were empty save for a few sets of collected sermons, which none of Abraham's descendants had wanted. The only other reading matter in sight consisted of piles of motorcycle magazines and comic books.

One window had been broken and crudely patched with a sheet of plastic. The few pieces of furniture looked beat-up; that may have been a case of all the better pieces' being taken away by the heirs.

One thing had been added. The living room had a huge fireplace, and over it ran a long stone mantel. On this shelf stood a score of helmets, of the sort worn in the Ring operas. The one in the center had a pair of metal wings, while all the others had horns. I suppose they were made of *papier-mâché* and covered with metal foil, but I had no chance to examine them closely.

"Sit down, gentlemen," said Nicholson. "Can we get you a beer?"

"Thanks," I said. As Vogel went out, Nicholson explained:

"You see, Willy—mind if I call you Willy?—this isn't just one more hell-raising gang of young punks, you know. They were that when I took 'em over, but now I've given them a goal, a direction in life."

"What direction?"

"Nothing less than national regneration—the restoration of the American spirit, making this a country fit for heroes. But you can't build a sound house of rotten wood, you know.

161

That means we've got to cull out the rotten material."

Vogel returned with three cans of beer. He served one each to Catfish and me and took the third himself. I asked Nicholson: "Aren't you having any?"

"No. I don't drink." The young man gave a nervous little laugh. "You might call me a kind of health nut. But to get back: You've got to have sound materials to build a sound structure, you know. This applies to human institutions just as much as it does to houses and bridges. You've got to cull out the unsound."

"Who are the sound and who the unsound, then?"

"Oh, come off it, Willy! As a member of an old Anglo-Saxon family, you ought to know. The sound are the old original Nordic Aryan stock, which came over from the British Isles and other parts of northern Europe and made this country what it is—or at least, what it was before we let in hordes of biologically inferior niggers and kikes and spicks."

When I sat silently, he continued: "The scientific evidence is overwhelming, only it's been smudged and covered up and lied about by the Marxists. But I won't go into all the angles yet. Most people have been so brain-washed by liberal propaganda that they think you're a nut if you tell them a few plain facts, you know. If I can continue this discussion latter, I'll prove my points." He turned to Catfish. "Charlie, I hear you've got the special powers belonging to some Indians. Is that right?"

Evidently, someone had already spread the word of my hiring an aboriginal shaman. How the news got out I do not know. Perhaps my garrulous aunt had told one of her friends over the telephone while I was out of the house. Knowing small towns, I should not have been surprised.

Catfish's round red face remained blank. He said: "I learned a few old-time prayers and ceremonies when I was young, yes."

"We can use a man like you in our movement. You people have valuable qualities."

"I'm not exactly a Nordic Aryan, Mr. Nicholson," said Catfish.

"Don't worry about that. When we take over, we'll make th Indians honorary Aryans."

162

I spoke up: "Nick, how do you expect to make friends and influence people by letting your gang terrorize my old aunt?"

"Why, we never terrorize anybody! We believe in being kind to old ladies, especially old ladies of sound Anglo-Saxon stock. But—" He hesitated. "—you know, when I took the club over, they were just like any other motorcycle gang. You've got to work with the material you have. You can't expect everybody to be a—a spotless Puritan and a perfect gentleman, just as you can't chop down a tree with a razor blade. I've brought 'em a long way, but they still get a little rowdy at times. That'll pass. If the boys knew you were among our supporters, I'm sure Mrs. Wilder wouldn't have any more trouble. Now, can we count on your help, you two?"

"I'd have to think it over," I said, and Catfish mumbled something to the same effect.

I rose without awaiting further argument and said: "It's been very interesting, Nick. Maybe we can look in on you again." When Nicholson opened his mouth as if to protest, I pointed to the mantelpiece, saying: "Those Viking helmets made me wonder. If you're so hot on the Nordic type, why do you call yourselves Huns? According to history, the Huns were Mongolians—little square, slant-eyed men in fur caps, who came galloping out of the Gobi Desert on shaggy ponies. Not at all Nordic."

"Oh, that," said Nichcolson. "The club called themselves Huns before I became leader. 'The Goths' would have been a better name, but I haven't yet been able to sell them on it. I will eventually. I'll also make 'em switch from Japanese bikes to Harley-Davidsons and Husqvarnas. If they're going to buy imports, at least they can import them from a Nordic country like Sweden."

"Thanks for the beer," I said, and went.

We left Nicholson and Vogel standing on the porch and staring after us. I led Catfish back to the highway and thence to the farm. When we had parked and gotten out, Catfish said:

"Jeepers! Felt like I'd put my hand into a hole and found it full of rattlers. You didn't kid 'em with your talk of thinking it

163

over. They know you've got your tomahawk out for them. And don't think they meant that crap about the noble red man, either. If I'm any kind of medicine man, they'll try to get in the first lick first."

"I suppose so," I said. "Here comes my aunt. Aunt Phyllis, this is Charles H. Catfish; Charlie, this is Mrs. Wilder."

Catfish, who had been looking solemn even for an Indian, grinned. "Delighted, ma'am. I was just telling your nephew that's the way I thought a woman ought to be built. If I didn't have a wife and five kids to support already, I'd take a shine to you myself."

Giggling, Phyllis Wilder led us into the house. Here, things were in disorder. Piles of old clothes and children's discarded playthings littered the rooms. I asked:

"Are you packing up already, Aunt Phyllis, before the place is sold?"

"No, Willy. But I am clearing out some of the junk collected by four generations. Here's one item." From a pile, she picked up a brown canvas hunting jacket with big pockets. "This belonged to Peter." (Peter Wilder was her late husband.) "Would you like it?"

I took off my own coat and tried on the jacket. "It fits fine," I said. "Thanks; this'll be useful." I told her about our visit to Floreando.

"Oh, dear!" she said. "They'll be up to some devilment. Can you help us, Mr. Catfish?"

"I can try," said Catfish. "Have you got a room where I can be let alone for the rest of the afternoon?"

"Sure. Right at the head of the stairs."

I helped Catfish to carry in three large suitcases. He shut himself in the room. Soon there came the tapping of a little drum and vocal noises, I suppose a chant in Seneca.

Aunt Phyllis and I sat downstairs, traded family gossip, and talked about the prospective sale of the Farm. The sun was low when Charles Catfish appeared at the head of the stairs. He came down slowly, and his voice sounded weak and husky. There was nothing of the jolly joker about him now.

"I've been in the spirit world," he said. "Eitsinoha will do what she can. She says the Huns got some spirit from across the water. Some name like 'Dawner.' That mean anything to

164

you?"

I thought. "Of course! She must mean Donner or Donar, the old Germanic thunder god. The Scandinavians called him Thor, but Wagner used the German form in *Das Rheingold*. What can your—uh—what's-her-name do for us?"

"Don't expect too much. The powers of spirits are limited, even big-league spirits like these. They can tell you things in dreams and trances; they can do things to the weather; they can fix cards and dice. But it's no use asking Eitsinoha to pick up young Nicholson and dunk him in the Black River. Oh, before I forget!"

Catfish brought out a flat pint whiskey bottle and set it down, saying: "I found this empty in one of them piles of stuff, Mrs. Wilder. Hope you don't mind me using it. Willy, what's in that there bottle looks and tastes like ordinary water; but, if you can get Nick to drink it, it'll change his attitude for sure."

I put the bottle in one of the pockets of the hunting coat. "How am I supposed to do that?"

"I dunno. You'll have to figure something out. Do I smell something cooking, ma'am?"

"Yes," said Phyllis Wilder. "Dinner will be ready in twenty minutes, praise be. Willy, you can be bartender. The stuff's in the cupboard to the left of the stove. Well, Mr. Catfish, what'll we do if—if they raid us again?"

"Do you keep a gun, Aunt Phyllis?" I asked.

"I have a little twenty-two, for woodchucks in my garden."

"Better think twice about using agun," said Catfish. "The way they got the laws fixed in New York State now, if you find a burglar climbing out the window of your house with his loot, you dassen't shoot him. If you do, they'll put you in jail for using 'excessive force.' Then if he dies, you'll take the rap for manslaughter. If he lives, he'll sue you for a million bucks and prob'ly get a judgment. We Indians were more practical. When we found some guy stealing our stuff, we killed him, and that was that."

I had gone to my room around eleven and was just beginning to undress when all hell broke loose. The roar of

165

motorcycles around the house was mingled with yells, whoops, and the crash of breaking glass.

I buttoned up and raced downstairs. Phyllis Wilder and Charlie Catfish were almost as quick.

"Aunt Phyllis, telephone the troopers!" I said.

Although fluttering and wheezing, she picked up the telephone. After a few seconds, she said: "Oh, dear me, it's dead! They must have cut the wires."

"Let me try," I said. She had been right.

Catfish said: "Tell me where the nearest barracks is. I'll drive over and get 'em, while you take care of Mrs. Wilder."

Phyllis Wilder gave directions, while the uproar outside. A bottle crashed through a window and landed at my feet.

Catfish ducked out into the car port but was back in a few minutes. "She's dead, too. Must have tore out the wires or pulled the distributor head. Suppose you try yours, Willy."

I did, with the same results. While I was explaining my failure, a stone whizzed through one of the windows and hit me on the forehead. I staggered and almost went down.

I am usually—if I say so myself—a pretty even-tempered, self-controlled man. In my business, one has to be. About once a year, however, the pressure builds up and I blow my top.

In the corner of the living room was a pile of disused toys, including a junior-sized baseball bat. As I recovered my balance, my eye fell upon that bat. In two steps I grabbed it up. Then I ran out the front door.

"Willy!" wailed Aunt Phyllis. "Come back! You'll be killed!"

At that moment, if I had been told that I faced execution by firing squad for use of excessive force, I would not have cared. I was an idiot, of course, but this is what happened.

When the first motorcyclist loomed out of the dark, I took him across the front of the helmet with the bat. I heard the plastic crunch, and the cyclist was flipped backwards out of his saddle. The motorcycle disappeared riderless into the dark.

Then they were all around me, their headlight beams thrusting like lances. The Huns could not all get at me at once because they were encumbered by their vehicles. I jumped about like a matador dodging bulls and whacked away. Some of the yells implied that I had gotten home. Then something hit me over the ear...

I awoke on the floor of the living room at Floreando. For a few seconds, I knew not where I was. I had an atavistic suspicion that I was in Hell; then I saw that the devils were merely the Huns in the horned helmets. My head throbbed like a forging hammer.

"Ah," said Nicholson's voice. "He's coming to."

I turned my head, wincing, and saw that Nicholson was wearing the winged helmet.

"Just what Donar ordered," continued Nick. "Hey, grab him!"

I had started to sit up. Four of them pounced upon me, hauled me to a chair, and sat me in it. They tied my wrists to the chair behind my back and my ankles to the front legs.

Now that my vision had cleared and my memory had sorted itself out, I saw that I had indeed done some execution among the Huns. One had his arm in a sling. Another had a bandage around his head under the helmet. A third was trying to staunch a flow of blood from a broken nose.

Many of them wore plastic protectors, like those of football players, on shoulders, chests, and knees. Together with the operatic helmets and the massive boots, the effect was startlingly medieval.

"Get the sacrifice ready, Truman," said Nicholson. "We'll use that old stump in the woodshed. Chuck, stoke up the furnace. Remember, we've got to burn up every last piece of bone or tooth. Carry him out, you guys."

The chair was hoisted and borne through the long hall to the kitchen and out the back door. Floreando had a huge woodshed, dating from the days when firewood was the only source of heat. Some ancestor had put in steam heat around 1900, but the woodshed still maintained a supply of wood for the fireplaces. Even in midsummer, the nights there get pretty cool.

A single light bulb illumined the area. The "stump" of which Nicholson had spoken was a cylindrical piece of tree trunk, about thirty inches high and the same in diameter. One of the Huns was whetting a double-bitted lumberman's ax.

"Now," said Nicholson, "you know the invocation to Donar. Gary, you keep hold of Newbury. He might try to wriggle away, tied up as he is, while we're looking elsewhere. Now, are you all ready with the responses? Great Donar, lord of the lightning—"

Overhead, lightning flashed and distant thunder rumbled.

"Hey, leader!" said a Hun. "He's got something in his pocket."

"Search him," said Nicholson.

From Uncle Peter's hunting coat, the speaker brought out the pint bottle. He chuckled: "Why, the old rumdum!"

"Throw it away," said Nicholson.

"No, Nick, wait!" said Truman Vogel. "No use wasting good booze." He unscrewed the cap and sniffed. Then he wet a finger and tasted. "Oh, shit! Seems to be plain water. Now what would he carry a bottle of water around for? It's not like he was out hunting or fishing."

The prospect of having one's head chopped off, and moreover by an amateur executioner who would probably make a messy job of it, is a wonderful stimulant to thinking. "Hey!" I yelled, although I suspect it came out as a croak. "Give me that!" The effort made my head throb.

"Won't do you no good," said Vogel. "What is this stuff, anyway?"

"I can't tell you. Catfish swore me to secrecy."

"Oh, yeah? We'll see about that. Gary, just tighten those ropes a little."

Gary obeyed. I put on an act—and not entirely an act—of a man bravely resisting torture and then succumbing to pain.

"Okay, I'll tell!" I gasped. "It's the magical Iroquois water. Their medicine men make it, to give their warriors the strength to overcome all their enemies. When they get enough, they hope to drive all the whites into the ocean."

"Oh," said Nicholson. "Well, maybe it'll work for us. I've got enemies to overcome, too. Let's see it."

He took the bottle from Vogel, sniffed, and tasted. "Seems harmless."

168

"Don't!" I cried. "You don't know what it'll do to you!"

"Fuck you, buster," said Nicholson. "You won't be here to worry about that, you know." He tilted up the bottle with a gurgling sound.

"Seems like good, clean water," he said. "Okay, on with the ceremony."

"And off with his head," said Vogel. A titter ran through the Huns. "Stan, you and Mike haul Newbury over to the stump."

"You want we should untie him?" said a Hun.

"God, no! He's no pushover, even if he is a gray-haired old geezer. Take the chair and all and put him so his neck is face-down on the stump—uh—well, you know what I mean."

I was dragged, still bound, to the stump and laid across it. By twisting my neck, I could still see what was going on. The Hun with the ax stood up and spat on his hands.

"Now repeat after me," said Nicholson: "Great Donar, lord of the lightning—"

"*Great Donar, lord of the lightning—*" said the other Huns.

"And god of the immortal, indomitable Nordic Aryan race—"

"*And god of the immortal, indomitable Nordic Aryan race—*"

"We sacrifice a man unto thee—"

"*We sacrifice a man unto thee—*"

There was a violet flash in the clouds overhead, and thunder rumbled.

"In return, we ask that thou smiteth our enemies with thy lightnings—" Nicholson's knowledge of Jacobean English grammar was weak. The Huns responded as usual.

"Beginning with Phyllis Wilder, Isaiah Rosen, and Paul Grier—"

"And that thou giveth us a sign—"

Again a flash and a rumble, but more faintly.

"Louder, we pray, great Donar!"

This time, the thunder was barely audible. Nicholson said: "He's not in a good mood tonight."

"Let's give Newbury the business, quick," said Vogel. "It's Thursday, and we can't wait a week for *his* day to come

169

around again."

"Ready with that ax, Frank!" said Vogel. "Wait till I give the signal. But—that's funny. *Was war ich*—what was I— going to say? I—ah—*ach*—" He stared about in a puzzled way. "*Was für ein Unsinn—*" He gasped and clutched at his throat.

"You been poisoned, Nick?" asked Vogel. The other Huns murmured excitedly.

Recovering himself, Nicholson shouted, gesticulating fiercely: "*Wir wollen wiederherstellen die Einheit des Geistes und des Willens der deutschen Nation! Die Rasse liegt night in der Sprache, sondern im Blute!*"

The Huns looked bewilderedly at one another. One said: "Hey, Truman, is he off his nut?"

"God, I dunno," said Vogel. "We can't take him to that Jew doctor—"

A Hun ran around the corner of the woodshed into the light. "The fuzz!" he shouted. "Split, you guys!"

With muffled exclamations, the Huns scurried away. I have never seen human beings scatter so quickly. There was a sudden glare of motorcycle headlights and the roar of motors. Away went the Huns, wheeling over lawns and through woods, as two state police cars turned into the driveway. By the time four troopers appeared around the corner of the woodshed, pistols at ready, the only persons present were myself, still tied to that chair, and Marshall Nicholson. The gang leader held his right upper arm out stiffly while the forearm pumped up and down with a clockworky motion, as if he were pounding an invisible desk with his fist as he ranted:

"*...Wer ein volk retten will, kann nur heroisch denken! Der heroische Gedanke aber muss stehts bereits sein, auf die Zustimmung der Gegenwart Verzicht zu leisten, wenn die Wahrhaftigkeit und die Wahrheit es erfordert!*"

"We left the house after they carried you off," said Charlie Catfish, "and hiked along the road till we found a place to 'phone."

"Oh, my poor feet!" moaned Phyllis Wilder.

We stood in Doctor Rosen's crowded waiting room, with

170

two troopers holding the handcuffed Marshall Nicholson. Jack Nicholson sat with his face in his hands. Young Nick was still orating in German. Questions in English brought no response.

Rosen finished his examination, or as much of it as he could do with an obstreperous patient. He said:

"Mr. Newbury, do you speak German?"

"A little. I got fairly fluent in Germany after the War, but I've forgotten most of it."

"I read it, but I don't speak it worth a damn. Ask him when he was born."

"Wann waren Sie Geboren?" I said to Nick.

He paused in his harangue. *"Warum?"*

"Tut nichts! Sagen Sie mir."

"Der zwanzigst April, achtzehnhundert neunundachtzig."

"April twentieth, eighteen eighty-nine," I told Rosen.

One trooper murmured: "That'd make him older than his father."

Rosen said: "Mr. Nicholson, what was your son's birthdate?"

Old Nicholson looked up. "April thirtieth, nineteen forty-five."

"Has he ever studied German?"

"Not that I know of. He never finished High."

Rosen stood for a minute in thought. "You'll have to commit him, Mr. Nicholson," he said. "I don't know any way around it. I'll get the papers. There's a good place in Utica..."

This happened before that court decision, that a loony must be allowed to run loose until he proves he is dangerous by killing somebody. After the troopers and the Nicholsons had gone, I asked Rosen:

"Doc, what was all that about birth dates?"

"Mr. Newbury, I've told you I don't believe for a second in supernatural stuff. But it is a strange coincidence that Adolf Hitler was born April 20, 1889; and that he killed himself in Berlin on the very day Marshall Nicholson was born. Moreover, I've read Hitler's speeches in the original."

"You have? That seems strange."

"Not at all. When you know somebody is out to kill you,

171

it's only sensible to learn all you can about him, so you can protect yourself. The German that Nick was spouting seemed to be nothing but excerpts from Hitler's speeches. I'd have to check—I can't remember them word for word—but it certainly sounded familiar. Mr. Catfish, what was in that water Mr. Newbury got Nick to drink?"

"Just tap water," said Catfish, "but I prayed to Eitsinoha to give it the power to take away a man's memory." To me he added: "Donar gave her quite a tussle, but every spirit's strongest on its home ground."

"You mean," I said, "that Nick is a reincarnation of Adolf Hitler? I can see how that might work. If you wiped out his memory of this life, that would leave him the memory of his previous life. So he'd think he was still Hitler and be very much confused. One moment he's in the bunker, getting ready to shoot himself; the next, he's in a woodshed in upstate New York—"

"Please, please!" said Rosen. "I've told you, I don't believe in that nonsense. My business is curing folks of what ails them, and for that I need a strictly scientific outlook. But I thought it might interest you. Do you need a lift home, now that your cars are disabled?"

"No, thanks," I said. "Trooper Talbot offered to drive us back to the Farm. He should be waiting outside."

"Well, good-night, then. And Mrs. Wilder, you simply must learn to resist the sweets and starches!"

The Purple Pterodactyls

I am as ordinary, commonplace a guy as you can find: middle-sized, middle-class, middle-aged; engineer by training, banker by circumstance; with a nice wife, nice kids, nice house, and nice car. But the damndest things happen to me.

When the children were grown enough so that they could take care of themselves in summer, Denise and I spent a vacation by ourselves at the shore. My cousin Linda, who has a house there, had been raving about Ocean Bay. So we rented an apartment in a rambly wooden-frame building, a block from the beach. This was before the waterfront sprouted a host of huge condominiums, like a plague of concrete mushrooms. You could walk on the sand without stepping on somebody or getting hit in the eye with a frisbee.

We swam, we sunned, and we walked the boardwalk. The second afternoon, Denise said: "Willy, my old, why do we walk not down to the park of amusement?"

She said it in French, since we speak it a lot *en famille*. It is her native tongue, and I try to keep mine up by practice. We tried to bring the children up bilingually, but it took with only one of them.

We walked a mile to the piers and concessions. There were the usual fun house, roller coaster, and shooting gallery. There was a fortuneteller who called himself Swami Krishna. There were concessions where you threw darts at rubber balloons, or threw baseballs at plywood cats, or tossed baseballs into baskets. These baskets were so set that, when you did get your ball in, it bounced right out again and did not count. If you succeeded in such endeavors, you won teddy bears, rubber pythons, and similar junk.

I am normally immune to the lure of such games. One, however, showed more originality.

You bought three rubber rings, four or five inches in diamater, for half a dollar. You tossed these rings over three little posts, a couple of feet high and a mere yard from the thrower. There were three sets of these posts, forming three sides of a square.

The upper part of each post was conical, and it was no trick to get the ring over the point of the cone. To win, however, the ring had to fall down the rest of the post, which was square in cross-section and barely small enough for the ring to go over it. Nearly always, the ring hung up on the corners at the top of the square section. You had to ring all three posts at once to win a prize.

The prizes were even more original: a flock of plush-and-wire pterodactyls. They came in several models and sizes, some with long tails and some with short, some with teeth and some with long, toothless beaks. The biggest were over a yard across the wings. They were made so that you could hang one from your ceiling as a mobile. If the wind was strong, you could lock the wings in place and fly the thing as a kite. They were all dyed in shades of purple.

"Purple pterodactyls!" I said. "Darling, I've got to have one of those."

"Oh, *mon Dieu!*" said Denise. "What on earth would you do with it?"

"Hang it in my study, I suppose."

"You had better not hang it where the people can see it. What do you like about these monsters?"

"I suppose it's the alliteration of the name. Only it's not a real alliteration, since you don't pronounce the *p* in 'pterodactyl.' That makes it just an eye-rhyme—I mean an eye-alliteration."

"In English, maybe. But in French we do pronounce the *p*: p'tero-dac-TEEL. That is what is wrong with the English; you never know when some letter at the beginning of a word is silent."

"Like 'knife,' you mean? Well, in French you never know when a letter at the *end* of a word is silent. Let me have a try at this."

The concessionaire was a short, tubby, bald man of about my age, with a big black mustache. The ends of the mustache were waxed and curled up, something like the *Schnurrbart* once worn by Kaiser Wilhelm II.

The man sold me a set of rings, and I threw....Ten dollars and sixty rings later, I was no nearer to getting my purple pterodactyl.

"Will you sell me one of those?" I asked the proprietor. "How much?"

The man ducked a little bow. "I am so sorry, sir," he said with a slight accent, "but they are not for sale. Either you win them with the rings, or you do not get any."

A look from Denise told me I had better not throw any more of the Newbury fortune, such as it was, after Mesozoic reptiles just then. As we walked off, I growled something like: "I'll get one of those things if it's my last...."

"You say we can't afford a Mercedes," she said, "but you throw away money on those hideous..."

"Well, anyway," said I to change the subject, "if we go right back to the house, we can get another swim before dinner."

"Willy!" she said. "You have had one swim today. The waves are big, and you will get the sunburn. Do not kill yourself, trying to prove your manhood! You forget we are middle-aged."

"I may be middle-aged," said I with a leer, "but I can still do some of the things young men do."

"Yes, I know. You did it just this morning. Some day you will try to prove your manhood once too often, and you will have the stroke in the middle of it."

"I can't think of a better way to go."

"But think of your poor wife! Aside from the fact that I don't want to be a widow, consider how embarrassing it would be to explain to the policemen!"

Next morning, we went out for our sun-and-swim. There on the beach was our friend of the purple pterodactyls, also soaking up ultra-violet. In bathing trunks, with his pod and his jungle of graying chest hair, he was a walking argument against nudism. He had been swimming, for the water had dissolved the pomade out of his mustache, so the ends hung down in Fu-Manchurian style. He was spooning sand upon himself with a child's toy shovel.

"Hello," I said, since you never know when the unlikeliest people might want to do business with your bank. "How's the pterodactyl business?"

"Business is good," he siad. "Three of my pterosaurs were won yesterday, so you see people do win sometimes. I regret that you did not. You must try again."

"I'll be back," I said. "Do you come out here every day before opening?"

"Yes. It is the only time I have, since I must be on duty from noon to midnight. It is not an easy business."

In answer to my questions, he told me something of the economics of boardwalk concessions. "Excuse me please," he said. "Permit me to introduce myself. I am Ion Maniu, at your service. I regret that I cannot give you my card."

"I'm Wilson Newbury," I said.

He repeated the name slowly, as if it really meant something to him. "Is there an initial?"

"Woodrow Wilson Newbury, if you want the whole thing," I told him, "but I haven't used the 'Woodrow' in years. When I see you this afternoon, we can exchange cards." I thought Mr. Maniu's formality a little quaint but did not mean to let him outdo me.

In the afternoon, my cousin Linda wanted to take Denise on one of those endless female shopping trips, looking at hundreds of wares in dozens of stores but probably not buying anything. On these safaris, my knees give out after the first hour, like those of an old prizefighter.

I begged off and sneaked back to Maniu's concession. All that got me was another five dollars down the drain.

I was to meet the girls at a souvenir and notion shop, combined with a branch post office, on Atlantic Avenue. While waiting, I looked over a bin full of junk rings, offered for a quarter each. They were little brass things set with pieces of colored glass, for the pleasure of vacationers' children. Some were elaborate, with coiled serpents or skulls and crossbones.

I pawed over this stuff, not meaning to buy—our own children were much too grown-up—but to pass the time and muse on the costs, mark-ups, and profits of merchandising

176

these things. Then I came upon one that did not seem to belong. I tried it on, and it fitted.

Although dull and dirty like the rest, this ring was more massive. It felt heavier than one would expect of a brass ring of that size. That proved nothing; it could be plated or painted lead. It seemed to have once been molded in a complex design, but the ridges and grooves were so worn down as to leave only traces.

The stone was a big green glassy lump, polished but unfaceted, with the original bumps and hollows preserved like those of a stream-worn pebble.

I gave the cashier a quarter, put the ring on my finger, and met the girls. Linda started to tell me about the women's club meeting, at which she had persuaded me, with some cousinly arm-twisting, to speak. Then Denise spotted the ring.

"Willy!" she said. "What have you done now?"

"Just a junk ring out of the bin there, but it appealed to me. For twenty-five cents, what did I have to lose?"

"Let me see," said Denise. "*Hein!* This does not look to me quite like what you call the junk. Look, we have just come from Mr. Hagopian the jeweller. Let us go back there and ask him what it is."

"Oh, girls," I said, "let's not be silly. You won't find a Hope diamond in a box of stuff like that."

"As you were saying," she persisted, "what have we to lose? Come along; it's only a block."

Hagopian screwed his loupe into his eye and examined the ring. "I won't guarantee anything," he said, "but it looks like real gold, and the stone like an uncut emerald. In that case, it could be worth thousands. It would of course take tests to be sure what this is... Where did you get it?"

"An unlikely place," I said.

"This is pretty unlikely, too. For four or five hundred years, practically all gems used in jewelry have been faceted. Before that, they just smoothed them off and tried to cut out obvious defects, while keeping as much of the material as they could.

"This kind of mounting goes back much further than that—unless somebody is making a clever imitation of a real ancient ring. If you would leave it a few days for assaying...."

177

"I'll think about it," I said, taking the ring back. Hagopian might be perfectly honest (in fact, I think he was), but before I left anything with him I would check up on him.

Next morning was overcast. When we went for our swim, there was Maniu, half buried in the sand, with just his upper body, arms, and head sticking out. He was ladling more sand over his torso. I asked:

"Mr. Maniu, if you want the sun, why bury yourself? The sun can't get through the sand."

"I have a theory, Mr. Newbury," he said. "The vital vibrations will rejuvenate you. Shall I see you at my concession today?" He grinned at me in a peculiar way, which led me to wonder if he slept in a coffin full of earth from Transylvania.

"If it doesn't rain, maybe," I said.

It did rain, so we did not go boardwalking. Denise wrote letters in the sitting room, while I took off my shoes and lay down on one of the beds for a nap.

Then a rhythmic, squeaky sound kept waking me up. After I had jerked awake three times, I hunted down the source. It came from an aluminum-and-plastic rocking chair on the little terrace of our apartment. Chair and terrace were wet from the drizzle. Nobody was sitting in the chair, but it rocked anyway.

Thinking that the wind was moving this light little piece of furniture, I moved the chair to a more sheltered part of the terrace and went back to bed.

The sound awoke me again. I stamped out to the terrace. The chair was rocking again, although there was no wind to speak of. The mate to this chair, in a more exposed place, stood still. I cast a few curses against the overcast heavens, turned both chairs upside down, and returned to the bed.

It seemed to me that I next woke up to find a strange man sitting on the other of the twin beds and looking at me.

He was a man of average size, very swarthy, with a close-cut black mustache. His clothes were up-to-date but what I should call "cheap and flashy": striped pants, loud tie, stickpin, and several rings. (But then, Denise is always after me to buy more colorful clothes. She says a banker doesn't

178

have to dress like an undertaker.) I also noted that the man wore a big, floppy panama hat, which he kept on his head.

What makes me sure that this was a dream is that, instead of leaping up and demanding: "Who in hell are you and what are you doing here?" I just lay there with a weak smile and said: "Hello!"

"Ah, Mr. Newbury!" said the man. He, too, spoke with an accent, although one different from Maniu's. "Peace be with you. I am at your service."

I stammered: "B-but who—who are you?"

"Habib al-Lajashi, at your service, sir."

"Huh? But who—how—what do you mean?"

"It is the ring, sir. That emerald ring from the Second Dynasty of Kish. I am the slave of that ring. When you are turning it round thrice on your finger, I appear to do your bidding."

I blinked. "You mean you—you're some sort of Arabian Nights genie?"

"Jinn, sir. Oh, I see. You were expecting me to appear in medieval garb, with turban and robe. I assure you, sir, we *jann* are keeping up with the times quite as well as mortals."

You might expect a suspicious, hard-headed fellow like me to scoff and order the man out. I have, however, come upon so many queer things that I did not dismiss Mr. al-Lajashi out of hand. I said:

"What does this service consist of?"

"I can do little favors for you. Like seeing that you are getting the choicest cuts of steak in a restaurant, or that you draw all aces and face cards in contract."

"Nothing like eternal youth for my wife and me?"

"Alas, no, sir. I am only a very minor jinn and so can do only small favors. The most powerful ones are all tied up with oil shaykhs and big corporations."

"Hm," I said. "If I knew which super-jinn served which corporation, it should affect the securities of that—'

"Ah, no sir, I am sorry; but that information is classified."

"How long does this service last? Is it one of those three-wishes-and-out deals?"

"No, sir. You remain my master as long as you keep the ring. When it passes to another, I pass with it."

"How do you like your job, Habib?"

Al-Lajashi made a face. "It depends on the master, like any other slavery. There is a jinn's liberation movement— but never mind that, sir."

"Is there any way you can end this servile status?"

"Yes, sir. If one of my masters is so grateful for services rendered that he is voluntarily giving me the ring, I am free. But that has not happened in three thousand years. You mortals know a good thing when you see it. You hang on to our service, even when you promise us liberty."

"Let's get down to cases," I said. "There's a concessionaire..." and I told Habib about the purple pterodactyls. "The next time I take a chance with Maniu's rings, I want to win one of those things."

Al-Lajashi took off his panama hat to scratch his scalp, disclosing a pair of small horns. "I think I can do it, sir. Leave it to me."

"Don't make it too obvious, or he'll get suspicious."

"I understand. Now, sir, pray lie down and resume your nap. I shall not disturb you again today."

I did as he said and woke up normally. I could see no dent in Denise's bed where the *soi-disant* jinn had sat. I did not think it wise to tell Denise about my experiences. Instead, I worked on my speech to Linda's clubwomen.

The next day was fair and breezy. Maniu was on the beach, all buried but his arms and head.

"Good-morning, Mr. Maniu," I said. "If you'll pardon my saying so, you give a slightly macabre impression."

"How so, Mr. Newbury?"

"You look as if somebody had put your severed head on top of that pile of sand."

Maniu grinned. "Come to my concession this afternoon, and you shall see that my head is firmly affixed to the rest of me."

So I did. My first three rings stuck at the square sections of the posts. Of my second three, one slipped down all the way. Of my third, two scored. The fourth time, all three rings fell to the base of the posts.

Maniu stared. "My God, Mr. Newbury, you certainly have

improved fast! Which pterosaur do you want?"

"That one, please," I said, indicating a long-beaked *Pteranodon*.

Maniu got down the prize, folded the wings, and showed me how to extend them again. "Come back tomorrow," he said. "You will never repeat this feat, ha-ha!"

"We shall see," I said. I bore my prize home, to the acute discomfort of Denise. She did not like the stares we got on the boardwalk, with that thing under my arm.

The next day, I was back, despite Denise's protest: "Willy, you big *pataud*, where would you put another of those monstrosities?"

"I'll find a place," I said. "This ganif has challenged me, and I'll show him.

And I did, coming away with a fanged *Dimetrodon*.

The following day, Maniu was not in his usual place on the beach. I took another nap after lunch and awoke to find al-Lajashi in the room.

"Mr. Newbury," he said, "shall you make another attempt on Mr. Maniu's prizes?"

"I thought of doing so. Why?"

"There may be difficulty, sir. Mr. Maniu is furious with you for winning two of his lizard-bats. He hardly ever gives one up."

"Stingy fellow! He told me three were won a few days ago."

"He lies. I doubt he has given out one all this season."

"So what?"

"He has rented the services of one of my fellow jann to protect him."

"Does that mean you won't be able to make the rings go over the posts?"

"Oh, I am thinking I can still do it, although not so easily. But this other fellow may make you trouble."

"What sort of trouble?"

"I do not know. But ibn-Musa can surely harass you."

"Why can't you protect me, as the other jinn does Maniu?"

"I cannot be everywhere at once, any more than you can. If he uses a phenomenon on the material plane over which I have no control, I cannot stop him."

"Where did Maniu get his spook? From another ring?"

"No, sir. He leased him from that astrologer on the boardwalk, Swami Krishna. The astrologer's name is really Carlos Jiménez, but no matter. He uses this jinn to make some of his little astrological predictions come true. Are you still determined to try your so-called luck again?"

"I am," I said.

When I bought rings from Maniu and began tossing, the rings did not fly so surely as before. They wobbled about in the air and hesitantly settled over the posts. I spent several dollars before I got my three rings over all three posts. When one ring started to fall to the base of the post, it fell partway, started to rise again, and bobbed up and down a couple of times before completing its descent.

Maniu watched it, chewing his lower lip. I could imagine two invisible entities struggling with the ring, one trying to push it down and the other, to raise it off the post.

I walked off with a fine *Rhamphorynchus,* the one with a little rudder on the end of its tail. The waxy spikes of Maniu's whiskers quivered like those of a cat.

I wanted to sail. The day after I won my third prize, I found the boat I wanted. It was a sixteen-foot centerboard sloop, the *Psyche,* which the Ramoth Bay Sailing Club had for rent. Ocean Bay is built on a long spit of land, with the Atlantic on one side and shallow Ramoth Bay on the other.

That day, however, there was a flat calm. Since the boat had no motor, there was no point in taking it out. Instead, I went back to the boardwalk and won another pterodactyl. Maniu hopped up and down with excitement.

"It is unheard of!" he said. "You must have supernatural aid!"

"Don't you want me to play any more?" I asked innocently. He knew perfectly well that I had the help of my jinn—ibn-Musa would have told him—and I knew that he knew.

To tell the truth, I was losing enthusiasm for collecting these bulky objects. I suppose some childish spirit of rivalry kept me trying to put one more over on this con artist.

I surmised that, however much Maniu hated to lose his pterodactyls, neither did he wish to lose the money that my visits brought him, not to mention the publicity. The prizes probably cost him no more than I paid in throwing fees.

Red-faced, Maniu mastered his conflicting feelings. "No, no, nothing like that," he said. "Come as often as you like. I am a fair man."

That evening was the women's club meeting. We got dressed up and had dinner at Linda's house with her and her husband. They brought us up on the local gossip: how one of the councilmen had been caught with his hand in the municipal till, and about the motorcycle gang suspected of local depredations. Then we went to the little auditorium.

I am no public speaker. With a written text, I can give a fair rendition, remembering to look up from the paper now and then and not to drone or mumble. But without a manuscript, rhetorically speaking, I fall over my own big feet. This time, I had my talk, written out, in the inside pocket of my jacket.

When the ladies assembled, there was the usual tedious hour while minutes were read, the treasurer's report was presented, delinquent members were dunned for their dues, committees presented reports, and so on.

At last the chairman (I absolutely refuse to say "chairperson") called me up and gave me a flowery introduction: "...and so Mr. Wilson Newbury, first vice president of the Harrison Trust Company, will speak to you on the importance of trusts to women."

I stepped up, put on my glasses, and spread out the sheets of my manuscript on the lectern.

The sheets were blank.

I may have goggled at them for only a few seconds, but it seemed an hour. I instantly thought: this is one of ibn-Musa's tricks.

Such reasoning, however, was of no help in getting me off the platform. There was nothing for it but to make the speech without this aid. I plunged in.

It was a pretty bad speech, even though I knew my subject. Even Denise, who is as loyal as can be, hinted at

183

that later. But I got through my main points:

"...Now—ah—let my tell you about—uh—reversionary living trusts. Umm. Ah. They combine some of the—ah—features of revocable and—uh—irrevocable trusts. This is—umm—a—er—a temporary trust, often called the—ah—the 'Clifford trust,' after a taxpayer who um—ah—in—uh—1934, fought the IRS to a standstill. Such a—ah—trust...."

I finished at last, submitted to the insincere congratulations of the ladies, and went back to the apartment with Denise. When I looked again at my manuscript, all the writing was back in place.

Next day, I went to Maniu's for revenge. I got it, too. I came away with *two* purple pterodactyls, leaving Maniu practically frothing with ill-concealed rage.

The following day, since the weather looked suitable, I called the Ramoth Bay Sailing Club to confirm our reservation of the *Psyche*. On our way thither, Denise kidded me some more about the vagaries of English, which insisted on pronouncing the name SIKE-ee instead of the more logical French psee-SHAY.

"I'm sure Socrates wouldn't have known whom you were talking about in either case," I said.

"Willy, darling," said Denise, suddenly serious. "are you sure you ought to take this boat out? The wind is pretty brisk."

"A mere ten to fifteen knots, and steady," I said. "You've sailed with me before, haven't you?"

"Yes, but—somehow I don't think this will turn out well."

I passed that off as women's intuition, which is wrong more often than not. People remember the times it works and forget those it fails.

We found the two young men in charge of the boats installing the sails, oars, life preservers, fire extinguisher, and other things called for by the maritime codes. In half an hour we were bowling along on Ramoth Bay under that brisk but soft, steady breeze abeam—a sailorman's ideal.

"Sun's over the yardarm," I said. "Let's break out the chow."

We had sandwiches, fruit, and enough whiskey to make

the world look good but not enough to interfere with conning the boat. Denise unwrapped and sorted and poured. I raised my paper mug and said: "Here's to my one true love—"

Then, from an easy twelve-knot breeze, it hit us. A tornado or hurricane must be something like that. It came without warning, *wham!*, whipped the tops off the little waves, and hit our sails broadside.

I was a couple of seconds slow in starting the main sheet. Denise screamed, and over we went. Away went lunch, whiskey, and all, and away went Mr. and Mrs. Newbury into the water.

Luckily, we came down on top of the mainsail instead of under it. As soon as I got myself untangled from the lines and sail and coughed out the water I had inhaled, I grabbed for oars and life preservers, which were floating away to leeward.

The blast had died as quickly as it had risen. We thrashed around, collected such gear as was still afloat, and held on to the hull, now lying peacefully on its side.

It occurred to me that all my sailing experience had been in keeled boats. Such boats cannot capsize, because the weight of the keel rights them again. A centerboard boat, however, easily overturns when a squall hits it, unless you are very spry at letting out the main sheet. And you cannot right the thing again while wallowing around in the sea.

All the Ramoth Bay sailboats are centerboard, because the bay is too shallow for keels. The place we had overturned, however, was too deep for us to stand on the bottom. There was nothing to do but hold on, wave, yell, and hope for rescue.

Soon the two young men at the club came out in a motorboat and hauled us aboard. They threw some tackle around the mast of the *Psyche* and had her right side up in a jiffy. One of them got aboard, struck the sails, and bailed out most of the water.

This took nearly an hour, while Denise and I huddled shivering in the motorboat. I do not think the young men had much sympathy for us. At last we returned to the pier, towing the *Psyche*.

It was still early afternoon by the time were dried, changed, and fed. I took a nap and, as I more or less expected, had another visit from Habib al-Lajashi. The jinn looked grave.

"Mr. Newbury," he said, "I know of your troubles with the boat."

"Ibn-Musa's doing?

"Of course. Now I must tell you that Mr. Maniu has ordered ibn-Musa at all costs to destroy you."

"You mean to kill me? Murder me?"

"That is what is meaning by 'destroy.'"

"What for? If he wants me to quit his damned game, why doesn't he say so? I have all the purple pterodactyls I need."

"You are not understanding the psychology of Mr. Maniu. He has many ideas that would seem to you strange. I understand them better, because many mortals have ideas like that in my part of the world. With him it is a matter of what he calls his honor, never to let another get the better of him. You have wounded his—how do you say—your wife would know the French expression—"

"*Amour-propre?*"

"That is it. When someone does that to him, he never forgives them. It does no good to give him back his prizes, or to let him win them back, or to throw his rings for a month without scoring. He has a—what is that Italian word?"

"A vendetta?"

"Thank you, sir; a vendetta against you."

"I guess ibn-Musa really tried to drown us this morning. Luckily, we're both good swimmers. Well, Habib, what can you do for me?"

"Not much, I fear. Ibn-Musa can, by a slight adjustment of the material factors on this plane, bring all kinds of bad luck on you. You step into the street just once without noticing the speeding car; or you neglect a little cut and get the blood poisoning."

"It's up to you to get me out of this, old boy," I said. "After all, you got me into it, in a way."

Al-Lajashi shrugged. "I will do what I can, since you command. But I guarantee nothing."

"Look," I said, "suppose I promised to give you the ring,

186

once I'm home free. Would that make a difference?"

Al-Lajashi pondered, lifting his hat to scratch between his horns. "If you will solemnly promise this thing, I do know one method that might work. It is risky, not only to you but also to me. But I am willing if you are."

"Don't see that I have much choice," I said. "Go ahead. I have to trust you, but you have impressed me as a pretty honest jinn."

Al-Lajashi smiled. "You are a shrewd judge of char-acter, Mr. Newbury; but in your business you have to be. Very well, I am starting this project at once. I cannot explain the method, but do not be surprised at anything."

"I won't be," I said.

I was not, however, prepared for the frightful shriek that came from the beach, around three or four a.m. that night. It woke up Denise, too. We looked out but could see nothing.

We finally got back to sleep. I do not remember my dreams, save that they were much less pleasant than having cozy chats with Habib al-Lajashi.

Next morning, the night's events had receded into a vaguely-recalled bad dream. After breakfast, we put on our bathing suits for our morning's beaching.

There was Maniu, lying under a mound of sand with his head and arms sticking out. He seemed to be asleep. He had buried himself below high-tide mark, and the incoming tide would soon wash over his mound.

"Somebody ought to wake him up," I said, "before he gets a lungful of Atlantic Ocean."

"How pale he looks!" said Denise. "With all the sun he has been getting, one would think—"

She stopped with a terrible shriek. I had glanced away towards a couple of kids flying kites. When I looked back, Maniu's head was rolling gently down the slope of his mound.

The head had been set, like a macabre grave marker, on the mound, which covered the decapitated rest of him. A wave of the incoming tide had lapped up to it and set it rolling.

Just how this happened was never established. The police rounded up the motorcycle gang. The tracks of their vehicles were found on the beach, and there were other bits of circumstantial evidence, but not enough for conviction.

I did not see al-Lajashi for several days. When he paid another visit, I did not wait for him to ask for the ring. I tore it off and tossed it to him before he could speak.

"Take it away," I said, "and yourself with it."

"Oh, thank you, sir! *Kattar khayrak!* You are my liberator! In the name of the Prophet, on whom be peace, I love you! I—"

"I'm flattered and all that. But if you really want to express your gratitude, Habib, you will scram. I want nothing more to do with the jann."

Then I really woke up. There was no jinn; only my darling in the other bed. The ring, however, had gone.

I drew a long breath. Denise stirred. Well, I thought, this is as good a time as any to prove my manhood again. At my age, one should not pass up a chance.

Dead Man's Chest

After I got rid of Habib the jinn, our boy Stephen, who had a summer job, arrived at Ocean Bay to spend a week end with his old folks. Stevie was full of a plan that he and his friend Hank had dreamed up, to hunt for pirate treasure with a World War II mine detector on an island off the Jersey coast. A local tradition claimed that Captain Charles Vane had once put in there to bury his hoard.

Stephen told me about it while we labored through a round of miniature golf, into which he had coaxed me. Tennis is my game, although as a banker I have to play golf in the way of business. But Stephen is too slow and dreamy ever to make a tennis player.

The miniature course had fancy decorations. There were models of space rockets, grotesque animals like dinosaurs, and mythical monsters, such as a life-sized statue of a fish-man like those my pulp-writing friend in Providence used to write about. It had fins running down its back and webbed hands and feet like those of a duck. It stood on a revolving turntable. I asked the ticket taker about it.

"I dunno," said this man. "It's one of them things that crazy artist who designed this place put in. Said he'd seen one alive once, but it was probably a case of the DTs. He's dead now."

We finished our round as Stephen wound up his account of their treasure-hunting plan. He looked at me apprehensively.

"I suppose," he said, "you'll tell me it couldn't possibly work, for some reason we never thought of."

"I don't want to spoil your fun," I said. "If you'd prefer, I won't say a word."

"No, go ahead, Dad. I'd rather have the bad news now than later, after we'd wasted our time."

"Okay," I said. "As I understand it, the routine on a

189

pirate ship was, as soon as possible after taking a prize, to hold the share-out. This was done, not by the captain, but by the quartermaster, normally a pirate too old for pike-and-cutlass work but trusted by the crew. The division was equal, except that the captain might get a double share and the other ship's officers—the doctor, the gunner, and so on—might get one and a half shares, according to the ship's articles. Anyone who held back loot was liable to be hanged or at least keelhauled.

"You see, the captain didn't get all that rich from a capture. When the ship got back to its base, the pirates spent their shares in one grand bust. Rarely did enough loot accumulate in the hands of any one man to be worth burying. Moreover, I thought the pirate Vane stuck pretty close to the Caribbean."

Poor Stevie's mouth turned down, as it always did when I shot down one of his wild ideas. The year before, he and Hank had talked of going to the Galápagos Islands to grow copra. Somehow that sounded glamorous. I had to explain that, first, those islands did not produce copra; second, that copra was nothing but dried coconut meat, which stank in the process of drying and was eventually turned into shampoo oil or fed to the hogs in Iowa.

As things turned out, Stephen had a chance both to see the Galápagos Islands and to hunt for treasure much sooner than either of us expected.

The following summer, my boss, Esau Drexel, took off in his yacht for one of his expeditions in marine biology. Before he left, he said:

"Willy, I can't take you on the whole cruise, because somebody has to run the trust company. But we're going to the Galápagos. Why don't you take Denise and the kids, fly to Guayaquil and Baltra, and meet me there? We can make a tour of the islands. It'll be a great experience, and you can be back in ten or twelve days. McGill can handle the business while you're gone."

It did not take much persuasion. Of my family, only Héloise, our undergraduate daughter, balked. She said her summer job was too important, she had promised her employers, and so on. I suspected that she did not want to go too far from the young man she was in love with. Stephen, who had just graduated from high school, was enthusiastic. An airplane put Mr. and Mrs. Wilson Newbury, with son Stephen and daughter Priscille, down on the island of Baltra, where Drexel's *Amphitrite* was moored to the pier. The two little ships that took tourists around the islands were both out, so the *Amphitrite* had plenty of room.

Drexel, looking very pukka sahib in shorts and bush jacket, with his white mustache and sunburned nose, greeted us with his usual roar. With him he had his wife, a little gray-haired woman who seldom got a chance to say much. There was another man, small, tanned, and white-haired, whom I had not met.

"This is Ronald Tudor," said Drexel. "Ronnie, meet Denise and Willy Newbury. Willy's the one who keeps the Harrison Trust from going broke while I'm away from the helm. Willy, Ronnie's the man who recovered the loot from the *Santa Catalina*, off Melbourne."

"Melbourne, Australia?" I asked.

"No, stupid; Melbourne, Florida. She was one of the treasure fleet wrecked there in 1715."

"Oh," I said, "Is that your regular business, Mr. Tudor?"

"Wouldn't ever call that kind of business regular," said the little oldster with a sly grin. He had a quick, explosive way of speaking. "I do work at it off and on. Right now—but better wait till we shove off."

"You mean," said Priscille, "you're going to find some treasure in these islands, Mr. Tudor?"

"You'll see, young lady. Since we're not sailing till tomorrow morning, how about a swim?"

We swam from the nearby beach, where the hulk of a World War II landing craft lay upside down and rusting to pieces. The children had fun chasing ghost crabs. These, when cut off from their burrows, scuttled into the water and buried themselves out of sight.

Back at the *Amphitrite*, we met the Ecuadorian pilot, Flavio Ortega, as he came aboard. Flavio was a short, broad, copper-colored man with flat Mongoloid features. While he must have been at least three-quarters Indian, he had the

191

Hispanic *bonhommie.* When I tried my stumbling Castillian on him, he cried:

"But, your accent is better than mine! *Usted habla como un caballero español!*"

He was a flatterer, of course; but one of life's lessons is that flattery will get you everywhere.

While we sat on the fantail nursing our cocktails before dinner, Esau Drexel explained: "The waters around these islands have got more rocks in them than the Democrats have in their heads. So we've got to have a local man to keep us from running into them."

"Well," I said, "how about Ronnie's great secret?"

When Tudor looked doubtful, Drexel said: "You can trust him as far as you can anybody, Ronnie. He's worked for me for over twenty years."

"Okay," said Tudor. "Wait a minute."

He went out and came back with a folder containing sheets of paper. In a lowered voice, he said: "Be careful; don't let water from your glass drip on these. They're only photostats, but we need 'em."

I examined the sheets. They were reproductions of three pages from an old manuscript, written in a large, clear longhand. The English had many obsolete usages, which put the document back two or three centuries. The sheets read as follow:

and so departed y^t Iland.

On June ye 6th, Capt. Eaton anchored in a Cove on ye NW Side of ye Iland, ye which Mr. Cowley hath named ye Duke of York's Iland. This Cove, which Mr. Cowley calls Albany Bay, is sheltered by a small, rocky Iland over against it. This little Iland hath a rocky Pinnacle, like unto a pointing Finger. Mr. Dampier assured us, y^t Water was to be found on ye larger Ilands, like unto y^s One, even during ye long Drought of Summer. Whiles ye Men went ashoar to seek for Springs or Brooks, Capt. Eaton privily took me aside and said: Mr. Henderson, ye Time hath come to bury y^t which lies in ye Chest. Sith I know you for a true Man, I will y^t ye and I, alone, shall undertake y^e

192

ticklish Task, saying Nought to Any. But Captain, I said, be ye determined upon yˢ Course? For by God's sir, it seems to me yᵗ yᵉ Contents of yᵉ Chest would, if used with Sense and Prudence, furnish us with a handsome Living back in England for yᵉ Rest of our mortal Dayes. If we ever get home, said Capt. Eaton; but with yˢ accursed Thing aboard, I doubt me we ever shall. A Curse lies upon it; witness our Failure to take yᵉ Spanish Ship whilst she had 800,000 Pieces of Eight aboard; so yᵗ all we gat for our Trouble was a Load of Flower, a Mule for the President of Panama, a wooden Image of yᵉ Virgin, and 8 Tuns of Quince Marmalade. Well, saith he, verily, our Men have a Plenty of Flower wherewhith to make Bread and of Jam to eat thereon, but we had liefer have yᵉ Money. The Men also be in Fear of what it may bring upon us and will be happy to see yᵉ Last of it.

So we went ashoar in yᵉ Pinnace with yᵉ Chest. Capt. Eaton and I carried yᵉ Chest inland from yᵉ Shoar and thence up yᵉ Slope towards yᵉ SW to yᵉ Top of yᵉ Cliff, which overlooks yᵉ Cove. At yᵉ Tip of yᵉ Point, which marks yᵉ western Limit of yᵉ Bay, we buried yᵉ Chest, and not without much hard Labour, for it was heavy to bear and yᵉ rocky Soil hard to dig withal. When we returned to yᵉ Ship

"Where did this come from?" I asked.

"Picked up the originals at an auction in London," said Tudor. "They're in a safe at home, naturally."

"Well, what does it mean?"

"Good God, don't you see, man?" Tudor exploded. "It's as plain as the nose on your face. This Henderson must have been one of the officers of Captain Eaton's *Nicholas*— the boatswain or the gunner, maybe—which stopped here in June, 1684."

"How do you know the year?"

"Because he mentions Dampier and Cowley, who were here with him in the *Batchelor's Delight* at that time. The buccaneer Ambrose Cowley gave the islands their first set of individual names, although the Spaniards later re-

193

christed them, and then the Ecuadorians gave them a third set. Gets confusing. Cowley called his island the Duke of York's Island. Then Charles Second died, and the Duke of York became James Second, so the island became James. The Spanish called it Santiago, and then the Ecuadorians decided on San Salvador."

" 'Santiago' ought to please everybody, since it means 'Saint James'," I said, "although I don't believe James the Second was very saintly."

"Most English-speakers still use 'James,' " said Tudor.

"Is this all there is to the manuscript?"

"That's all. Did some sleuthing—British Museum and such—to try and locate the rest, but no dice. Probably somebody used it to light a fire. Couldn't find any other record of Henderson, either. But this is the important part, so what the hell."

"All right, assuming the document refers to the present James or Santiago Island, do you think you can find this chest from these scanty directions? I thought James was a large island."

"It is, but the directions are as plain as a Michelin guidebook. This bay is what we call Buccaneer Cove. All we have to do is land there and follow Henderson's directions. With a metal detector, it ought to be a breeze."

I thought. "One more thing, Ronnie. The paper doesn't say what was *in* the chest. How do you know it's worth going after?"

"It wasn't money, or it would have been divided in the shareout. It was something of value, as you can tell by Henderson's comment. Evidently one single thing, not divisible. Must have been something of religious or super-natural significance, or the crew wouldn't have gotten spooked. My guess is, some fancy religious gewgaw—a jeweled crown for a statue of the Virgin, or maybe a golden religious statuette, which the buccaneers stole from one of the Catholic churches along the coast. But what the hell, we'll see when we dig it up. It's worth the chance."

Esau Drexel glanced over his shoulder and spoke in a low voice. "We need your help, Willy. I don't want to let the crew in on it, for obvious reasons, but this takes a bit of

194

muscle. You remember how Henderson found the chest hefty to carry. Now, I'm too old and fat for hauling a couple of hundred pounds around rough country, and Ronnie's too old and small. There'll be some digging, too. But you're an athletic type, and your boy has pretty good muscles.

"Ronnie and I have agreed to go halves on whatever we find. If you'll come in with us, I'll give you half of my half, or a quarter of the total."

"Fair enough," I said. Drexel had his faults, but stinginess with his considerable wealth was not one of them.

At this time, the Galápagos Parque Nacional had been established only a few years, and things were not so tightly organized as they became later. Nowadays, I understand, the wardens would be down on you like a ton of gravel if you tried anything like treasure-hunting.

The next week we spent in cruising the southern islands. We saw the frigate birds and the blue-footed boobies on North Seymour. We were chased along the beach on Loberia by a big bull sea lion who thought we had designs on his harem. On Hood, we watched a pair of waved albatross go through their courtship dance, waddling around each other and clattering their bills together. We gauped at swarms of marine iguanas, clinging to the black rocks and sneezing at us when we came close. We admired the flamingoes in the muddy lagoon on Floreana.

On Plaza, Priscille, the strongest wild-life buff in the family, had the thrill of feeding some greenery to a big land iguana. That would not be allowed nowadays. On Santa Cruz (or Indefatigable) we visited the Charles Darwin Research Station. They told us of breeding tortoises in captivity, to reintroduce them on islands whence they had been exterminated.

We dropped anchor in Buccaneer Cove on James, behind the islet with the rocky pinnacle of which Henderson had written. The four treasure-hunters went ashore in the launch, leaving young Priscille furious at not being taken along. Denise was more philosophical.

"Have yourself the fun, my old," she said. "For me, to sit on a cactus once a trip is enough."

195

We left Flavio Ortega in charge of the boat, having told him we were looking for a brass marker plate left by Admiral de Torres in 1793.

"Be careful, gentlemen," he said. "There is said to be a— how do you say—*una maldición*—?"

"A curse?" I said.

"Yes, of course, a curse. They say there is a curse on this place, from all the bisits of the wicked pirates who preyed on us poor Esspanish peoples. Of course, that is just a superstition; but watch your steps. The ground is treacherous."

We headed inland. Stephen carried the shovels and I, the pick and the goose-necked wrecking bar. Tudor toted the metal detector and Drexel, the lunch.

The weight of my burdens increased alarmingly as we scrambled up the rocky wall that bounded the beach. Above this rise, the sloping ground was fairly smooth, but parts of it were a talus of dark-gray sand made from disintegrated lava. Our feet sank into it, and it tended to slip out from under us.

There was a scattering of low shrubs. Higher, the hillsides were covered with an open stand of the pale-gray *palo santo* or holy-stick trees, leafless at this time of year. Even the parts of these volcanic islands with a plant cover have an unearthly aspect, like a lunar landscape.

A narrow ravine cut through the terrain on its way to the bay. We had to climb the bluff on the eastern side of this gulch, and our goal lay on the west side. The ravine was too wide to jump, and its sides were too steep to scramble down and up. So we had to hike inland for a half a mile or so until we found a place narrow enough to hop across. Drexel and Tudor were both pretty red and winded by that time.

The day was hotter and brighter than most. Although right on the equator, the Galápagos Islands (or Islas Encantadas or Archipielago do Colón) are usually rather cool, because of the cold Humboldt Current and the frequent overcasts of the doldrum belt. I smeared sun-tan oil on my nose.

I could also not help thinking of Ortega's curse. Most of my friends consider me a paragon of cold rationality and common sense, never fooled by mummeries and superstitions. In my business, that is a useful reputation. But still,

196

funny things have happened to me....

On the western side of the ravine, we hiked back down the slope. Then we cut across towards the tip of the western point, keeping at more or less the same altitude. When we neared the apex, we stopped to let Tudor set up the metal detector.

As he thumbed the switch, the instrument gave out a faint hum. Tudor began to quarter the area. He moved slowly, a step at a time, swinging the head of the detector back and forth as if he were sweeping or vacuum-cleaning.

Drexel, Stephen, and I sat on the slope and ate our lunch. A handbill given us at Baltra warned us not to leave any litter. Nowadays they are still tougher about it.

The detector continued its hum, getting louder or softer as Tudor came nearer or went further away. It made me nervous to see him close to the tip of the point. The surface on which he was working was fairly steep, so that walking took an effort of balance. If you fell down and rolled or slid, you might have trouble stopping yourself. This slope continued down to the top of the cliff, which here was a forty-foot vertical drop into the green Pacific.

At last, when Tudor was twenty-five or thirty feet from the edge, the hum of the instrument changed to a warble. Tudor stood a long time, swinging the detector.

"Here y'are," he said. "I'll eat my lunch while you fellas dig."

Since Stephen and I were the muscle men, we fell to. There was no sound but the faint sigh of the breeze, the scrape of the shovels, and the bark of a distant sea lion. Once Stephen, stopping to wipe the sweat from his face, cried: "Hey, Dad, look!"

He pointed to the dorsal fin of a shark, which lazily cut the water out from the cliff. We watched it out of sight and resumed our digging. Having finished his lunch, Tudor came forward to wave his detector over the pit we had dug. The warble was loud and clear.

We began getting into hardpan, so that we had to take the pick to loosen stones of increasing size. Then the pick struck something that did not sound like another stone.

"Hey!" said Drexel.

We soon uncovered the top of a chest, the size of an old-fashioned steamer trunk and much distressed by age. Drexel, Tudor, and Stephen chattered excitedly. I kept quiet, a dim foreboding having taken hold of me. Somehow the conviction formed in my mind that, if the chest were opened, one of us would die.

Tudor was nothing to me; I distrust adventurer types. I should be sorry to lose Drexel, a friend as well as a boss. But the thought crossed my mind that I might succeed him as president of the trust company. I was ashamed of the thought, but there it was. For myself, I was willing to take chances; but that anything should happen to Stephen was unbearable.

I wanted to shout: stop, leave that thing alone! Or, at least, let me send Stevie back to the ship before you open it. But what argument could I offer? It was nothing but an irrational feeling—the kind of "premonition" we get from time to time but remember only on the rare occasions when it is fulfilled by the event. I had no evidence.

"Tired, Willy?" said Drexel. "Here, give me that shovel!"

He grabbed the implement and began digging in his turn, grunting and blowing like a walrus. Soon he and Stephen had the chest excavated down below the lower edge of the lid.

The chest had a locked iron clasp, but this was a mass of rust. The wood of the chest was so rotten that, at the first pry with the wrecking bar, the lock tore out of the wood. Stephen burst into song:

> "Fifteen men on a dead man's chest,
> yo, ho, ho and a bottle of rum!
> Drink and the devil had done for the rest,
> yo, ho, ho and a—"

He broke off as Drexel and Tudor lifted the lid with a screech of ancient hinges.

"Good God!" said Ronald Tudor. "What's this?"

In the chest, face up, lay a fish-man like that of which a statue stood in the miniature golf course at Ocean Bay. The thing had been bound with leather thongs in a doubled-up position, with its knees against its chest. Its eyes were covered by a pair of large gold coins.

"Some kind of sea monster," Drexel breathed. "Oh, boy, if I can only get it as a specimen for the Museum...."

Tudor, eyes agleam, shot out two skinny hands and snatched the coins. He jerked away with a startled yelp. "The goddam thing's alive!"

The fish-man's bulging eyes opened. For one breath it lay in its coffin, regarding us with a wall-eyed stare. Then its limbs moved into jerky action. The leather thongs, brittle with age, snapped like grass stems.

The fish-man's webbed, three-fingered hands gripped the sides of the chest. It heaved itself into a sitting position and stood up. It started to climb out of the excavation.

"Jesus!" cried Tudor.

The fish-man was climbing out on the side towards the sea, which happened to be the side on which Tudor stood. Tudor, apparently thinking himself attacked, shoved the coins into his pants pocket, snatched up a shovel, and swung it at the fish-man.

The blade of the shovel thudded against the fish-man's scaly shoulder. The fish-man opened its mouth, showing a row of long, sharp, fish-catching teeth. It gave a hiss, like the noise a Galapagos tortoise makes when it withdraws into its shell.

"Don't—I mean—" cried Drexel.

As Tudor swung the shovel back for another blow, the fish-man moved stiffly towards him, fangs bared, arms and webbed hands spread. Tudor stumbled back, staggering and slipping in the loose, sloping soil. The two moved towards the cliff, Tudor dodging from side to side and threatening the fish-man with his shovel.

"Watch out!" yelled Drexel and I together.

Tudor backed off the cliff and vanished. The monster dove after him. Two splashes came up, in quick succession, from below.

When we reached the top of the cliff, Tudor's body was lying awash below us. We caught a glimpse of the fish-man, flapping swiftly along like a sea lion just below the surface and heading for deep water. In a few seconds, it was gone.

"We've got to see if Ronnie's alive," said Drexel.

199

"Stevie," I said, "run back to the top of the little cliff just this side of the ravine. Call down to Flavio, telling him to bring the boat. Don't mention the monster—"

"Aw, Dad, I can get down that little cliff," said Stephen. He was gone before I could argue. He slithered down the cliff like a marine iguana and leaped the last ten feet to sprawl on the beach. In a minute he was in the launch, which soon buzzed around to the place where Tudor had fallen.

Stephen and Ortega got Tudor into the boat, but he was already dead. He had been dashed against a point of rock in his fall.

"Maybe," said Ortega, "there is a evil esspell on this place after all."

"Well," said Drexel later, "at least we know now what Captain Eaton meant by 'this accursed thing.' "

We sailed back to Baltra and arranged for the local burial of Ronald Tudor.

"He was kind of a con man," said Drexel, "but an interesting one. Let's not put anything in our report to the local authorities about the monster. We don't have a specimen to show, and the Ecuadorians might think we had murdered poor Ronnie and were trying to cover it up with a wild yarn."

So we said only that our companion had met death by misadventure. While I had not much liked the man, his death cast a pall on our vacation. Instead of rounding out our tour by visiting Tower, Isabela, and Fernandina Islands, we cut it short. Drexel sailed for the Panama Canal, while the Newburys flew home. After we got back, it was as if Ronald Tudor and the fish-man had never existed.

But, although I have been back to Ocean Bay several times since, nobody has ever again inveigled me into playing a round at that miniature golf course. To have the revolving statue of a fish-man goggling at me while I was addressing the ball would give me the willies. No pun intended.

The Figurine

The off-black statuette from Guatemala was five inches high and two inches thick at its widest. It also seemed to interfere with our television reception.

This figurine represented a squatty, sexless little person, with a large, wide head on which knobs stood for ears. It had a snub nose, slitty, slanting eyes, and thick lips set in a look of cosmic disgust. It reminded me of the Billikens that decorated the homes of my parents' generation, albeit its expression was far less amiable.

The statuette had been made of a lump of either brick or red sandstone, shaped with a jackknife and a couple of files and painted black. After poking at the base with a tool, I guessed sandstone.

I got the object when, for almost the only time in our married lives, Denise and I took separate vacations. The Museum of Natural Science, in which I have a family membership, offered archaeological safaris to Central America in March and April. The Newburys wanted to look at Mayan ruins; but, with two children in college and another in high school, we did not feel we could both leave at once. While our children have been pretty good, the great youth revolt of the sixties was boiling. We had heard too many horror tales of bourgeois parents who left adolescents in charge of their houses and returned to find the houses savaged by their children's scruffy friends.

I took the first of these field trips, and Denise took the second. I won't give a travelogue, save to say that I got through without a case of the trots and was devoured by mosquitoes at Tikal while sitting in the jungle watching for wild life. There had been a yellow-fever epidemic among the monkeys, so I saw none. I did, however, smell a big cat—a puma or a jaguar—in one of the so-called temples, where this feline had made its lair. But it had cleared out in advance of our coming.

Our bus stopped at Sololá, by Lake Atitlán, on market day, to view the colorful crowd of Guatemalan Indians. They still wore the distinctive costumes of their villages. Some of the little brown men were in pants and some in kilts. Each, no matter how poor he looked, wore a spotless new straw sombrero. Someone must have once sold a lot of surplus nineteenth-century hussar jackets hereabouts. Many wore monkey jackets obviously copied from that pattern. They were made of coarse brown cloth, embroidered in black with frogs, like those worn in the charge of the Light Brigade.

As we were getting off the bus, an urchin piped up: "Buy esstatues! Ancient pagan gods of Indians! Bery reasonable!"

The boy had set out a row of little uglies on the sidewalk. They sell many of these at Chichicastenango. Evidently this boy, learning that we should stop first at Sololá, meant to steal a march on his competitors. I must have looked like a good prospect, for he glued himself to me and uttered a flow of sales talk.

Much as I admired his enterprise, I remembered that Denise does not like filling the house with strange-looking souvenirs. So I fobbed the boy off with "No ahora, gracias; mas tarde, acasa"; and other ambiguities. Perhaps, I thought, he would have gone away when we returned to the bus.

He and most of his idols, however, were still in place. When I still declined to buy, he set up a cry: "But you promised, Meester! All Norteamericanos keep their promises!"

"Oh, all right," I said, secretly glad of an excuse to buy a souvenir of my trip. I paid a dollar for the figurine. "What's he called?"

"No name. Just ancient god."

"Well, what's your name?"

"Armando."

"Fine; this ugly little fellow shall be called Armando."

When I got home, I put Armando on the desk in my home office. Then the children began complaining of television reception. The tube was full of snow, failed to hold the vertical, and displayed other malfunctions. The service man could find nothing wrong. When the set was taken back to the shop, it worked perfectly, but nothing seemed to fix it at home. The repair man guessed that some neighbor might be operating a citizen's-band transmitter.

Priscille said: "It's that hideous little idol Daddy brought back from Guatemala."

"It might have a radioactive core," said Stephen.

"No," said Héloise, "because then we'd all be dying of radiation disease."

"I don't mean that," said Priscille, who seems to have an instinct for these things. "The god is sore at not getting his daily sacrifice."

"Whom would you suggest that I eviscerate with a flint knife?" I asked.

"Well, there's my geometry teacher—but I guess that isn't practical. Maybe you'd better buy a rabbit or chicken or something. If you'll hold it, I'll cut its throat in front of the idol, if you're too squeamish."

"Not over my nice oriental rugs!" cried Denise.

"You bloodthirsty little monster!" I said. "Maybe Armando will be satisfied with an offering of flowers."

"The flowers will not be out till next month, my crazy dears," said Denise.

"You could buy them from a florist," said Héloise.

"With whose money?" I said. "Look, why not use one of those wax flowers that fellow sold your mother last year? Okay, darling?"

Denise shrugged. "It is all to me equal. *Amusez-vous donc.*"

So a couple of waxen flowers were placed at the feet of Armando. At once the snow disappeared from our tube.

Denise departed on her tour. A few days later, Carl telephoned to say that Ed and Mitch were both in town, and couldn't we arrange an old-time get-together?

These three and I had been cronies back in the thirties, when we were young bachelors. We used to gather for a weekly poker game—penny ante with a quarter limit, and a case of beer. It made each of us feel like a hell of a fellow.

203

Then came the war. Afterwards, Ed and Mitch moved to other parts. Besides, I had discovered that I did not really get so much pleasure from the game itself. It was, rather, the talk and the camaraderie that I enjoyed. One could have those without the distraction of cards.

Carl, however, urged the real old thing. Since his house was being painted, I invited the others.

On the Saturday of my party, our television set acted up again. Since I had counted upon the machine to keep my offspring out of my hair while I entertained my old pals, I was concerned. Priscille said:

"Armando's sore again, because you've left those same old wax flowers in front of him for a week without changing them."

"He's an ungrateful little spook," I said. "The wax flowers keep indefinitely, which real ones don't."

"Well, there's your evidence. You'd better take away those and give him some others."

"Oh, nonsense!" I said. "You know it was just a coincidence."

Nevertheless, when none of the children was looking, I removed the first pair of waxen blossoms and put another in their place. The television set cleared up at once.

Carl, Ed, and Mitch arrived with a quarter-century quota of bald heads and potbellies. Since I, by dint of diet and exercise, had kept my shape the best, they kidded me about my gray hair.

"My hair turned gray fifteen years ago," I said, "when I found I'd authorized a bad loan by the bank; but at least I still have it. Draw for deal."

"King deals," said Ed.

We did not argue over the form of the game, for we always played simple draw—not even five-card stud, let alone spit-in-the ocean or other female aberrations with wild cards. We were purists who allowed nothing fancier than jack pots. The draw-poker party is one of the last stands of the heterosexual all-male social group.

On the first hand, my kings beat Mitch's jacks.

On the second, my aces and treys beat Ed's queens and fives.

On the third, Carl drew to a pair and made three tens. Since I seemed to be having an exceptional run, I drew to an inside straight. I would never do that ordinarily, having better sense; but I, too, made it.

On the fourth, I had nines up and Ed, queens over deuces. He discarded his low pair with the odd card, which is usually sound tactics, and made three queens. I dropped my odd card only and made a full house.

After a few rounds, the others had to buy more chips, even at our minuscule stakes. They looked uncomfortably at each other.

"Where have you been the last twenty-seven years, Willy?" said Ed. "Las Vegas?"

"No," said Carl. "A banker is used to carrying figures in his head. He's got all those probabilities memorized."

"No," said Mitch, "he got the dope from those statistics courses at M.I.T. He was always a pretty sharp player, and he's just refined his skills."

"Then why sit behind a desk in a bank, Willy?" asked Carl. "Wouldn't it be more fun and money to gamble for a living? You could have all the booze and broads you wanted—"

"Me?" I said. "Look, you guys, don't you know a banker has ice water in his veins instead of blood? I can take my booze or leave it. As for broads, I find one about all I can manage—"

"He had enough blood in his veins to get three kids," said Mitch.

"Assuming he didn't have to call in outside help," said Ed.

We went on with the game, with the same results as before. No matter who dealt, at least one of my guests had a bettable hand, while I always topped him. After a while, not wanting to be suspected of sleight-of-hand, I began losing deliberately, failing to draw when I had an improvable hand, dropping out when I had a pat hand, and folding when I would normally have called or raised.

We had our coats off. When I went out to the kitchen for more beer, I quietly rolled up my shirt sleeves. At least, they could see that I had nothing in those sleeves.

About eleven, the game died by unspoken mutual consent. I suppose they realized, as I had from the start, the futility of trying to recapture one's lost youth. Even when one goes through the same motions, the feeling is never the same.

Instead, we drank more beer and told of our careers. Having moved to California, Mitch was full of the virtues and faults of his adopted state.

"I have to go out there next month," I said. "One of our trust accounts just died, in a place called San Romano."

"I live thirty miles from there," said Mitch. "You must come and see us."

Carl put in: "Isn't that where all the college kids have been raising hell lately?"

"One of the places," said Mitch. "No worse than you've got back here. Look at Columbia—"

"Ought to machine-gun the lot," growled Ed. "Damned long-haired, loafing, dope-shooting bums—"

"I'll tell you about it when I get back," I said. "I'm staying with my brother-in-law, who's a professor there."

"Damned yellow, cowardly professors," said Ed. "Haven't the guts to can these young thugs when they act up, when they're not red revolutionists themselves. Now, when I went to college, if you presented the prexy with a list of non-negotiable demands, he'd have thrown you out the window without first opening the window."

The party ended soon after midnight. Middle-aged men are less charmed by the small hours than once they were. There were good-nights and badinage. As the other two started out the path to Carl's car, Carl turned back and quietly asked:

"Willy, tell me something. Why the hell did you drop when you had four queens? I looked at your discards."

"Must have been plain stupidity," I said. "I probably mistook them for queens and jacks."

"Don't give me that! Anyone can see you're just as sharp as ever."

"I'll try to explain some other time," I said. "It has to do with the way my television set has been acting, but it's too complicated to tell you now."

"You mean radiations from it?"

"Something like that. Good-night, Carl."

When Denise returned from her safari and I was packing for California, on an impulse I put Armando in with my socks. In the late thirties, I should have scorned such superstition. There was no harder-boiled materialist than I; I rejected Marxism as too mystical and not materialistic enough. But with all the funny things that have happened to me...

My brother-in-law is Avery Hopkins, Ph.D., professor of Middle English. He and my sister had one child, a boy of the same age as my Héloise and a student at the local college. I had not long been in the Hopkins house when I caught the tension.

"We're so worried," said Stella. She was a willowy blonde, an inch taller than Hopkins—a little round, bald man, sweet-tempered and gentle. He and Stella seemed to get along well enough. My sister continued:

"With all these demonstrations and things, you never know when the police will cut loose with their guns. Robert might be killed."

"It's the fault of the municipal government," said Hopkins. "The police shouldn't have guns. The students are only exercising their constitutional right of assembly."

"Okay," I said, "but I think the Constitution says: peaceably to assemble. When somebody heaves a rock, as usually happens, you assembly isn't peaceable any more."

"But, don't you see? If the system hadn't produced so many injustices and oppressions, there wouldn't be all this resentment to incite people to throw missiles—"

"Ever hear of a human system that didn't have injustices and oppressions? Besides, the world is full of people who, if they got to Heaven, would complain about the tune of the harps and the dampness of the clouds. And some like to throw rocks for the hell of it. Why don't you just lower the boom on young Robert? Tell him he may not, repeat not, take part in these marches and riots?"

"Oh, my!" said Hopkins. "We should never think of dealing with him by such authoritarian tactics. We don't believe in them. Besides, he's threatened to run away and become a real bum, a drifter, begging and stealing for his living."

Stella said: "You know, Willy, we always thought you were kind of a Fascist, the dictatorial way you brought up yours. Now I'm not sure."

I shrugged. "At least, they seem to be turning into hard-working squares, so we must have done something right. But now I've got to run over to the First National to see Evans."

I took the car I had rented at the airport and went to the bank, the entrance to which was flanked by a pair of big date palms. Evans, the treasurer, and the bank's lawyer met me. We three spent the afternoon going through the contents of the late Mary Trumbull Hammerstein's safe-deposit box and bank-account statements. I had to be there in person because the estate was in litigation, with a contested will and lots of money involved. A local judge had ordered the bank to turn Mrs. Hammerstein's papers over only to an official of my bank, which was the executor of the decedent's estate.

When five o'clock came, the lawyer was finished, but Evans and I still had work to do. Evans suggested that he and I come back at eight, so that we could complete the job and I could take my 'plane the next day.

Back at the Hopkinses', I met Robert Hopkins, whom I had not seen for several years. He was a small, pale, weedy, hollow-chested youth, with enough hair to qualify as the Dog-Faced Man in a circus. He wore clothes of such ragged denim that he might have been a castaway recently rescued from an uninhabited island.

He gave me a limp hand, saying: "Oh, yeah, you're my Uncle Willy. Do I understand you're—like—a *banker?*" He made it sound as if he were accusing me of mass murder.

"Yes," I said. "That's how I earn my living, such as it is."

He looked at me as if I had crawled out from under a flat stone and turned to his parents. "Say, when do we eat? I gotta get back to the campus. Big rally tonight."

"Please, Bob dear," said Stella. "Your father hasn't had time to serve the cocktails yet."

Robert snorted. "Okay, if you want to fool around with that middle-class crap. But I got business. Gotta eat by six-thirty at the latest."

"We'll try to hurry, Robert," said Avery Hopkins,

208

nervously pouring. "Here's yours, Willy. *Wæs hail!*"

"*Drink hail!*" I responded, pleased with myself for being able to return his verbal serve. Robert was silent during our hasty cocktail hour. When Stella had served dinner, I asked him:

"What's this rally you're attending?"

"Why, the usual thing. To protest, like, this obscene, immoral war, and pollution of the ecology—"

"Excuse me, Robert," said Avery Hopkins, "but I think you mean 'pollution of the environment.' 'Ecology' is the science of the environment, not the environment itself."

"Oh, who cares, Dad? Anyway, we're gonna protest pollution and racism and Fascism and sexism and capitalism and imperialism and grading and intelligence tests and—"

When Robert paused for breath, I said: "That's a pretty broad spectrum of complaints. Don't you think you'd get further if you concentrated on one thing at a time?"

"Oh, you wouldn't understand, Uncle Willy. You're on the other side of the barricades from us."

"Some of my banking friends consider me a bright pinko liberal," I said mildly.

"Oh, that's worse than a real conservative! You guys are always trying to damp down the class conflict, but we gotta have class struggle if we're ever gonna smash the System. We need it to raise the revolutionary consciousness of the masses. I mean, like, you may be a decent sort of guy in your private life, but you belong to the oppressing class. Also, you're an old man past forty, so you just couldn't understand us young progressive types. Might as well be talking Greek."

"Well," I said, "I have at least read Marx's *Capital.* Have you?"

"Marx? Naw. He's not relevant any more. The Communists have become, like, just another bunch of bureaucratic squares. All they want is to take over the system and run it for their own benefit. But we gotta overthrow the system, smash it to pieces, and start over. Now if you'd read Marcuse—"

"I have; that is, one of his books."

"What ja think?"

"I thought it the worst lot of rhetorical balderdash since *Mein Kampf*. All about how Man wants this and needs that and ought to do the other thing. He throws around a lot of abstractions having no connection with the real world—with what any real man or group of men wants—"

As I spoke, Robert became more and more excited. Now he jumped up from his half-eaten dinner, shouting:

"All right, we'll show you old mother-fuckers! We'll get you, like we got that reactionary sociologist! You're all parts of the system that's grinding down the people. You talk about our violence, but you use violence against us all the time, like sending your Fascist pig cops to beat us up! You're too yellow to do your own dirty work, so you hire the pigs to do it! Well, fuck the system, and fuck you, too!"

He slammed out, leaving Avery, Stella, and me staring. It was one of the more uncomfortable moments of my life. Avery Hopkins muttered:

"Willy, I can't tell you how sorry I am that you should be subjected to such barbarous discourtesy—"

"My fault, I'm afraid," I said. "I should have shut up instead of needling him."

After groveling apologies all around, I asked: "Who was the reactionary sociologist?"

"Oh," said Hopkins, "he meant Vincent Rosso, the one who had his office blown up. Lost his right foot and all his scientific data."

"I read something about that in the Eastern papers. What was his offense?"

"He believed in heredity, so that made him a racist, an imperialist, and other dreadful things."

After I had helped with the dishes, I collected the things I needed for the evening session at the bank. Looking at Armando, lying amid my socks, I thought: if you ever need supernatural help, Wilson Newbury my lad, now is the time, with a horde of young idealists on the rampage. I put the statuette in my brief case.

Evans awaited me in front of the First National. The watchman, a white-haired ex-cop named Joshua, let us in.

After another hour, we were just wrapping up the transfer

of the Hammerstein papers to my custody. We worked in an inner office, so as not to be seen through the picture windows. It has always seemed foolish to me to build large expanses of glass into the walls of a bank, which ought if anything to resemble a medieval fortress. But the First National of San Romano was some architect's dream, with vast panes of plate glass outside and fancy wooden paneling within.

Joshua knocked on the door. When told to enter, he came in with Robert Hopkins, the latter breathing hard. The watchman said:

"Mr. Newbury, is this your nephew? Says he's Professor Hopkins's son."

"Yes, Josh, he is. What's up?"

"There's a big crowd outside, making a holler. So this young man came to the door and asked me to let him in. He wants to warn you."

"Yes, Bob?"

"Uncle Willy! You and Mr. Evans better split. The comrades are gonna destroy this symbol of repression, and if you're inside—well, I'm sorry I blew my top. Like, I didn't mean I really wanted to see you fried alive."

"Good God!" said Evans. "I'll call the cops."

"Won't do any good," said Robert. "The fuzz are already out there, but they're not doing anything. You guys better get the hell out while you can."

"That damned city council!" said Evans. "They told the police to handle the students with the utmost restraint, because they didn't want any more of the bad publicity the town got from last February's bust. Let's go."

I quickly stuffed the remaining papers into my brief case. We had hardly left the inside office when a terrific crash came from the front. At once the crowd noises, which had been barely audible in the office, became loud.

Joshua opened the door to the foyer and stepped through. There was a dull impact, and he staggered back. He had lost his uniform cap, and blood ran down his scalp. A brick had hit him. Bottles, bricks, stones, and pieces of concrete were raining into the foyer through the picture windows, most of whose glass lay in fragments on the tiled floor. One of the date palms by the entrance was burning briskly.

"Keep back!" said Evans. "It's suicide to step out there."

"Has this place a back door?" I asked.

"Yes. Let's try it."

When we came to the back door, however, it transpired that it had to be opened by two keys, and Joshua had only one of them. None of the others on his ring fitted. After Joshua had fumbled in a dazed sort of way, Evans took the keys from him and tried them with no more success. The door was a solid affair, with a steel frame and small panes of laminated glass, so we could not hope to batter our way out. I said:

"If we went back to the front and put out the inside lights, so they couldn't see us to aim, we might make a break."

Robert Hopkins, looking as if he were about to faint, staggered after us. When we got to the foyer again and put out the lights, the rain of missiles continued. The floor was ankle deep in stones, bricks, and broken glass. I do not know where the rioters got such an inexhaustible supply.

With the lights out, we could see our assailants. About a third or a quarter were girls, and all were in the ragged barb that symbolized rejection of bourgeois values. They formed a loose semicircle in front of the bank. Off to the left I saw the gleam of brass buttons, but the police stood idly by.

To escape, we should have to bull our way through the line. While throwing things, the rioters chanted some slogan, which, after a while, I made out to be: "*Fuck the system! Fuck the system!*"

"Oh, boy," snarled Evans, "if I only had a machine gun and plenty of ammo!"

Little flames appeared in the ragged line. One of the flames soared up in a parabola and struck the outside of the building. There was a burst of yellow flame.

"Fire bombs," I said.

Another gasoline-filled bottle, with a lighted wick, sailed sparkling through the air. This one came in through one of the gaping picture windows and spread its flame around the foyer. Papers and curtains began to burn.

"Now we'll be roasted for sure," said Evans. "I said there was too much goddam wood in this building. What'll we

212

do?"

Another Molotov cocktail whizzed into the building. The heat became oppressive, and the smoke made us cough. Beyond the flames, I saw firemen wheel up a truck and run a hose out to a hydrant. No sooner had they attached it, however, than several students attacked it with axes and machetes and soon had it in shreds. The firemen retreated from the shower of missiles.

"Goddam cops!" breathed Evans. "Look at 'em, standing back and just watching? They're afraid to do anything, because then every pinko journalist in the country will tell how the brutal Fascist pigs killed some innocent children who were just having fun."

"We'll have to take our chance and run through the fire and rocks and everything," said Robert Hopkins, shivering. "Maybe, if I yell I'm one of them, they'll let us through."

Crash! went the missiles, while the flames flashed and crackled.

"Just a second," I said. I stepped aside, turned my back, and fished Armando out of my case.

"Armando," I muttered, "if you get us out of this with whole skins, I'll sacrifice a rabbit to you."

Hardly had I spoken when there was a brighter flash and a deafening crash of thunder. It seemed to come from right overhead. In my part of the country, when that happens, you look out to see if a nearby tree has been struck by lightning. Then came a terrific down pour, with more lightning and thunder.

The idealists scattered in all directions. The firemen attached another hose. A couple ran up and sprayed the gasoline fires with chemicals, while others hosed down the outside of the building and then the foyer. Coming out, we got hosed, too, and emerged dripping, coughing, and sputtering. I did not mind, even though it meant leaving San Romano a day late.

As a Northeasterner, I was used to thunderstorms. I did not then realize that, in most of California, they are so rare that when one occurs, people telephone radio stations to ask if there has been an earthquake. Therefore it was not surprising that the mob dissolved quickly in the face of the strange meteorological assault.

Young Robert was subdued as I drove him home; fortunately nobody had thought to burn my car. Perhaps he learned something from the experience.

That, however, was not the end of the tale of Armando. When I got home, I put the statue back on my desk. At once our television set acted up again. Placing waxen flowers in front of the statue did no good.

When the real flowers burst into bloom, I tried a sprig of forsythia on Armando, and then some lilacs and azaleas. The television set still balked, nor could the service man fix it. Priscille said:

"Daddy, he's mad about something. What did you do to stir him up?"

I thought. "Come to think of it, when we were trapped in that burning bank building, I promised to sacrifice a rabbit to him if he's save us. He did, but I haven't made the sacrifice."

"Then we've got to give it to him or do without the TV. Go buy us a rabbit. I'll help you kill it."

"Damned if I will! No five-inch piece of rock is going to tell me what to do."

The television remained out of action. In addition, we had a run of accidents and petty disasters. I sprained my ankle at my regular Sunday morning game of tennis and limped for a fortnight. Our lawn tractor broke down. So did our clothes washer, our electric stove, our dishwasher, our vacuum cleaner, and our furnace. The Buick developed a flat. It was a revolt of the robots.

I decided to take the statue to the archaeology department of the Museum of Natural Science. I told an archaeologist there, Jack O'Neill, how I had come by the figurine, adding:

"I was sure it was a modern fake, or I wouldn't have bought it. I don't want to encourage clandestine digging. But I do want to know what I've got."

"Leave it here a few days," said O'Neill. When I went back the following week, he said: "This is a funny one, Mr. Newbury. On your time scale, it's a real antique; but on mine, it's a modern fake."

"How do you mean?"

214

"All our tests—chemical, fluorescent, and so on—indicate that this thing was made about the mid-nineteenth century. It's a common pattern. I can show you dozens, almost identical, in our storage vaults.

"The catch is that the originals were made in pre-Columbian times. In the sixteenth century, the Spanish forcibly converted the Quiché peoples to Catholic Christianity, so the making of these idols stopped. It was revived in the present century as a means of making a fast quetzal off the tourists. Some peasants dig up the original molds used in casting the ancient figurines and cast new statues in them."

"That would make the new casts only fifty per cent fake," I said.

O'Neill smiled. "It's better than having them dig up the real old ones and ruin them as evidence. But in the nineteenth century, Guatemala had been Christian for four centuries, while on the other hand there weren't enough tourists to furnish a market."

"Do you suppose some pre-Conquest cult had survived in the hills and continued to make these things?"

He shrugged. "Maybe. Or perhaps some enterprising Quiché farmer made it to sell to John Lloyd Stephens or Zelia Nuttall or one of their successors, when archaeologists began poking around the Mayan ruins in the last century." O'Neill looked thoughtful. "Would you sell this?"

"I don't know. For how much?"

"A thousand dollars."

But for my banking experience, I might have started and shouted "*What?*" A thousand is a nice, round sum, even in these inflated days, especially when the statue had cost me one dollar. But experience has made me cautious.

"Really?" I said. "Is it worth that to the Museum?"

O'Neill seemed to go through an internal struggle. "It's not the Museum," he said at last. "It's a private party, who came to us a few days ago for help in tracing his statue. He says it was stolen from him. He traced it to Sololá and learned that one of your group had bought it last March. He didn't know which, but he posted this reward and promised the Museum a donation if we'd help him locate his idol."

"Who is this man?"

215

"Agustín Flores Valera, a Guatemalan."

"Where is he now?"

"Back in Guatemala, but he left word for us to cable him."

"Why does he want it so badly?"

"He's a professional gambler; says it's his good-luck charm. Silly of him, but I don't see why we shouldn't help him out at that price."

"I'll think about it," I said, putting the statue back in my brief case.

I took Armando home and thought. I had nothing against Señor Flores, although his occupation was not one that our bank would consider a good credit risk. He had doubtless figured out how to butter up Armando so as to make the cards shuffle, the dice roll, and the roulette ball drop just right. It was hardly fair to his opponents, but I have never had much sympathy for the victims of gambling sharks. If they were not trying to get something for nothing, they would not expose themselves to being taken.

If I kept Armando, I should have to give him his promised sacrifice. Otherwise he would keep on sending us bad luck. If I yielded to him, he might throw some good luck my way; but he would also want more of the same. I could imagine what it would do to the Harrison Trust Company if the story got out that the vice-president was performing pagan blood sacrifices in the dark of the moon. Before the war, when I was a young engineering graduate, desperately job-hunting, I would have taken Armando to my bosom, sacrifices and all. Now, however, things were different.

I was still pondering the problem a week later when, one rainy Sunday afternoon, my doorbell rang. Stephen called:

"Man to see you, Dad."

The man, small and dark, introduced himself as Agustín Flores Valera. I showed him into my home office and seated him.

"It is a great pleasure, a great honor, to meet you, sir," he said, bouncing in his chair. "You have a beautiful place, a beautiful wife, beautiful children. I am overwhelmed. I am enchanted."

"Very kind of you," I said. "I suppose you've come about

216

that statue?"

"Ah, yes indeed. I see him there on your desk. The good Doctor O'Neill tells me that he has explained the circumstances to you? A great scientist, a great man, Doctor O'Neill."

"Well, Señor Flores?"

"You know my offer?"

"Yes, sir."

"Are you prepared to accept?"

"Not yet. I want more time to think it over."

"Oh, please, Mister, I need my esstatue now. In my business, one needs all the luck one can get. I am on my way to the casinos at Puerto Rico...Look. I tell you. I have here another esstatue of the same kind. Genuine antique, not a modern fake."

Flores whisked out an idol much like mine. When he set it beside Armando, it took a second look to tell them apart.

"There you are, Mister," he said. He was standing at my desk and leaning over me. He had the Latin American habit of getting within inches of the person one is talking to, and he had a breath that would knock over a buffalo.

"You will never miss the one you have now," he went on. "Besides, I have here one thousand in cash." From another pocket, he produced a wad of hundreds and flapped them in my face. "Come! It is a deal, no?"

Although he had not done anything really offensive, I disliked Señor Flores more and more. Before he arrived, I had almost decided to let him have Armando; but the hard sell always gets my back up. I run into that sort of thing all the time from promoters and developers who want to try out some grand scheme on our depositors' money. I said:

"No, sorry. I want more time to think this over."

"How about fifteen hundred? I can go that high."

"No, Señor, I meant what I said. I am not yet prepared to sell. *Mas tarde, puede ser.*"

"Oh, you esspeak the Esspanish! Excellent! One can see that you are a man of great culture. But now really, Mr. Newbury, I must have that esstatue, now. Do not make it difficult for us. I will even offer two thousand."

I sighed. "Señor Flores, I have said my say, and that's

217

that. When I've had time to think it over, if you will write me, I'll give you an answer."

He stood for a minute with tight lips. I could see a vein in his temple throb and thought he was about to burst into a tirade. He controlled himself, however, put away the money and the substitute statue, and said:

"Bery well, Mr. Newbury, I will not take more of your time. Perhaps we will be in touch again soon. Pray convey my compliments to the beautiful Mrs. Newbury and the beautiful Newbury children. A pleasant good day to you, Mister."

He bowed formally and went. As he disappeared into the waiting taxi, Priscille called from inside:

"Hey, Daddy, the TV's working again!"

So it was. Struck by a thought, I went back to my office and picked up Armando. Only it was not Armando. It was the near-duplicate that Flores had placed beside my statue.

This one, as I soon ascertained by digging through the black paint, was made of gray clay, not red sandstone. Moreover, it had been cast in a mold—one could see the parting lines—and finished by filing, instead of being sculptured from solid stone. Flores had shuffled the two on my desk and coolly picked up mine. I should have known better than to let a professional gambler work his sleight-of-hand on me.

What hurt the most was the two thousand, which, had I not let a petty personal dislike sway my actions, I could have had for the asking.

I never heard of Flores Valera again, nor did the Museum receive his promised donation. I have often wondered: was Armando so eager to get someone to make a blood sacrifice to him that he engineered his own abduction? Did his new possessor submit to his demands? If the gambler balked, Armando was in a position to ruin him by a few bum steers.

I sometimes miss the ugly face of my little Quiché godlet, but perhaps it is just as well he is gone. In financial transactions and human relationships, I find it hard enough to estimate the most favorable probabilities, without having also to take into account the whims of a bloodthirsty and temperamental deity!

Priapus

I like my brother-in-law but, after what has happened each time I have visited him, I am wary of going there again. The first time, when I was in California on business, I was almost roasted alive in a burning bank building. The second time...

The winter our son Stephen was a sophomore, I came down with the flu, which left me as limp as a wet noodle. The president of the Harrison Trust, Esau Drexel, said:

"Willy, take the rest of the month off and go somewhere warm. Business is slow, and we can handle it. Take Denise with you."

"And leave those three kids alone in the house?"

"Oh, forget about being the heavy father! They're old enough to manage, and they're about as well-behaved as you can expect of kids nowadays. Why, when I was your boy's age..."

Having wangled an invitation from Avery and Stella Hopkins, Denise and I flew to San Romano and the Californian sunshine. True, we arrived in the middle of a two-day winter downpour, but then things cleared up to let us get some tan and tennis.

My skinny little nephew Robert Hopkins, as hairy as ever but more subdued than the year before, was a senior at the local college, where Avery Hopkins was Professor of Middle English.

"You know, Uncle Willy," said Robert at dinner, "all that stuff about burning banks and such was attacking the problem from the wrong end. I see that now. Like, if you really want to change the System, it does no good to use the same material means that the oppressing class does, because you end up just a materialistic as the oppressors. That's where the Communists went wrong. You've got to approach it on another plane, like you was making an end run in football."

219

"As if you were making an end run," said Avery Hopkins.

"Okay, okay, as if you were making an end run. Not that I'm any kind of jock."

"I never suspected that of you," I said. "How do you get to this other plane?"

"That takes special knowledge. There's a little study group working on it right now. We're figuring out a scientific way to use love as a weapon."

I glanced a question at Robert's parents. My sister Stella said: "It's some occult group that Robert has joined. We don't think much of their ideas; but they got Bob to give up marijuana, so they can't be all bad."

"So long as he keeps his marks up," said Avery Hopkins, "it's his business what ideological vagary he pursues. The young are always careening from one extreme belief to another. As Aristotle says, they despise money because they don't know what it is to be without it."

Remembering Robert's antics of the previous year, I expected a tantrum or at least an outburst. Instead, he smiled benignly.

"You'll learn," he said. "Uncle Willy, would you and Aunt Denise like to attend one of our ceremonies? I've tried to get Mom and Dad to go, but they won't touch it. The Master Daubeny's promised us a climax."

"I might," I said. "As for Denise, ask her."

"I might, also," said Denise. "My great big stubborn idiot of a husband needs me to keep him out of the trouble."

Next day, Stella took Denise on a round of the shops of San Romano. Avery Hopkins asked if I should like to see his campus. Nothing loath, I submitted to his guided tour. Since I am an engineer by training and a banker only by circumstance, the scientific laboratories interested me most. In the Worth Biology Building, Hopkins met a young instructor.

"This is Jerry Kleinfuss," said Hopkins. "My brother-in-law, Wilson Newbury. What's new, Jerry? Has anybody put piranhas in the swimming tank again?"

"Good God!" I said. "Has some poor devil been devoured while taking a swim?"

"No," replied Kleinfuss. "Some undergraduate did put a few of these fish in the tank and then spread the story during a meet. You should have seen the swimers leap out of the water like seals! But these piranhas were of a harmless species. What puzzles us now is: who stole one of our *Urechis* worms?"

"Your what?" I said.

"*Urechis*, a large marine worm. We got several for experiments from the coast near Santa Barbara. Now somebody's pinched one, tank and all."

"Why should anybody do that?"

Kleinfuss shrugged. "We have no idea, unless the thief wanted to fry and eat it. I don't thing the result would be anything to write home about."

"Could I see one of these worms?"

"Sure. Right this way."

Kleinfuss led Hopkins and me into a room lined with small glass tanks, containing various marine organisms. Some had jointed legs, some tentacles, and some other appendages.

"Here they are," said Kleinfuss.

In each of the tanks, a large pink worm was moving slowly about in the water. Each worm was a cylinder, about eight or nine inches long and an inch in diameter. It was just the color of human flesh, which it amazingly resembled. It even had little blue veins visible through the skin. The effect was startling.

I burst out laughing. "I see the organs," I said, "but where are the organisms?"

Kleinfuss smiled. "You're not the first to notice the resemblance. Anyway, that vacant place in the row is where our missing worm was. We called him Priapus. The others are Casanova, Lothario, and Don Juan. To catch them, you stick a length of rubber tube down the burrow. The worm swallows the tube and swarms up it, forming a kind of fleshy sleeve on the outside of the tube. Then you have only to pull out the tube and scrape off the worm."

That evening, the Hopkinses had another couple to dinner. These were Associate Professor Marvin Held, from

221

the Language Department, and his wife Ethel, an assistant professor of psychology. Held, a big, bushy-bearded chap who taught Romance languages, defended Latin and bewailed its disappearance from modern high-school curricla.

"I don't know," I said. "I've forgotten most of my high-school Latin. I'd rather have put the time on a widely-spoken modern language, like Spanish."

"Oh, you're both wrong," said young Robert in his squeaky voice. "I know people who've been all over the world, and they always found somebody who spoke English if they hollered long and loud enough."

Held snorted. "No wonder we're becoming a nation of illiterates! First the kids demand a say in college policies, and our spineless administration gives in. Then they find there's nothing duller than committee meetings to decide if full credit shall be given for French 1-A from Primeval Baptist College of Mud Creek, Mississippi. So they stop coming around. Next, they don't want to have to learn any history, or any foreign languages, and so on. Then they ask credit for what they call 'life experience.' What they really want is a diploma for merely existing, without any work at all."

"Instead of studying nine tenths of the irrelevant crap you guys give us," said Robert, "it would be more to the point, like, to spend the time learning to use the unseen forces of the universe."

"For my money," I said, "languages are the main unseen force around. Just get stuck in Iraq, as I once did, not knowing any Arabic beyond 'Yes,' 'No,' and 'Where's the toilet?' and you might change your mind."

Denise added: "No one can call himself a civilized, educated man without at least the French."

Ignoring her, Robert said: "That's not what I meant at all, Uncle Willy. Come to the big do of the Agapean Association day after tomorrow, and you'll see. We're gonna invoke the spirit of love."

Marvin Held said: "Bob, I've heard rumors about this outfit. Could Ethel and I come, too? It might be of professional interest."

"So you can look at us like bugs under a microscope?" said Robert. "Okay, come along. You might decide that the bugs have got the right idea and join us."

After the Helds had gone, Avery Hopkins said to me: "Willy, I think I ought to warn you. The rumor is that these people put on orgies."

"Really?" I said. "I've always wanted to attend an orgy. I don't know how Denise will take it; she was strictly brought up by a very proper French Protestant family. What sort of cult is it?"

"One of these sex-and-magic things that are springing up, now that the youth revolt has begun to run out of steam."

"Well, the state has always had a fine climate for nuts. I'm a little old for organized orgiastics myself, but I still want to see. I'm an old wild-life watcher, and such excesses make *Homo sapiens* a fascinating species to watch."

Early in this century, a man named Bannister made a mint in oil and built a mansion in San Romano. The Agapean Association had leased this mansion, which stood on an estate-sized lot, surrounded by palms, acacias, and pepper trees. The house was a huge, rambly place, pseudo-Spanish outside and medieval German baronial within. It had run down since the days of the Bannister family but was not yet decrepid enough to be really spooky.

Marvin and Ethel Held drove us to the mansion, since we might have had trouble finding it in an unfamiliar city by ourselves. Robert Hopkins was not with us. Having promised to meet us at the Bannister house, he had gone to fetch his own girl friend.

There was a delay getting in. A pair of muscular Agapeans in black robes guarded the front door. They would not admit us until Robert came to vouch for us, and Robert was late. When the formalities had at last been complied with, we were shooed into the huge living room just as the lights were being turned down for the big show.

"Sandy and I gotta get dressed," whispered Robert. "Visitors sit in the last row. You go ahead and sit; we'll be with you in, like, half a minute."

The seats were arranged in concentric crescents. We found four vacant chairs at one end of the rear row. Thence we could see many of the others present, either in profile or in three-quarters full-face.

As our eyes became accustomed to the dim light, Denise gasped. The front rows, composed of sofas, divans, and ottomans placed end to end, were occupied by thirty-odd people, in couples. Most were young, and all were naked. Some were petting.

Robert Hopkins, looking like a plucked chicken without his clothes and followed by his equally naked girl, stole in from the other side and took seats at the end of one of the forward rows. Robert's idea of "getting dressed" was not what most would understand by the term.

Denise whispered: "Willy, I do not think we ought to stay here. *C'est une indécence, donc!*"

"Oh, come!" I whispered back. "You took me to that nudist place in France."

"That was different—the clean, healthy nature. This is a depravity."

"Stick around," I said. "Nobody claims we have to strip, too."

Denise subsided. In front of the seats, a temporary wooden dais rose a foot from the floor. On this platform, a stand upheld a small glass tank. In the tank was water and something pink and wriggly. I recognized a urechis worm, doubtless the one stolen from the biology laboratory.

At each end of the dais, a huge candle burned in an oversized brass holder, standing high above the floor. To one side, an incense burner sent up a thread of fragrant smoke.

A man in a red robe strode out of the shadows and took his stance on the dais, behind the tank with the worm. He was a slight, balding man of about my age, with a thin film of black hair combed across his bare cranium.

"Good evening, companions in transcendental adventure," intoned the Master Daubeny. "May infinite love be yours. Tonight we shall undertake the greatest of our magical operations, to secure for ourselves and for all of factious mankind the infinite blessing of love. We shall invoke love in its purest, most concentrated form, the form of the god Priapus, the god of the ultimate act of love, personified by this marine creature before me.

"By the laws of sympathetic magic, an invocation directed at this animal, which by its form symbolizes the outstanding characteristic of the god, will draw the god himself unto us. We shall then perform the appropriate—here, here!" He spoke chidingly to Robert and Sandy, who had been fondling each other's persons and gave every sign of being about to jump the gun. "You must wait till after the god manifests himself. Patience, patience!

"To continue. We shall perform the ultimate act of love as a reverent tribute to the god. For what ails mankind today? Why wars, crimes, and strikes? Because there is not enough love. With the help of Priapus, we shall, by our command of the occult currents, instill more love, first into our fellow countrymen and then into all the world..."

He went on for half an hour, talking about the different planes of existence, the materialization of spiritual abstractions, and the need for transcendental currents of love throughout the seven-dimensional universe. These currents were to be set flowing by a mass act of communal copulation.

From what I could see of the young men in the audience, they were ready to perform their roles in the rite. The soldiers of my outfit in the Second World War never stood up straighter. All the couples were kissing and fondling. I itched to grab Denise and join the revel, but her expression of stern disapproval squelched that idea. She whispered:

"Willy, I will not stay here longer, to see the beautiful making of the love turned into a circus!"

"Oh, come on!" I said. "What they do won't hurt us. Besides, if you left me here, who knows what mischief I might not get into?"

On the other side of her, a similar argument had broken out between the Helds. With them, however, it was the man who wished to leave and the woman to stay. As a psychologist, Ethel Held did not want to miss anything.

At last the sermon was over. Daubeny pulled a wand out of his baggy sleeve and began to utter his incantation. He faced in various directions, moved his wand as if he were leading an invisible orchestra, and chanted.

225

The Master's voice rose to a shout. From an occasional word, I realized that he was speaking Latin. He ended with a scream:

"*Veni, magistre venereonum! Veni, veni, veni!*"

I was braced for a bit of conjuring or other hocus-pocus but not for what happened. The flames of the two big candles shrank to mere points, glowing like stationary fireflies. Then came a brilliant flash of cold, white light and a clap of thunder.

A young woman stood at one end of the dais, facing the Master Daubeny. Tall, slim, dark, and aquiline-nosed, she wore a knee-length Classical chiton, which left one small, virginal breast bare. In her left hand she bore a strung double-curved bow. A quiver of arrows hung at her back from a leathern baldric.

Standing in the darkened room in a blaze of light from no source that I could see, the maiden stared at the Master, then at the audience. The naked worshipers were sitting up, their foreplay forgotten. They stared—I suppose "aghast" is the word.

"So!" she said in a ringing alto. "You calla me for your—how you say—your *comissatione turpi*—your obscena misbehaviors?"

It had not occurred to me that Diana—for such I presumed our transcendental visitor to be—would speak English with a strong Italian accent.

"Willy!" said Marvin Held in a low, tense voice. "Let's get the hell out of here, pronto! I'll explain outside."

He rose. So did Denise and Ethel Held. Being at the end of the row, I had to rise, too.

"Quick!" said Held. "Don't argue; I'll tell you later." I meekly accompanied the others of our quartet.

"So," continued the apparition, "I fixa you *dissolutos!*"

We stumbled out into the entrance hall. As we reached the front door of the mansion, the spectral presence ripped out a long sentence in Latin. I caught only the final words: "...*cum impotentia, sterilitate, et frigore!*"

We were on our way to the Helds' car when a call of "Hey!" made us pause. It was Robert and Sandy. Robert wore his shirt and ragged blue jeans but had fled barefoot;

226

the girl was equally disheveled.

"What—what happened?" he panted. "All I know is, Sandy and I couldn't wait, so we split to the bedroom and were screwing away when the big boom came. It kind of, like, took our minds off what we were doing. When I stuck my nose in the meeting hall, there was this dame on the platform, hollering in some language, and the four of you running out. So I grabbed Sandy, and we high-tailed it out of there. What happened?"

Held explained: "Your wizard invoked Priapus, the phallic god, but got Diana instead. Being the goddess of chastity as well as of the moon and of hunting, she was outraged by what she saw. Therefore she cursed everybody in the room with impotence, sterility, and frigidity. Knowing the Classical myths, I guessed what might be coming."

(According to what the older Hopkinses wrote us later, the curse worked. I don't know if the effect ever wore off.)

"Oh, man!" wailed Robert Hopkins. "D'you suppose the curse reached as far as us?"

"I don't know," said Held. "You'll have to wait and see."

"How come the Master goofed?"

"Didn't know his Latin. In his invocation, he said *magistre venereonum*. In the first place, he thought *magistre* was the vocative of *magister;* but only second-declension nouns in -*us* take that ending. In the second, there's no such word as *venereonum*. He formed a genitive plural from a non-existent third-declension noun *venereo*, which would be the ablative—" Ethel Held poked her husband in the ribs. He concluded: "Anyway, he meant to say *magister venerariorum*, 'master of the lovemakings.' With his bad pronunciation, what he actually said sounded like *magistra venationum*, 'mistress of the hunts,' and it naturally fetched Diana."

"Professor Held," said Robert in a small voice, "do you think I could switch to, like, a language major next year?"

"Come to my office tomorrow and we'll talk it over."

Late that night, Denise gave a happy sigh. "At least, my old one, we know that the curse did not reach so far as us. But when I tell you that it is time to leave a place, do not argue with me, but come along à l'instant!"

"Yes, dear," I said.

THE PURPLE PTERODACTYLS
by
L. Sprague de Camp

The First Edition of THE PURPLE PTERODACTYLS is limited to fifteen hundred copies, two hundred of which have been signed and numbered by the author in a special, boxed edition.